Home Sweet {tiny} Home

Center Point
Large Print

Also by Melody Carlson and available from Center Point Large Print:

Home Sweet {tiny} Home

MELODY CARLSON

CENTER POINT LARGE PRINT
THORNDIKE, MAINE

This Center Point Large Print edition
is published in the year 2022 by arrangement with
WhiteFire Publishing.

The text of this Large Print edition is unabridged.
In other aspects, this book may vary
from the original edition.
Printed in the United States of America
on permanent paper.
Set in 16-point Times New Roman type.

ISBN: 978-1-63808-177-7

The Library of Congress has cataloged this record under
Library of Congress Control Number: 2021946631

Chapter 1

Less is more, less is more, less is more. Kate Burrows muttered these three words to herself as she gazed blankly at the spacious great room she'd once loved. But that was when it had been filled with family and friends, light and life and music. But then Kenneth passed away, and the kids went off to college. For several years she'd known that 5,280 square feet was too much house for her, but at the same time she'd had no choice. But today she felt trapped.

Kate paused the TV show that had her mesmerized, staring in wonder at the charming tiny home featured in this segment. The proud owner of the pint-sized bungalow was frozen too, but the three simple words she'd just proclaimed seemed to still hang in the air. "Less is more." And Kate couldn't help but agree with the young woman. Less did seem like it could be more. But how did someone like Kate reach that place?

Kate sighed as she laid down the remote. Time for a break from what had turned into an embarrassingly long TV show binge. But as she wandered through her oversized house, she just sadly shook her head. Would she ever feel at home in this oversized McMansion again? And was it her imagination or were these spaces actually growing larger right before her eyes? *Less* was growing more and more appealing.

As Kate carried a half-eaten carton of mocha-fudge ice cream back into the cavernous great room, she put the blame on her college-aged daughter. A couple of weeks ago, Zinnia had texted Kate about an architect friend featured on *Teeny, Tiny Home*, begging her to record it. Naturally, Kate had agreed, and not knowing which episode to record, she'd set her DVR for "unlimited" and then forgotten about it.

So this weekend, which just happened to be Mother's Day weekend complete with a deluge of rain, Kate had abandoned her plans to work in the yard. Feeling slightly depressed by the weather, and slightly neglected by her kids, Kate turned on her first episode of *Teeny, Tiny Home*. That was all it took. She spent all of Saturday glued to her big screen TV, obsessively blasting through show after show after show. After all, wasn't bad weather the perfect excuse for a good long TV binge?

But by Sunday morning the storm had passed and Kate's neglected palette of perennials remained sequestered in her oversized three-car garage. Kate shamelessly remained in her *I Love Lucy* flannel pajamas, remote in hand, skipping commercials, and soaking in every single episode of *Teeny, Tiny Home*. For the whole day! By that afternoon, her shoulder-length auburn hair, which needed a good shampoo, resembled Bozo the Clown. But she no longer cared.

Kate couldn't quite grasp why she was so fascinated by these thirty-minute shows. Maybe it was just plain boredom. But something about these energetic souls in search of a scaled-down lifestyle was inexplicably compelling. Equally intriguing were the tiny structures that became their new abodes. From quaint recycled cabooses and old school buses to tree houses and seaside yurts, it seemed that everyone was hopping onto the tiny house bandwagon. And she became even more convinced that less really was more.

By early Sunday evening (which still happened to be Mother's Day—without a word from either of her children) Kate began to seriously envy these optimistic carefree souls of all ages and backgrounds, bravely turning their backs on traditional oversized housing. They seemed to have a spring in their step as they walked away from the excess of "too much stuff." Boasting about how freeing it was to live the simple life. It was all strangely liberating. Kate realized (after the first dozen or so episodes) there was a certain "formula" to these shows. Still, it didn't bother her—maybe she was hooked.

Each show began by showing how a single person or couple—and occasionally a family— were dissatisfied with a lifestyle that had gotten too big, too busy, or simply too costly. They would then decide upon a tiny home that suited their needs and voila—by the end of the thirty-minute episode, the smiling people would triumphantly move into a perfectly adorable and highly efficient miniature house where, Kate assumed, they were sure to live happily ever after.

By late on Sunday evening (still nothing from Jake or Zinnia) Kate knew a real sense of desperation. Unlike those liberated tiny home-owners, she felt imprisoned. Except her "jail cell" was an enormous, luxurious home. And she felt slightly ridiculous—who would pity someone living in this large, lovely house—complete with vaulted ceilings, hardwood floors, home theater, cook's kitchen, spa-like bathrooms?

But get real, why did she need four and a half baths? She only used two of the toilets but still had to clean the other three to keep them from getting a water ring. And her kitchen . . . She used to enjoy cooking, but she probably hadn't cooked a real meal since last Christmas—nearly six months ago. She didn't need that six-burner stove any more than she needed the oversized refrigerator. And she wasn't even sure what she had stashed in the multitude of extra tall cherry cabinets—clever culinary contraptions that she probably couldn't even remember how to use. And what about the "acres" of cold, hard black granite countertop? Good grief, she spent more time dusting the surface than using it. It was all so ridiculous. Why did one woman need so much?

Kate glanced at the TV screen, pausing it once again in order to study the interior design of a particularly well-constructed tiny home. This one was a contemporary design, with excellent craftsmanship, and very clever. Every inch of the 280 square feet looked fully utilized—and yet the small space didn't seem crowded or cluttered. She stared at the little washer-dryer unit, tucked neatly beneath the loft ladder—noticing that it even had a miniature pull-down clothes-drying rack above it. So handy.

Kate cringed to think of her own laundry room. Oh, sure, she had been grateful for the extra large room when the kids were small. The deep sink and granite countertops with storage shelves for the kids' stuff. But as she considered the hike from her second-floor master bedroom, clear down to the finished basement, well, it just made her tired. Plus it reminded her that she still hadn't done laundry.

Tuning her attention back to the TV, she pushed "play" and watched as the new homeowner, a divorcee a bit older than Kate, climbed the ladder into her cozy sleeping loft. Showing her built-in bookshelves, filled with interesting novels, and her handy reading light, the woman looked happy as a clam. She pointed out the ledge created to hold her coffee mug then leaned back into a pile of fluffy colorful pillows and, gazing up through the skylight above her, she let out a long contented sigh. "It reminds me of the tree house I had as a child," she said blissfully. "I never want to leave this place."

"Well, I sure want to leave *this* place." Kate tossed the remote down—making a different kind of sigh. Had this mad binge watching messed with her head? The more she'd watched, the more discontented she'd become. Like the proverbial kid with her nose pressed to the candy-store window. Filled with a desperate longing for less stuff, less ownership, and more simplicity— she suddenly despised her stupid big house. She felt lost in the cavernous great room, over- whelmed by the tall rock fireplace that Kenneth had insisted upon. And the twenty-foot ceiling— who needed it? The thought of facing the future in a house that would never feel cozy wasn't just overwhelming—it was pathetic.

It was nearly midnight when she finished the last episode and finally went upstairs—only to be reminded that the spacious master suite no longer felt cozy. Not since losing Kenneth. The vaulted ceiling and hardwood floors made it feel cold up there. And her "spa-like" master bath was too big and drafty for a nice warm bath, not to mention she got chilled every time she emerged from the oversized shower. And as for that "rain" showerhead, she was tired of getting her naturally curly hair wet every time she took a quick rinse.

Kate paced back and forth in her bedroom, mulling everything over, wondering what she might do to make her home cozier. But, really, wouldn't it make more sense to move into something smaller? *Like a tiny house?* She grabbed the remote for the master suite TV and, feeling a bit like an addict grasping for her next fix, turned the DVR back on and rewatched another *Teeny, Tiny Home* episode.

As it ended—happily of course—she noticed the time and remembered tomorrow was a workday. But after getting in bed, her thoughts were still racing and tumbling, visions of tiny homes seemed to dance through her brain. And so, as usual when she couldn't sleep, she prayed. She begged God to lead her, to direct her path, to help her find a new and satisfying life. It was high time. Suddenly, she knew what she needed to do. And this had nothing to do with Mother's Day neglect.

In one simple split second, her mind was made up. Even if friends and family questioned her sanity—and she suspected they would—she was determined to do this.

Kate Burrows was going to reinvent her life. And she was going to do it with a tiny house.

Feeling an incredible sense of wonder, relief, and great expectations, she texted her realtor friend Jennifer, simply stating that she wanted to sell her house. *As soon as possible.* Feeling guilty for texting at this late hour, she apologized and promised to call first thing the next morning. And then she leaned back and closed her eyes and—for the first time in a long time—felt happy and hopeful and peaceful. Her life was about to get better.

Chapter 2

But it was Jennifer who called Kate early the next morning. The realtor's voice sounded light and cheerful and fully awake. "This is wonderful news, Kate! So exciting."

Caught off guard and groggy with sleep, it took Kate a moment to remember the text she'd sent very late last night. "Exciting?" she muttered.

"Yes! I can't believe the timing. That you're finally ready to sell," Jennifer said brightly. "Because I'm almost certain I have a buyer for you. That's exciting!"

"Seriously?" Kate blinked and, climbing out of bed, shuffled toward the bathroom.

"I have a family from California looking for a house exactly like yours, in a neighborhood just like yours. It's, like, providential."

"That's, uh, great." With slight heart palpitations, Kate listened as Jennifer went on about what great timing this all was and how she had cash buyers and how it could all close very quickly.

Finally, Kate explained she needed to get ready for work and, after saying good-bye, she tried to convince herself that she was making the right decision. As she brushed her teeth, she told herself that selling a home was no big deal.

People did it every day. As she hurried to dress, she reminded herself how most of her monthly salary went to house payments, taxes, insurance, and maintenance. And the funds from Kenneth's life insurance wouldn't last forever. Really, selling was the sensible thing to do. But then what? Was she really ready for a tiny house? Or had she simply been brainwashed?

Instead of obsessing over the machinery she'd set in motion, Kate drove to work. She hated this commute. Would selling her home somehow free her from this? Hadn't she prayed about this last night? Hadn't it seemed God was leading her?

As she pulled into a parking spot, she felt certain she was on the right path. Okay, it might be a bit shaky at the moment, but she believed it would all work out in time. As she entered the building, she determined to do something she'd dreamt of doing for years. Kate sat down at her desk and wrote a resignation letter. She knew that her pragmatic boss would question what would probably appear to be an impetuous decision. But having this letter ready would help show Marion her resolve.

Despite her few hours of sleep, Kate grew strangely energized as she walked the letter to Marion's office. Imagining that she was being filmed for an episode of *Teeny, Tiny Home*, she held her head high as she strolled through the design firm where she'd worked for the last ten years. She even smiled as she handed her boss and good friend her official letter of resignation.

Clearly shocked, Marion stared down at the announcement of two weeks' notice without even speaking.

"It's not that I haven't been happy here," Kate said after Marion looked up again. "It's just that I need a change."

"Are you absolutely certain about this?" Marion's brow creased with concern as she laid the letter down on her desk.

"Yes." Kate nodded firmly. "It's time."

"I know you've talked about doing something different for a while now." Marion adjusted her glasses, studying Kate closely. "And I encouraged you to wait, to give yourself time. After losing Kenneth, well . . . I just didn't want to see you make a knee-jerk decision." She cleared her throat. "Or a mistake."

"And I appreciate that," Kate assured her. "But it's been more than five years since Kenneth passed away. And really, I'm ready to move on now. I'm going to sell my house and—"

"Seriously?" Marion looked more than a little concerned. "This seems like a lot—all at once. Are you certain?"

"You've been to my McMansion. You know it's way too big for me. I just rattle around and—"

"But don't your kids still come home to

visit? What about summers? What if you have grandchildren some day?"

Kate waved her hand. "Grandchildren are a long way off. Trust me on that. And after graduation, Zinnia plans to spend her summer in Seattle. She's been accepted for an internship with an online fashion magazine. And Jake has his job, his life." Kate smiled brightly, hoping to make her understand. "Really, Marion, it's time for me to do this. And I'm really excited about it."

Marion nodded with a sage expression. "Yes, I can see that. But what will you do? Where will you go? Do you have another job lined up? A place to live?"

Kate went ahead and spilled the beans, explaining her plan to buy a tiny home.

"You can't be serious!" Marion's jaw literally dropped.

"I am serious. I've been, uh, studying up on it. It's a simpler way of life. And I feel I'm ready for it." Of course, Kate was making this up as she went along. But it's not that it wasn't true.

"A tiny house? Here in the city?"

"No. I plan to put my tiny house in a small town. You know I grew up in a small community, and I've always missed that."

"So you are quitting your job, selling your house, and relocating?" Marion's eyes were wide. "Have you really given this much thought?"

"I need a change."

"But how will you support yourself in a small town?"

"I think I'll open a florist shop."

"A florist shop?" Marion frowned.

"It's probably a silly old dream," Kate confessed. "But you know how much I love my flower garden in the summertime. And how I bring in arrangements for the office and for friends' birthdays and whatnot."

"You do have a knack," Marion conceded. "But that's not the same as running a business."

"I know. But I believe I can learn."

"Won't a business startup be expensive?"

"It'll probably take my savings, but it's an investment in my future. It's a risk I have to take. My mind is made up."

Marion still looked dumbfounded. "That's, uh, very interesting. I, uh, I don't even know what to say."

"How about *good luck?*"

"Well, yes, of course. I certainly want you to succeed, but are you sure you've given this enough thought?"

Kate didn't want to lie to Marion, but she wasn't comfortable admitting that the idea had hit her rather quickly—like two days ago quickly. And so she mutely nodded.

Marion sighed. "We will miss you here. You've been a good designer and a good team player."

"I'll miss you too. It's been a great job." Much of it had been great . . . but some of it, not so much. Kate would not miss everything about working for a corporate design firm.

Marion got out from behind her desk and, opening her arms wide, gave Kate a big, warm hug. "I do wish you good luck—the best of luck," she said. "In some ways I almost envy you being able to do this. Sometimes I want to jump off this treadmill too." She sighed. "Honestly, this morning's traffic made me want to pull my hair out."

"I sure won't miss that commute." Kate tried not to sound overly smug, although it did feel slightly euphoric to realize all the hours that would no longer be spent behind the wheel. "Hopefully you'll come visit me in my new life."

"Count on it." Marion's phone rang and, waving Kate away, she picked it up.

Kate felt relieved that had gone as well as it had. And with only two weeks to wrap up her projects, she focused on her work. But as she went through her day, answering work friends' questions about her decision to quit, she couldn't stop smiling. It was as if all her reservations were evaporating. The more people she told, many of whom expressed a longing to do something similar, the more lighthearted she felt about her decision.

To think that in just two weeks, she'd be

starting her new and improved, and soon-to-be downsized, life. Well, it was downright exhilarating.

She just hoped she could pull it off.

Chapter 3

Still riding the high of her upcoming down-size, Kate signed a real estate agreement with Jennifer after work, even taking a moment to show Jennifer a website she'd found with some very innovative tiny homes and explaining her plans.

"You really think you could live in something that small?" Jennifer looked even more doubtful than Marion had been.

Kate simply nodded.

"You're talking a major downsize." Jennifer set the paperwork aside. "Are you sure you wouldn't rather do this in steps? I have some lovely smaller homes I could show you. There's a charming thousand square foot cottage over in West View that—"

"My mind is made up," Kate declared as she stood. "I want to live in a tiny home." Although a part of her was curious about the cottage, she'd already told too many people about her tiny home plans to back out now.

"I suppose you can always size-up later," Jennifer teased. "And I promise not to say I told you so."

Kate shook her head. "I really think I can do this. You'll see."

"I'd like to see." Jennifer opened the door. "The buyers from California would like to tour your house on Wednesday, if that's not too soon."

Kate assured her this was doable and, for the next two evenings, got her home ready for the prospective buyers to view. She even planted the pansies and petunias in the big flowerpots by the front door. By Wednesday morning, the place looked so good that she was almost having regrets. Except that it was too big for one lonely widow.

That same evening, Jennifer called with a full-price offer, which Kate nervously accepted. The buyers wanted to move in as soon as possible, which Kate also agreed to, but her fingers trembled a bit as she signed the electronic document. Was this crazy? Still, she experienced a wave of relief when she hit "send." It was done. Her first big step to a simpler life.

The next morning, she used her break time to make an appointment with a representative from the tiny house company. The plan was to look at some completely finished model tiny homes on Saturday morning. She was just putting her phone away when Leota stopped by her desk.

"I can't believe you're really doing this, Kate. Quitting your job, downsizing into a tiny home." Leota's brown eyes grew wide with wonder. "It's so daring and exciting."

Kate smiled. "It is pretty exciting."

"I wish I could do something like that." Leota sighed with a dreamy expression. "I watch that tiny house TV series and I love the idea of living in a tiny house."

"Why don't you do it?"

Leota's brows arched. "Honestly, I wouldn't know where to begin. I mean I've been saving for some kind of home where I don't throw my money away on rent. But even if I bought a tiny house, I wouldn't know where to put it."

"I didn't really know that myself, but I think it will all work out. I'm just putting one foot in front of the other and moving forward."

"You make it sound so simple."

"That's what it's supposed to be . . . simple." Kate reached for her coffee mug.

"Well, maybe you're the pioneer, bravely venturing out into the tiny world." Leota giggled. "Maybe I'll learn from you."

"I'm not really a pioneer. Lots of people have done it—are doing it. You've seen them on that TV show."

"Sometimes it feels a little unreal. And I don't know anyone personally who's downsized like that. Well, except you."

"You want to go with me this weekend? To see the model tiny homes?"

"I'd totally love to!"

So it was arranged, Kate would pick up Leota on Saturday at ten. And, knowing that her young coworker was very artistic, she thought having a second opinion might actually be helpful.

Leota wasn't only helpful on Saturday morning, she made the whole experience more fun. Her enthusiasm and honest but provocative questions about things like toilets and hot water heaters really got the young salesman engaged. His name was Kirk and he seemed to have taken a fancy to Leota, eagerly answering all her questions. But it actually helped Kate to decide on which model she liked best. Her favorite was a midsized design called the *Chalet*. With 240 square feet on the first floor and a loft of eighty more feet above, it was cozy without being too tight.

"This one seems just about perfect," Kate told Kirk as the three of them stood in front of the gable-roofed house. "I love the Dutch door and paned windows and shutters. And the window boxes will be great since I plan to grow lots of flowers. Really, other than the exterior paint colors, I could totally live with this."

"The paint colors are easy to change." Kirk pulled out a folder with lots of paint color choices. "You pick 'em, we paint 'em."

"And how long would it take for a house like this to be completed?" Kate asked.

"We could easily have it ready within the week." He grinned.

"A week?" She was stunned. "I thought you said there was a wait for these houses."

"That's true for most of them. But this one happens to be available now."

"You're saying I could have this very house?" she asked. "I don't have to order it from the factory?"

"That's right. We've discontinued the Chalet so we're letting the model go at a discounted price."

"Oh?" She frowned. "Discontinued? Is something wrong?"

"Don't worry. It's just fine. And everything— stainless appliances, hardwood flooring, quartz countertops—it's all top of the line," he assured her. "That's how we do our model homes. It's just we're getting more orders for the contemporary styles. The younger market is hot for mid-century modern right now. And the younger market is really into tiny homes. Lucky for you, the *Chalet* appeals more to you older folks." He grimaced. "Not to say you're old."

"Well, I am old." Kate confessed. "Older than both of you, anyway."

"But you're not old," Leota insisted.

"I could be your mother," Kate grimly reminded her.

"Except you're the wrong color," Leota teased, holding out a smooth coppery arm next to Kate's pale freckled one.

"We might not match." Kate laughed then

hugged her. "But I'd be proud to be your mother." She knew from breakroom chatter at work that Leota's family hadn't been exactly supportive of her or her career. Especially after she'd moved a few hours away to work at the design firm. But Leota was always an optimistic delight and, of all the people at work, besides Marion, Kate would probably miss Leota the most.

With Leota's help, Kate picked out paint colors. Olive green for the siding and rusty red for the shutters and door, with creamy white for the narrow strips of window trim.

"I'd stick with that neutral shade for the interior." Leota pointed to the pale taupe wall inside the door. "It'd be a good backdrop for your other colors."

"I'd brighten it up with curtains and dishes and art and rugs."

"I can just imagine how great it will look."

"So it's settled." Kate handed the paint swatches back to Kirk, showing him her choices as he wrote them down. And next he wrote up the sales contract and took her down-payment. "You can pay off the balance when you pick it up next week. I think it should be ready for pick up by Friday."

"Pick up?" Kate frowned. "Uh, how does one do that?"

"Well, short of a 350 Super Duty, which I'm guessing you don't have, I'd recommend a professional with a semi to haul it for you. I have some great guys I can set you up with. Where are you putting your house? If it's not out of state, we're happy to arrange the transport for you?"

Kate cringed. "I'm not exactly sure yet. I mean, not out of state, for certain. But I'm still figuring it out. I guess I didn't expect everything to fall into place so quickly."

He looked concerned. "You don't have a place to set it up?"

"Not exactly. But I'm thinking of Pine Ridge."

"Pine Ridge would be nice," Leota said. "I love that little town."

"So do I." Kate smiled. Yes, Pine Ridge would be the perfect place to live. She was surprised she hadn't thought of it before. Well, except that everything was happening so fast. She promised Kirk she'd let him know as soon as she knew. "Hopefully that will be very soon." She thanked him, but as she and Leota left the tiny home sales lot, her head was spinning.

"This is so exciting," Leota said as Kate parked in front of Leota's apartment complex. "And even though I'm kind of envious, I'm really happy for you."

"Thanks." Kate smiled. "And thanks for your help."

"That was just plain fun." Leota opened the door.

"Hey, what about going to Pine Ridge with me tomorrow? Or maybe you have plans."

"Plans?" She rolled those big brown eyes. "I haven't had plans since Daniel the dirty dog broke up with me a couple months ago. It probably didn't help our relationship when my little brother Erik showed up out of the blue—on the same night I was fixing dinner for Daniel. Erik was high as a kite and he and Daniel nearly got into a knockdown drag out fight. Not pretty."

"I heard about that." She wasn't sure how much to say. Daniel worked for their firm but wasn't highly respected by many—including Kate. "But I, uh, I do think you might've missed a bullet there."

Leota brightened. "Yeah, me too. Still, it stings to be dumped like that. I mean I'd rather have done the dumping myself."

"I know." Kate smiled. "So if you want to go with me, I was planning to leave around nine and make a full day of it."

Leota eagerly agreed. "Maybe I will adopt you as my mother. But that tiny house is probably too small for the both of us."

"Then you get one for yourself and we can be neighbors," Kate teased.

Leota laughed and waved, promising to be ready by nine. As Kate drove home, she still felt a bit overwhelmed. In one short week, she'd sold her house and made the down payment on a tiny house. Now she needed to find a place to put it. Feeling a rush of panic to imagine her sweet Chalet parked alongside the freeway, she shot up a quick prayer, once again asking God to direct her path.

Chapter 4

To Kate's disappointment, Leota had to bow out of accompanying her to Pine Ridge. "I want to go more than you can imagine," Leota sadly told her the next morning. "I honestly feel like I could live vicariously through you—I mean just imagining life in a tiny home in Pine Ridge, well, it's so dreamy."

"Then why don't you come along?" Kate urged.

"My older sister Clarissa." She groaned and lowered her voice. "Showed up unexpected late last night. The girl is a hot mess. And as usual, she needs money."

"Oh."

"But she's family, and I have to deal with it. Hopefully, we'll get her on her way soon. I can't have her staying here at my apartment for more than a week or two. My lease won't allow it."

"I'm sorry you can't come with me." Kate sighed. "But you're a good sister, Leota."

"Yeah, I guess."

"Just, uh, don't let Clarissa take unfair advantage of your sisterly relationship. I mean it's none of my business, but if you were *my* daughter . . . well, I'd give you the same advice."

"I'll keep it in mind. You have fun in Pine Ridge."

"Thanks. And maybe I'll find a good place for my tiny house and then, after I get settled, you can come visit me."

"Yes! I would love that. Maybe spend a whole day there with you. That'd be awesome."

"Plan on it." Kate hung up, and even though she hadn't planned to leave this early, she felt antsy to get on the road. Disappointed she'd be doing the trek alone, she stopped for a latte to go then headed out through the back of town. But as she drove, she felt anxious—would she be able to find the perfect spot for her tiny house? And if not, what would she do? Rent a lot from a place like that? She frowned at a run-down mobile home park. That was *not* what she wanted.

Determined to de-stress, she slid a smooth jazz CD into the player while waiting for the light to turn green. This trip was supposed to be relaxing and fun. Before long, she was on the back highway, snaking through rural country-side, and going back in time. This was the same route she and Kenneth used to take when the kids were little. Back when they'd had idyllic dreams of living in a town like this someday. But jobs and school and life . . . well, it had gotten in the way.

Pine Ridge was two hours and another world away. Situated in the foothills of the Cascades, right next to a clear blue mountain lake, it had always been a magical sort of town. After the kids got older, it was the place she and Kenneth had imagined retiring to . . . someday. It was hard to think about those old dreams; they'd seemed to evaporate when she lost Kenneth. But as she drove today, she pushed unhappy thoughts away from her. Like her grief counselor had often reminded Kate, the best way to honor her deceased husband was to remember the happy times—to celebrate all the goodness he'd brought into her life.

And somehow she knew Kenneth would be glad for what she was doing right now. Not just making this trip to Pine Ridge, although that was good. But he would like that she was finally taking some initiative, exercising some control over her future. Making a plan for simplicity, happiness . . . peace. Kenneth would approve.

Trying to focus on happier thoughts, Kate recalled another trip to Pine Ridge. It had been a summer Saturday, and she'd gotten up early to pack a picnic lunch, hiding it in the trunk, along with towels and swimsuits and camp chairs and things, while the kids were still in bed. Then she and Kenneth pretended like they were going to the big box store to stock up on groceries—a chore Zinnia and Jake despised. But instead, Kenneth turned the opposite direction, taking the highway to Pine Ridge. The kids were ecstatic, and the four of them spent a long, almost perfectly happy day at Pine Ridge Lake. Well, until Jake got stung by a wasp. But even that made it memorable.

They went to Pine Ridge at other times of the year too. Like in late August to buy fresh produce. Or in October, they'd trek over for the harvest fair and bring home pumpkins and apple cider. And at Christmastime to see Santa Claus and the town all lit up with Christmas lights, often with snow. As the kids grew older and busier, the long car trips lost some of their charm. But she and Kenneth were never disappointed. From the old-fashioned ice cream parlor to the quaint little tourist shops, the small town had always drawn them in.

As she got nearer town, she realized it'd been close to six years since she'd been here—shortly after Kenneth's diagnosis of stage-four pancreatic cancer. They hadn't even told the kids the devastating news yet, needing time to process it themselves. It had been a somber drive over, just listening to quiet jazz music. But then Kenneth perked up once they were in town. And Kate tried to keep things upbeat, swallowing back tears as they strolled about, reminiscing about previous visits there with the kids.

But they'd both known their lives were about to change forever. Kenneth slept all the way home. She sighed to remember how quickly his health had gone downhill from there. But then she reminded herself—that was then, this was now. She needed to move forward.

Kenneth had been great at moving forward. Between the two of them, he was usually the best planner, and the dreamer. In fact, it had been his dream to buy their oversized home—back when the kids were starting grade school. With both of them working, it was affordable, but it had been slightly overwhelming to Kate. Even back then. But because of Ken's optimism, she had bought into the dream. And then it had ended.

But now, for the first time, she was chasing after her own dream. And she knew that if Kenneth could see her now, if he could somehow watch from heaven, he'd be cheering for her. She could imagine his wide grin, giving her two thumbs-up as she drove into town. It was almost as if he was with her.

Kate was surprised to see that Pine Ridge had grown quite a bit in the past six years. There were several new shops and restaurants. But for the most part, it was the same. Charming, quaint, slow-paced. And no florist shop. Her dream, back when she'd worked at a nursery while attending art school, was to be a floral designer—to run her own florist shop. Kenneth had encouraged her to pursue that dream when Jake and Zinnia were teens. But with college tuition around the corner, the prudent thing was to remain with the design firm. But now that Jake was graduated and Zinnia only had one more term, well, times were changing.

As Kate parked her car in front of Rosie's Deli, she realized she still needed to tell her kids about this downsizing decision. For some reason she was not looking forward to that. And the best plan seemed to be to have her ducks in a row before she broke the news. It would be harder for them to discourage her if she had everything all figured out.

Rosie's used to be her and Kenneth's favorite breakfast and lunch spot and, although there were some changes and improvements in the deli, she was not disappointed. Although it felt slightly awkward to be there alone. Still, she hadn't taken time for breakfast and needed more coffee to clear the cobwebs out of her head. So instead of allowing herself time to wallow in old memories, she made small talk with a mother and daughter at the table next to hers while she waited for her order.

"I'm hoping to relocate here too," Kate confided after the older woman, Aileen Marten, explained how she'd recently retired and moved here to be nearer her daughter Jessie. "It's such a sweet town."

"I adore it here," Aileen told Kate. "Although I'm not so sure Jessie and Ryan are so happy about having me as their *full-time* houseguest. That hadn't been our plan."

"We love having you here," Jessie reassured her mom then turned back to Kate. "This town is growing fast right now. Retired baby boomers seem to be coming by the boatload. So real estate is limited. Mom's still looking for a place."

Kate quickly explained her plan to live in a tiny house and, although Aileen looked interested, Jessie admitted she couldn't imagine downsizing like that. "Especially with my three kids."

"I can understand that, but I think it'll be liberating for me," Kate declared as her breakfast sandwich arrived. "Like they say, less is more."

"Hey, remember that development south of the lake?" Jessie said to her mom. "Didn't you check it out when you first moved here?"

"Yes. It was beautiful, but they didn't have a single vacancy. Although I did get on a waiting list for a tiny home. Not that I've heard back."

"Do they have any lots available?" Kate asked eagerly.

"They seemed to have quite a few at the time. The owner said he was waiting on tiny homes. And they had quite a few houses already in place. It was all very nicely done. And the lake view! I wouldn't have minded living there. Even if it was only temporary."

Kate explained about her own tiny house. "It'll be ready in just a week."

"Then you should go look at this place." Aileen wrote the name of the development on the back of their receipt. "Although I'll warn you the lots are pretty small and close together."

"Oh?" Kate wasn't too sure about that. "I was hoping for a bit of ground, you know, to garden. I'd love a lot inside the city."

"Good luck with that." Jessie frowned.

"Yes, good luck," Aileen said. "I looked into lots. I thought I'd get a manufactured home placed. Not a single lot for sale."

"What about Uncle Hank?" Jessie said to her mom.

"But doesn't he own a farm?" Aileen asked.

"Yes, but it's a small farm. At least that's how Hank describes it. And Ryan just told me he's been talking about selling. Or even dividing it." She turned to Kate. "Hank is my husband's uncle. His property is right on the edge of town."

"I doubt that Kate wants a farm," Aileen told her daughter. "Even a small one."

"A farm would be too much for me." Kate shook her head.

"You never know." Jessie pulled out her phone to search for the number. "Uncle Hank might want to split it with you. It's rich farmland. A great place to grow things."

"How big is it?" Kate asked with growing interest. "I was hoping for enough room to grow flowers. Maybe have a greenhouse."

"There's plenty of room," Jessie assured her as she wrote a phone number on the back of the receipt. "Ryan said the only thing Hank's been growing is alfalfa. I'm guessing it's about fifty acres."

"Oh, well, fifty acres is way too much for me." Kate laughed.

"Here it is, just in case." Jessie handed her the receipt.

By the time Aileen and Jessie left, Kate had already plugged the tiny house development information into her phone. After finishing her late breakfast, she was eager to check it out. According to her phone's map, this place was on Pine Ridge Lake and not far from the state park they used to visit.

The drive was less than five minutes, probably short enough that she could ride a bike from there to town. And having an old fashioned "flat-lander" bike was another part of her downsized dream. Not that she wouldn't keep her car. But it would be fun to have a bike with a big basket in front. She could just imagine herself pedaling back and forth on this country road. Perfect!

Seeing the sign for the development— WELCOME TO PINE RIDGE ESTATES—she parked her car then got out. Feeling almost like a kid at Christmas, she walked over to where quite a few homes were already in place. Like Aileen had said, they were very close together, although they did have nice views of the lake. She did think it was odd that they looked so similar. Did this place have CC&Rs? She'd looked forward to being free from a homeowner's association.

Still, the location was spectacular. She couldn't help but smile as she strolled down the path that ran between the houses and the lake—like being at summer camp. And there seemed to be quite a few empty lots. Just waiting for their tiny homes. Maybe her house could be put in over by the water.

Although the houses all had identical siding that resembled stained cedar shakes, some of their trim colors were different. Green, red, or blue. The designs varied ever so slightly too. Some had a second floor, but most were just one level. But all had nice little porches. In some ways, they weren't so different from her tiny house. And despite the closeness, they did have the lake view. Like a mini resort. Kate felt herself being drawn in—she suddenly wanted to join this community.

"Hello?" A young woman with short blonde hair came over to her and, smiling, stuck out her hand. "I'm Kerry Stryker. I manage Pine Ridge Estates. Can I help you?"

Kate introduced herself, then quickly explained her interest, enthusiastically telling Kerry about how she'd just listed her home, was quitting her job, and was eager to live in a tiny house. "This location is just perfect," she told her. "How much are the lots going for?"

"The lots aren't for sale," Kerry explained. "They're leased."

"Leased?" Kate considered this.

"And we don't actually have anything available at the moment."

Kate pointed to the empty lots. "What about those?"

"Those are already contracted for lease and they'll have tiny houses set up within the next six months."

"So you have nothing available?"

"We might have a house available by the fall."

"I don't want a house." Kate explained about her own tiny house. "I just need a place to put it. And it's so pretty here."

"We only place our own houses here. And they're leased too. But if you're interested, I can put you on our waiting list for one if you like."

"No thanks. I don't *need* a house," Kate repeated herself, suppressing aggravation.

"Well, that's great. Hopefully you'll find a place to put your house. Real estate is pretty tight in town. If you change your mind, you can always call and get on our list for one of our houses."

Kate looked longingly toward the lake. "It is a lovely location."

"Tiny homes have become quite the trend." Kerry chuckled as if she knew an inside joke. "Although it doesn't take long for some people to discover that it's not for everyone. It's not as easy as people assume. We have a fairly high turnover rate. I already had two tenants give notice just this month. Of course, the people on our waiting list are thrilled to hear it. Eventually, it all works out."

"Right." Kate knew she was in the wrong place. "Thanks for your time."

"No problem. We're not everyone's cup of tea. But it seems to be working. My dad's the owner and developer. He thought leasing was a good way to give people a chance to discover what tiny home living is really like."

Kate felt keen disappointment. "That makes sense, but it's not for me. I want my house on my own land."

"It's possible we'll eventually sell some of the homes." Kerry shrugged. "In the meantime, I just play by Dad's rules."

"Right." Kate stared longingly at the lake.

"You do understand that the real estate in town moves extremely fast?" Kerry asked abruptly. "It's a seller's market. What few homes are available sell as soon as they're listed. Not only that, but rentals are extremely scarce in town. That's why we've become so popular out here."

"Well, I only just got to Pine Ridge. This has been a recent decision for me." Kate didn't want to admit how recent—or how she obviously hadn't thought everything through. What if she couldn't find a place for her tiny home?

The buyers for her house wanted to close in less than two weeks. Why had she agreed to cut it so close? Two weeks from now she could be literally homeless.

"Lots of people are retiring here. My dad speculates real estate will only get scarcer. That's why we're so fortunate to have all this property out here. And lakeside too." Kerry seemed a bit smug, although she made a good point.

"Well, maybe I should put myself on your list. Just in case." As Kate gave Kerry her information, she chided herself for not having researched her plan better. What if she couldn't find any place to live in Pine Ridge? What then? Would she have to park her tiny home in front of a Walmart? She'd heard that RVers parked there sometimes. Or perhaps she'd have to back out of buying it and come out here to rent one of these tiny homes. But she needed to figure something out. The clock was ticking.

Chapter 5

Kate stopped in town again, this time going into a realtor's office where she was told a similar version of what both Jessie and Kerry had said. Pine Ridge real estate, thanks to baby boomers fleeing city living, had become a very hot commodity. And bare land was even more scarce than houses.

"But I do have some properties that might interest you," the realtor reached for some flyers, first showing her an "affordable fixer-upper" in town, and a manufactured home on two acres, five miles from town. "You might be able to place a tiny home on the one outside of town."

Neither option appealed to Kate. "I really just want a bare lot," she explained for the second time, "in town or very close. That I can place my tiny house on."

The realtor grimly shook her head. "I'm not even sure you can do that in town. And there's nothing like that available right now anyway. But leave me your name and number, and I'll get back to you if something comes up."

Once again, Kate wrote down her information, but as she left the office, she felt deflated. Or even like someone had stuck a big fat pin into her beautiful balloon and her hopes of living in a tiny home in sweet little Pine Ridge and running a florist shop had exploded right in her face. Besides disappointing, it was slightly humiliating. What was she going to tell Marion? Or her colleagues? Or Leota? That she hadn't done her homework? Nothing was going as planned. Nothing was as simple and easy as on the tiny home TV show.

Kate felt ready to give up as she got into her car. What made her think she could take on something this big? And why did owning a tiny house suddenly feel so "big?" Was it too late to change direction? But then she remembered praying for God's direction, and she'd felt such a peace. Had she missed something? She leaned her head against the steering wheel and, closing her eyes, muttered another "please, show me the way," prayer. "Please, direct my path. Amen."

As she opened her eyes, a slip of white paper on the floor caught her eye. She reached for what turned out to be the deli receipt Aileen and Jessie had penned their tips onto. Besides the tiny home development, which had been a bust, was the name *Hank Branson* with a phone number. But hadn't they said fifty acres or something like that? No way could she use or even afford that much land. She wadded the paper then paused when one of Kenneth's favorite phrases wafted through her mind.

Leave no stone unturned.

"Really?" she said to herself, but she reached for her phone. She punched in "Uncle Hank's" phone number and, imagining a gray grisly farmer in overalls and straw hat on the other end, she waited.

"This is Hank," a gravelly voice said.

Kate quickly explained meeting his niece-in-law and her mother. "They seemed to think you might have property for sale," she said tentatively. "It's probably too large for what I want, but—well, I'm feeling a little desperate just now." Her voice trailed off. Really, this was ridiculous. She should just hang up.

"Desperate? What do you mean?"

She explained about her tiny house and dream of living in Pine Ridge and how she'd quit her job and wanted to grow and sell flowers—and everything. "I'm sorry. I'm sure this is what my daughter would call TMI."

"TMI?"

"Too much information."

He chuckled. "Well, you're right, my property is probably too much for you. But you're welcome to come out and see it if you want. I've considered partitioning, and I'm in the UGB so it's feasible."

"UGB?"

"Urban growth boundary. That's for land bordering the city limits. And that means it can be rezoned. Especially nowadays with the scarcity of real estate in town. I've been approached more times than I can count about selling for a subdivision. But having a bunch of tract homes out here doesn't interest me."

"So you're pretty close to town then?" She felt a trickle of hope.

"Just a ten minute walk from the edge of my land."

"And you'd really consider selling just a section of it?" It seemed too good to be true.

"I might. Under the right circumstances. But let's not get the cart ahead of the horse here. You haven't even seen it yet. And I'd need to hear more about your plans for using it."

"I'd love to see it."

"I'm out here right now if you want to stop by."

She assured him she did, and he gave her directions. Within minutes she was driving down a long, graveled driveway, surrounded by a bright green crop of what she assumed was alfalfa. Up ahead, she spotted a two-story log home and a big red barn. A very well maintained and attractive setup. And obviously way beyond her price range. Not that she'd be interested in buying the house and barn. But property like this—even just a few acres—wouldn't be cheap.

Parked in front of the house was an old olive green pickup with a lanky guy climbing out. Like she'd imagined, he wore a straw hat, but it was a cowboy hat. And instead of overalls, he had on worn blue jeans and a faded plaid western shirt with the sleeves rolled up to the elbows. And he wasn't old. But not young either. Maybe fifty-something? She parked her SUV in front of the house and got out.

"Hank?" she called out as she approached him, but before he could answer, a flash of black and white fur streaked around from the other side of the pickup, racing toward her and barking wildly.

"It's okay," she said, trying to keep her voice calm as she extended her hand, palm and fingers toward her. "I'm friend not foe."

"Chester, stop!" The man whistled sharply, and the dog came to a halt just a couple feet from her.

"He won't hurt you," he called out. "Come, Chester." He continued toward her with a friendly smile. "He likes to announce visitors. It's his most important job. Sit, Chester." He snapped his fingers, pointing downward and—just like that—the dog sat, head erect, as if at attention.

"Mr. Branson?" Kate asked the man, trying not to act as rattled as she felt.

"That's me." He stuck out his hand. "Just call me Hank."

"I'm Kate Burrows." She shook his hand and then knelt down by the dog. "You're a good boy, Chester. You mind really well." She glanced up. "Can I pet him?"

"Sure, but Chester can be a little standoffish with strangers."

She reached down to pet his smooth head then ran her fingers through the long silky fur around his neck. "You're a good watchdog, Chester."

The tail switched back and forth and then he licked her hand a few times.

"Well, Chester seems to approve." Hank chuckled. "You never can tell."

Kate stood, taking a moment to study the tanned face. He had attractive creases at the edges of his sky-blue eyes—either from the sun or perhaps he smiled a lot. His sandy colored hair had some gray streaks and curled around his ears below the cowboy hat in a boyishly attractive way. Although this guy was not a boy. Kate suddenly felt herself blushing to realize he was super good looking.

"Welcome to my little ranch." He waved his hand toward a green field. "I only grow alfalfa these days. The older I get, the more I want to scale down. *Need* to scale down."

"You don't seem that old." She instantly wished she hadn't said that.

But he just smiled. "I turn sixty in August. Seems plenty old to me."

"Oh." She nodded. "Well, you don't look sixty."

He chuckled. "I guess hard work either keeps you young or makes you old. Not sure I've got it all figured out just yet."

Worried she was staring at him, she glanced

out over his farm. "It's a beautiful place. But I'm guessing way out of my price range. I mean even just a little piece of it. Not that you'd want to sell just a little piece. But like I told you, I only need enough room for a tiny house. I should probably be looking for a small lot. But there really aren't any in town. I was just at the realtor's. It all seems pretty hopeless." She knew she was babbling now, but it was her way of covering up the nervousness rustling around inside of her. She was way out of her element.

"How about we take a walk," he suggested. "I'll show you the portion of land I've been considering partitioning." With Chester trailing them, Hank led her along a fence line until they reached a metal gate that he opened for her. "I used to keep cattle out here, but that got to be too much work. Especially in winter. And I'm not really a farmer. Not a full time one anyway. I guess I'm what they used to call a gentleman farmer, but that's always seemed like an oxymoron to me. Especially when you're out there in the pouring rain, chasing cows that broke through a fence." He chuckled. "Nothing gentlemanly about that."

"Sounds exciting."

"The kind of excitement I can live without. Especially with a bad back."

"Bad back?"

"Old injury from rodeoing as a kid. Nothing

too serious. Mostly just aggravating. Especially as I get older."

"Uh-huh." She watched as Chester ran toward a grove of trees up ahead. "That's a pretty scene."

"Those aspens got planted nearly thirty years ago. My wife wanted them along one side of the irrigation pond to create a shady oasis in the summertime. It's a nice spot, but I've considered selling."

"Wouldn't you miss it? It's so lovely."

"My wife had wanted me to build our house closer to the pond, but I liked it back there where it is. You get a better view of the mountains over there." He turned around and pointed. "See, they're visible from here too. Just not as good."

"Oh, wow, that's really beautiful." She felt incredulous. "You wouldn't *really* sell this piece of your land, would you? And, if so, why? Is there anything wrong with it?"

"Not really." He rubbed his chin. "Good question." His brow creased as he started walking again. "So, tell me more about you? Why Pine Ridge? Why a tiny house?"

As they continued toward the aspens, she explained about being widowed and her grown kids, and how she longed for a change. "To be honest, it was ignited by binge watching this tiny house TV show one rainy weekend. It's like I got hooked or something."

"No kidding." He laughed.

"But I think I was simply ready for something different." She explained about quitting her job, selling her house, and purchasing the tiny home that was getting painted next week. "I haven't even told my kids any of this yet." She grimaced. "And most of my coworkers think I've lost my mind. But my house was way too big. Something smaller sounds good. And I've always wanted to live in Pine Ridge. I'd love to have a bit of land. Not a whole farm, mind you. And probably not enough to make sense of you dividing your acreage. But I'd like enough land to grow flowers and build a good-sized greenhouse." She explained about wanting to have a florist shop in town.

"Sounds like you're a real dreamer."

She sighed. "To be honest, that was my husband's gift. I was always the practical one. Stick to the plan. Don't take risks. He was the one with big dreams."

"How did he die?"

She explained about the pancreatic cancer. "It all happened so fast. In a way, I guess it was a blessing because he didn't suffer for long. And yet we all had time to say good-bye. Still, it was hard. He was only fifty-two." A familiar lump rose in her throat.

"How long ago?"

"Little over five years."

"I'm sorry."

They were in the aspens now, shady and cool. In front of them was what appeared to be a large manmade pond, but very natural looking. "This is really lovely," she said quietly. "A lot bigger than I imagined. It looks more like a small lake than a pond."

"It was just an old irrigation pond when we bought the place, but my wife—the dreamer in our family—anyway, she planted all these trees. Elizabeth wanted to make this spot into something very special. She had the pond dug deeper and bigger. There's a natural underground spring that feeds it. She envisioned this as a glorious getaway where our kids could come for picnics and catch frogs. Swim in the summertime. Maybe stock the pond with trout. And in the autumn, she imagined how we'd make bonfires and invite friends out. Maybe the kids would ice skate on it in winter, if it froze hard enough." He sighed. "Not that it ever happened."

"It never froze hard?"

"No, no, we've had plenty of hard freezes. I meant Elizabeth and I never had kids, or too many of those other fun times she dreamed about. Not like that anyway." He let out another sigh as he sat down on an old wooden bench that looked like it could collapse at any given moment. Meanwhile, Chester sank to his belly in a soft looking patch of cool green grass.

"Oh." Kate wasn't sure what to say and

wondered if it was safe to sit on that rickety bench. For some reason, she felt like an intruder now. As if this was a sacred spot. And, somehow, she knew something bad must've happened between Hank and Elizabeth. Had they split up?

"It's okay." He patted the bench seat next to him. "It's sturdier than it looks."

She gingerly sat, unsure of her next move, but fairly certain that Hank was caught up in some gloomy memory.

"You see, I lost my wife to cancer too," he spoke quietly. "I guess we're in the same sort of boat."

"Oh." She sadly shook her head. "I'm so sorry."

"It's only been three years for me." He leaned forward, elbows on his knees, slowly shaking his head. "Longest three years of my life."

"I know what that feels like." She gazed across the pond's glossy surface, seeing the quivering green leaves of the aspen trees reflected there.

"But Elizabeth's cancer dragged out a lot longer than your husband's. She was in her thirties when she got her first diagnosis. But she battled it and we thought she won. She was in remission for six years. Then the cancer came back—even worse than the first time. But she believed she could beat it again. She was really brave . . . but she lost the battle."

"I'm so sorry. That must've been hard."

"Yep." He slowly exhaled. "What was that

acronym you used on the phone? TMI? I guess I'm guilty of that too. Weird because I don't usually go on like this about Elizabeth. Maybe there's something in the air today. Or being out here. I never come out here much. I used to call it Elizabeth's pond."

She listened to the birds singing in the trees. "It's a beautiful spot. I can't imagine you'd really want to sell it."

"I do. And I don't. I mean, you're right, it's pretty enough out here. But it always makes me sad. So, really, what's the point? Besides, I do need the money. Still paying off medical bills, trying to get myself set up for retirement . . . someday."

"Oh." Kate wondered if that would cut her out. She didn't have a ton of money to invest in bare land. Not if she wanted to start her florist business.

"Elizabeth would've been almost fifty by now." He sighed. "Ten years younger than me."

That would make her four years younger than Kate. Only forty-seven when she died. Too young. A heavy cloak of sadness encompassed Kate. She felt sad about Elizabeth. And sad about Kenneth. Sad that Hank still seemed to be in pain. And sad that this beautiful property probably wasn't right for her. Not such a desirable location if it was so full of sorrow, unrealized dreams. Heartache. She stood up, swallowing against the growing lump in her throat. "Well, I appreciate you taking the time to show me the pond." Her voice choked with emotion. "I—I'm sorry if it sent you to a dark place."

Hank stood too. "I'm the one who should be sorry. I apologize for sounding so morose. Honestly, I'm not usually like this. I guess it's being out here caught me off guard."

"It's okay. I understand." She took in a deep breath. "I have my ups and downs too. I know it sounds trite, but it does get better with time. I've had five years."

"One of my buddies keeps telling me to go to grief counseling. But I sort of feel like I just did that now." His half-smile made the edges of his eyes crinkle. "How much do I owe you, ma'am?"

"Not a penny." She brightened. "My therapist says there's nothing better than just honestly talking about our feelings. Good, bad, and ugly. It helps to flush things out. And eventually helps us move on."

"Uh-huh." He sounded doubtful. "So anyway, back to your tiny house plans? I'd be willing to partition off a smaller parcel. Say, five acres? That'd give you plenty of room to grow flowers. Do you think you could be happy out here?"

"Are you kidding? I'd be ecstatic to live in such a beautiful place."

He pointed to a fence line alongside the road. "That borders the city, so after annexation, you'd have to figure out your utilities with them. But I can assure you, they'll be happy to work with you. They're pretty eager to bite into the UGB."

"So, you're saying this is really doable?" She could hardly believe it. And although she had no idea what five acres of this lovely land would go for, she doubted she could afford it. Even if she had to eat beans and rice for a year or two. It'd be worth it.

"You're sure you'd be okay living out here all by yourself? It's pretty isolated. Might be a little lonely."

"I'll admit it'd be a big adjustment for me." She glanced around, wondering what it'd really be like to have her tiny house out here all by itself. At Pine Ridge Lake Estates the tiny homes might've been squeezed tightly together, but at least there were neighbors.

"Maybe you could invite a few others to join you. Start yourself a regular tiny house community."

"Tiny house neighbors?" She considered this idea—and liked it. "Do you really think that would be okay? I mean you'd agree to something like that? A few other tiny homes?"

"Don't see that I'd even notice. Thanks to the barn and positioning of the house, this area isn't even visible from over there."

"Would it even be allowed? Would the city have some sort of ordinances or anything?"

"I'm actually an architect—well, most of the time anyway." He smiled. "So I'm fairly familiar with city building and developmental codes. Although I wouldn't call myself an authority on zoning, I'm pretty sure tiny houses are considered temporary-use structures—because they're moveable. And, naturally, they can't be too big, hence the term tiny home. But I suspect if you stayed within the city's parameters, they wouldn't object."

"So maybe I could have a few neighbors? I mean if I were to buy five acres from you. You'd really be okay with a few more tiny homes? Like maybe three or four more?" Suddenly she imagined several tiny houses situated here and there around the pond. It all seemed rather charming.

"I actually think it's an intriguing idea. As long as it's done right." He tipped his head to one side. "I'd want thoughtful planning behind it."

"Of course. So would I."

"And I'd like to see it drawn out on paper first, but I could do that myself."

"And I could maybe do some artist sketches to show you what I'm thinking," she offered. "I'd want it to be attractive as well."

"You're an artist?"

"Sort of. Mostly I've been a designer. But I dabble some. I'd really love to put my creative energies into flowers."

"Plenty of sunshine here. They'd probably do well."

"It'd be fun to have the pond be like the centerpiece for this development."

"I agree. Have you seen the development out by the lake?"

"Just this morning. What a gorgeous location. But this could be pretty too."

"This is going to sound crazy, but the idea of a tiny house development on my property is turning out to be kind of appealing."

"Seriously?" She blinked.

"Yeah. When I first saw that one at the lake—a friend of mine, Glen Stryker, had just started to develop it—well, it sort of piqued my interest. But Elizabeth was really sick around the same time, and I had enough on my plate. Still, I thought Glen could be onto something. For a while I actually toyed with the idea of designing some tiny homes myself. I even did some research on it. But life got busy." He frowned, and she suspected he was referring to Elizabeth's illness again.

Not wanting to see Hank grow blue again, Kate told him about her visit to Pine Ridge Lake Estates, and how disappointed she'd been to discover they were only leasing the houses. "That excludes people like me who own their tiny home. Wouldn't it be fun to create an attractive place where people could park their own tiny homes? Naturally, you'd want some control. You know, so it didn't look junky or get out of hand. But you could still allow for different designs and personalities."

"And you'd want roomier lots. The ones by the lake are too small." He told her more about his friend. "Glen bought that land more than thirty years ago. Steal of a deal too. He did some early on development then just sat on it for years. I'll admit that I thought it was kind of a nutty idea when I first heard about the tiny house development. But when I went out there to see it for myself, when he was just starting it up, well, I was pretty impressed. Glen seemed to be doing it right."

"Right for him maybe. But it's not for everyone. Not for me anyway. And your niece's mother Aileen—"

"You know Aileen?"

"I just met her. She looked out there too, put herself on the waiting list."

"Do you think she'd want a tiny home out here?" He rubbed his chin. "Maybe we need to dream bigger. Maybe my land has the potential to be a real tiny house community."

"Would you seriously want to do that?" She felt a flash of hope. If Hank was willing to create a tiny house development, it would take the pressure off her. Besides, he was an architect and probably understood these things much better than she did. Still, a part of her wanted to be involved. Yet, at the same time, the thought of building something like that was overwhelming. And how long would it take for it to get rolling? And what about her? She needed a place to park her tiny house—ASAP!

Chapter 6

As they walked back toward the house, they both were tossing out ideas—left and right, fast and furious. One would suggest an idea and the other would hitchhike on it. Both were enthused and clearly on the same page. Kate was astonished over how fully on-board Hank seemed. By the time they were standing in the driveway, they had a solid beginning of a rather interesting plan.

"I can imagine twenty to thirty pie-shaped lots." He used his hands to show her. "Encircling the pond like this. All faced toward the water with the narrow part of the lot in front and the wide part in back. Then we could create a walking trail to circle the pond, both for strolling and for connecting the houses. Access to the development would come from the east end, right into the main road. Just minutes to town."

"Would people have places to park cars?" she asked.

"What about a holding area? People could park vehicles away from the tiny houses. That would reduce engine noise and exhaust fumes."

"Although it would require some walking." She imagined herself carrying groceries in the middle of winter. "It could be a hardship for some."

"That's true. We might have to rethink."

"But I do love the idea of having the homes situated in a quiet and peaceful sort of place." She opened her car door.

"I think Glen uses golf carts at Pine Ridge Lake Estates. Maybe we'd want something like that to help folks get around."

"Not a bad idea."

"In fact, I'd love to go pay old Glen a visit. Pick his brain a little."

"Will he see you as competition?"

Hank shrugged. "Seems to me he's got all the business he can handle. Waiting lists and a lack of real estate in town. His hands are full. Besides, our place would be different."

"What about pets? I noticed in the Pine Ridge Lake Estates brochure that it's a no pet zone." She reached down to pat Chester's head. "And I've been dreaming of getting a dog."

"You should get a dog." He nodded eagerly. "Our place will definitely be pet friendly. Don't you think?"

"Absolutely."

"And we'll allow fenced yards," he said. "Maybe we'll fence them first. That way people would have privacy too."

"I like that, but all this takes money," Kate spoke slowly now. "I have some to invest, but not enough for all that. And you did mention you have medical bills." Were they both just sharing an impossible pipe dream?

"If we sell leases on the lots, that should cover a lot of the initial expenses—like water, electric, sewer. Plus the city might have some incentives since we'd be providing some much-needed affordable housing options. I have tractors and tools to do a lot of the development myself. And my nephew Zeb will probably want to help out. He's my right-hand man on the farm. I bet we could come up with lots of ways to save money and cut some corners. Then, once we're up and running, there'd be monthly income to cover more improvements and maintenance, as well as some profits to share."

She nodded. "That does make sense."

"Plus I could always sell off another portion of my land. Not for tract houses though. But I had considered portioning some bigger parcels for larger homes. Maybe ones of my own design. If this whole thing is done right, it could be pretty nice."

She glanced over to his log home. "Will you keep your beautiful house?"

He shrugged. "I don't know. I like it, but part of me doesn't really care. It's way too big for me. Even with my nephew, it's way more than we need. Maybe I'll want a tiny house too."

She laughed. "I guess it's contagious."

"I can actually imagine the whole thing." His eyes sparkled with enthusiasm. "It could be pretty cool, Kate. To be honest, it's been lonely out here these past few years. But I just haven't wanted to give up on it. Not completely."

Kate wasn't sure what to do next. Did they need to shake hands or get something in writing? How did one go about setting up a business venture like this? And was she being foolish? Good grief, she'd barely met this man—and now she was considering partnering with him on what was probably a risky investment venture? Yet, it felt right. And it was exciting.

"Come on up to the front porch for some tea or lemonade and we can hash this out some more," he suggested. "I really think we're onto something big." He laughed. "That is, if you can call a tiny home big."

As they drank lemonade, Chester lay his head on Kate's lap, and Hank got out some drafting paper. First he drew up some sketches of how he saw the development. She made some suggestions and, with his architectural skill and her design background, it didn't take long to have a rough draft laid out before them. Even with some dimensions.

Kate blinked. "This actually seems really doable, Hank. I'm kind of in shock."

"It is doable. But it'll take work. Are you sure you want to partner with me on this?" He looked at her. "I mean, we hardly know each other . . . and yet I feel like I do know you. Like I can trust you."

"I feel the same." She nodded nervously. "And if you're willing to invest in this, I am too."

"I'll talk to my lawyer tomorrow. I'll ask him to draft some kind of agreement to protect both of us." He neatly rolled up the large pieces of paper containing their plans and notes.

"Yes, good idea."

"Then I'll talk to the city about incentives and permits and utility hookups."

"I feel guilty now. It seems like you're doing all the work."

"Maybe for now. But once you get moved here proper, you can roll up your sleeves too." He put a rubber band around the paper roll. "Speaking of moving. Didn't you say you needed a place to park your tiny house? By next weekend?"

"Yes." She nodded. "But I can't imagine our development will be ready that soon."

He laughed. "That's for sure. But you could park it over there." He pointed to a concrete pad next to the barn. "You'd have water and electric to connect with. It's not as scenic as by the pond, but it'd be a place to live."

"You wouldn't mind?"

He smiled. "I'd like to have a neighbor." He nodded at Chester, his head still resting on Kate's lap as she petted his ear. "And he seems to approve of you too."

She stuck out her hand. "It's a deal then. I'll

have my tiny home transported here. Maybe as soon as a week from now, if that's okay."

"Perfect." He grasped her hand in a handshake and, as their eyes locked, Kate experienced an electric-like shiver shooting through her. A sensation she hadn't experienced since Kenneth. It was both thrilling and frightening. She quickly pulled back her hand.

"I, uh, better be on my way. It's a two-hour drive." She stood, awkwardly knocking Chester aside. "And I have work in the morning."

He nodded. "And I still have some engineering reports to go over before tomorrow's meeting with a client."

"Thanks for everything." She smiled. "I have to admit, I'm a little overwhelmed. I can't believe we're really going to do this. It's kind of amazing."

"Well, it was sort of your idea." He stood. "I just kind of hitchhiked onto it."

As he walked her to her car, he promised to be in touch with any news from his attorney or the city. "I'll keep you fully informed."

She waved as she drove down the driveway, watching him in her rearview mirror and wondering, *Is this really real?* The whole thing had a weird, dreamy quality to it—and it was a bit unnerving. And yet, it was exhilarating. Kate took in a slow deep breath. Whatever this was, it promised to be an exciting ride.

• • •

The farther Kate got from Pine Ridge, the more doubtful she became. Oh, sure, Hank had been interesting, charming, and handsome. But what did she really know about the man? Certainly not enough to become a partner in a major development like this. What had she gotten herself into? How would she get herself out of it? At least there'd been no contracts signed, no exchange of finances. Not yet anyway. Not too late to pull the plug.

As she turned into the city, she recalled horror stories she'd heard of older women being scammed for hundreds of thousands, even millions. Not that she had millions. But she did have a nice little nest egg . . . and her house sell money by the end of next week. Usually those nasty phishing scams happened online, usually by someone from Nigeria pretending to be someone who looked like Hank Branson. But Hank Branson had stolen no one's identity. She'd actually met his niece-in-law Jessie and her mother Aileen. They'd seemed nice and normal.

Still, she couldn't be too careful. What if she was in over her head? What if she lost everything in this harebrained scheme? Partnering in a tiny home development with a perfect stranger? *Oh, he was perfect, wasn't he?*

"Stop it, stop it!" she scolded herself out loud as she turned into her own neighborhood. For a moment she was shocked to see how all the oversized homes looked freakily similar—her house was almost unrecognizable to her. As if she'd been gone for a long time and barely remembered her home. Although it wasn't really her home. New buyers wanted occupancy by the following weekend. Was that even possible?

Oh, dear, she really was in over her head. How was she going to pull this whole thing off? It was nearly five o'clock, and all she wanted was a nice long nap. But seeing the state of her house, with stuff she'd started to sift and sort all over the place, she knew it was time to get to work.

So instead of napping, Kate returned to the overwhelming task of sorting through her house. She had a lot to get done in one short week. How was she going to do it all? She started with the kitchen, where she'd already emptied a few of the cabinets. She began to set things she thought she could use in her tiny home on the island and everything else on the counters. But what would she do with all of it? She had no idea.

It was nearly midnight by the time she got ready for bed—and her kitchen and great room looked like a natural disaster had hit . . . or maybe just a poorly organized garage sale. As she got into bed she thought maybe that's what she needed—a great big honking garage sale. Except there just wasn't time. Why hadn't she considered all this sooner—before she'd set the works in motion to move into her tiny home?

Kate had never been a particularly impetuous person before. What had she gotten herself into? But as she dozed off, she had a thought that encouraged her. Hank. At the end of this chaotic week of packing, storing, and getting out of her oversized house, there was Hank and his beautiful farm. And Chester.

Chapter 7

By Tuesday night, Kate knew she was in way over her head. Despite renting a storage unit and reserving a moving truck for Saturday, and growing stacks of packed boxes piled in her garage, she knew this task was impossible. Just the sight of her house, now turned upside down and inside out, made her feel ill.

Even so, she got up early the next morning, determined to get some sorting, sifting, and packing done. Except that it felt useless. It was too much. She couldn't do this. So, before going to work, she called Jennifer, begging her for an extra week before the buyers moved in.

Jennifer reminded her that she'd signed a contract. "And the buyers would've loved to have moved in even sooner. Did I mention they're staying in a hotel downtown? With three kids under the age of seven? Can you imagine?"

"No." Kate looked around her disaster of a house. "But I also can't imagine getting this place cleared out by the weekend for them."

"There are other houses like yours on the market. If you start backing out of this deal, we could lose our buyers. Our eager cash buyers. Do you want to risk that?"

Kate thought about her sweet tiny house getting

painted this week, and about Hank's lovely farm. "No, I guess not."

"Then you don't want to rock their boat by breaking, changing, or extending the sales contract, do you? Because, don't forget, they plan on taking occupancy on Saturday afternoon. No ifs, ands, or buts."

"I haven't forgotten, and I'm doing my best. But I have so much stuff. An accumulation of nearly thirty years of marriage and children. How do you get rid of all that in a few days? I already have a huge donation pile, and I've called Salvation Army to pick it up. But there's the kids' stuff to sort through. And Kenneth's things—all the memorabilia, family heirlooms, collectibles—it's overwhelming." Kate choked back a sob.

"That's what happens when you move," she said gently. "But you're a strong woman, Kate. You can handle this. Just take it one step at a time. You know what they say about eating an elephant. It's one bite at—"

"My house is a total freaking mess! I don't mean a little cluttered disarray. I mean it's a complete, wall-to-wall, horribly hopeless mess." She explained in a bit more detail, but Jennifer still acted as if this was perfectly normal, par for the course.

Kate let out a choked sob. "I'm afraid I've made a huge mistake. I never should've quit my job and sold my house so quickly. It's just impossible to—"

"Tell you what, I'll pop over this morning and give you some suggestions."

"But I have to go to work."

"You're kidding? You're trying to work and move at the same time? By yourself? Oh, Kate, that is insane."

"Thanks for your encouragement." Kate sniffed.

"You need serious help."

"Mental health help?" Kate said weakly.

"No, silly, hands-on help."

"My friend from work offered to help, but I honestly wouldn't even know how to direct her. It feels like every single item in this house needs me to think and decide. And there are thousands, maybe millions, of items. My poor brain is just muddled. It's because we're moving too fast. Can't we please beg the buyers for more time? Just an extra week or two? Or shut it down completely."

"How about I come over after work. If you've really truly made a mistake, we'll pull the plug on the sale. It won't be easy, but it's doable. Although I really believe you're just having the home-selling jitters. And if not, well, we'll just deal with it. See you around five-thirty. And I'll bring food."

Kate thanked her and, after hanging up the

phone, blew her nose on a paper towel. But she did not feel a bit better. As much as she appreciated Jennifer's attempt to talk her off the ledge, Kate knew clearing this house by Saturday was impossible. Selling was impossible. Living in a tiny home was impossible. She had failed. Sure, it would be hard to admit this to others, but Kate knew for certain that she was not cut out for downsizing. Even the lure of Hank's lovely farm had lost its initial appeal. Kate felt helpless . . . and hopeless.

Barely home from work, Kate had just changed into sweats when Jennifer arrived. She was dressed in jeans and a T-shirt and armed with pizza and coffee. But instead of coming in, she simply stood in the foyer, staring around her with an astonished expression. "You weren't kidding, were you?"

"Welcome to my world," Kate said in a flat tone.

Jennifer came into the great room, and her eyes grew even wider. She slowly shook her head with a look of utter disbelief. "Wow, this is a lot of stuff."

Kate sighed. This was not encouraging. "Be careful." She watched nervously as Jennifer navigated through a heap of sporting goods debris. Hopefully she wouldn't trip and break her neck. That would be awkward. "I tried to warn you."

"Just because this is, well, a great big fat mess—that doesn't mean we can't do this, Kate. Don't give up on your goal just because of this. You wanted to downsize. Remember? And it takes work to get there."

"Tell me about it." Kate cleared off a box of office supplies from the sectional so Jennifer could sit. "I'm just so frustrated." She swept a pile of holiday table linens off the ottoman to make room for the pizza box.

"I'm not surprised." Jennifer handed Kate the coffee carrier and set down the pizza box. "But you can't let your frustration drive your decision."

"I know." Kate removed a cup of coffee. "I'm just worried I jumped into this too quickly."

"That's quite possibly true," Jennifer said in a pragmatic tone. "But I happen to believe some of the best decisions are ones we make quickly." She reached for a piece of pizza. "So remind me of your goals. What first motivated you to sell your house?"

Kate sheepishly admitted binge-watching the TV show. "I wanted to live simply."

Jennifer nodded with an amused smile.

"It was like I was obsessed," Kate continued. "I could really imagine myself being happy in a tiny house. I dreamed of a fresh start. Living in a small town. Running a florist business. It all felt so right." Kate told Jennifer about getting a good deal on the model tiny home and her trip to Pine Ridge. She even told her about meeting Hank and their spontaneous plans for a tiny house development on his farm.

"How exciting! That really does sound wonderful. It seems like a lot of pieces are already falling into place for you. I can't believe you're willing to let that dream go."

"I guess I'm not. Not really."

"But you sounded like you wanted to pull the plug on the sale."

"I just wanted an extension," she said hopefully. "Just another week."

"I already told you that would probably kill the deal. And, honestly, you don't want to go back to your old job, do you? Or to remain here in your oversized McMansion? And, really, you don't want to keep all this stuff?" She plucked a sad looking wreath from a box of dusty holiday decorations. "You'd give up your dream for this?"

"No! Of course not!" Kate exclaimed. "It's just that I'm overwhelmed. I don't think I can do this. Not this fast anyway. Every time I get started on packing, it seems to unravel. I get distracted. I can't make up my mind about what to do with everything."

"I get that. And that's why I'm here instead of home cooking dinner for Rod and the kids."

Kate felt guilty now. It seemed her problem had

become Jennifer's problem. But then, Jennifer didn't want to rock the buyers' boat by asking for another week, so maybe it really was her problem.

Jennifer took in another slow look at the great room then grimaced. "I think we need to get you some serious help." She pulled out her phone. "I have a friend who's an organizational guru. And she owes me a favor."

"Do you think she'd be—"

"We won't know unless I ask." Jennifer was already calling her. "Hey, Rose, we really need Superwoman. Are you available?" She held the phone out so Kate could hear the laughter on the other end. "You are too Superwoman," Jennifer continued. "And I have a friend who needs to downsize in a big way. And she needs it pronto. I mean like right now. Or tomorrow morning at the latest. Any chance you could help out?" She explained the urgency and about Kate needing to work then waited for an answer, eventually breaking into a huge smile. "Thank you so much!" she exclaimed. "That's fabulous." She gave Rose the address and hung up.

"Good news?" Kate felt a smidgeon of hope.

"Not only is Rose coming, she's bringing her assistant, Seth. They'll be here by seven tomorrow so they can talk to you before you go to work." She took a sip of coffee. "But I should probably warn you about a few things."

"Warn me?"

"I've done organizational projects with Rose before. You need to grasp that she's no-nonsense when it comes to organization. She hates wasting time. And she has zero patience for whiners."

Kate considered this. "Well, I'm not usually a whiner."

"Rose can be relentless. Some people call her ruthless. Plus she expects you to trust her judgment. Quite honestly, she can come across like a bulldozer at times. But she does get the job done."

"So she'll do this while I'm at work?"

"You'll have to give her some instructions, get her on the same page. And I wouldn't leave anything out that you don't want disposed of because you never know."

Kate took in a deep breath, mulling over this information. "I probably do need someone like Rose."

Jennifer grinned. "And we're lucky she's available—and that she owed me a favor. So that gives us this evening to get things ready for Rose to do her magic tomorrow. She's really amazing."

Kate nodded nervously, imagining a loud-mouthed bossy woman wearing a Superwoman cape and driving a bulldozer through Kate's great room while swinging a fist in the air, declaring, *"Less is more!"*

• • •

Even with Jennifer's help in preparation for Superwoman, Kate's house still looked like a disaster area by the time she went to bed—again around midnight. She was so exhausted and sore from carrying stuff downstairs and into the garage, she doubted she'd be able to get up in the morning. And after she got in bed, all she could see in her mind's eye was cardboard boxes. And the word "downsize" sounded like a very bad expletive.

But when she jolted awake at 5:13 a.m., muttering, *"Less is more—less is more,"* she could hardly breathe. Was she having a heart attack? Then she remembered her claustrophobic nightmare—she'd been trapped in a windowless storage unit, piled to the ceiling with soggy, mildewed boxes. Unable to breathe, death was inescapable. With her heart still pounding and panting like she'd just sprinted a mile, Kate sat up in bed.

Once again, she felt certain she'd made a huge mistake. She should simply cancel her house sale. Pay the buyers whatever fees were necessary to shut this thing down. Jennifer wouldn't like it, but she'd said it wasn't impossible.

Unable to return to sleep, and aware that Rose and Seth would be here by seven, Kate crawled out of her king-sized bed, which was still heaped with a mountain of clothes that she needed to sift through. She pushed through a dangerous mound of shoes and boots clogging the doorway of her walk-in closet, trying to find her bathrobe, which seemed to be AWOL. No question about it—less really could be more. If only she could figure out how to get there from here. Or else just pull the plug.

Like going through a minefield, Kate picked her way through her oversized house which had never looked worse. Thanks to Jennifer's help, every cabinet, closet and storage area had been emptied last night. Piles of beach towels, bed linens, Halloween decorations, and miscellaneous toiletries were heaped on the dining room table. The foyer looked like a sporting goods mark-down sale of tennis racquets, golf clubs, baseball bats, lacrosse sticks, ski boots.

What once had been her family's orderly peaceful domain now appeared to be sick, as if the whole house had regurgitated onto itself. If someone snuck in here to take photos, they could probably lure one of those hoarding TV shows to feature her house. And quite honestly, she wasn't sure she'd even mind—as long as they helped her to get rid of all this stuff. But then she remembered, oh yeah, that's why Rose and Seth were coming. Maybe it wasn't as hopeless as it looked.

As Kate kicked a deflated soccer ball toward the front door, she wondered why she'd been chosen to become the "keeper of the stuff." Most of this junk wasn't even hers. Snowboards, skateboards, bicycles, roller skates—why was it up to her to manage Jake's and Zinnia's and Kenneth's old stuff? And yet she wasn't ready to tell her kids about what she was up to . . . not yet. And she'd already set aside the items she knew they wouldn't want to part with to go into storage. But that still left a lot to do. And the buyers wanted to move in this weekend. Kate glanced at the stove clock, realizing she had about ninety minutes to do more sorting before Rose and Seth got here.

One of her priorities was to make sure she had what she'd need in her tiny home. She had a special spot in the garage designated for that. But it had gotten rather full. And she knew that even that needed some serious pruning. But pruning, while simple with rosebushes, was another matter altogether with household goods. Perhaps she could leave that for later.

Right now, the important thing was to glean any of her kids' items that she wouldn't want to disappear. It was okay if they got buried in her storage unit. Jake and Zinnia could sort through all that later. Maybe this summer. But as she picked her way through the house and their old bedrooms, all she saw was heaps and piles of junk. Junk, junk, junk. Did they or anyone else really want any of it? She couldn't think.

Hoping caffeine might help clear her head,

Kate returned to the kitchen. Shoving aside a small mountain of storage containers to look for the coffee maker, she felt certain those little plastic boxes must've multiplied in the corners of her cabinets over the years. Finally, she unearthed her coffee maker, but it took several minutes to locate the bag of coffee beans, and she had no idea where the grinder was hiding. She looked behind Crock-Pots, a bread-maker, and the never used fondue pot until she finally found the grinder. At least she knew where these items were going. She would definitely want her coffee making supplies in her new tiny home. She'd be sure to tell Rose that.

With a strong pot of coffee brewing, which she hoped would jumpstart her brain, Kate began to assemble yet another packing box. Never mind that she had a dozen boxes sitting around half filled. But perhaps this box would change the tide. She would use it for any last items that she wanted to be spared from Rose's ruthless organizational skills.

Then thinking she should utilize this time to keep packing, she picked up a chipped milk-glass candy dish that anyone else would probably just toss. But Kate wasn't so sure. It had been given to her by her grandmother. As a little girl, she'd kept pennies in it and had held onto it for close to fifty years. How did you just throw something like that away? And yet she didn't want it, didn't need it, probably wouldn't even miss it.

Why was it so difficult to sort through these belongings? Why did she keep getting waylaid? Like now, about to get some momentum, she was suddenly launched into a sentimental journey down memory lane. This was not an efficient way to get rid of stuff. But she couldn't seem to help herself.

And so she assembled even more empty cardboard boxes, stacking them on top of each other like building blocks. As she stacked, she tried to remember the "sorting" plan Jennifer had explained to her last night. Ways to determine what should be saved. Did she love it or lose it or use it or need it? It was all mixed up in her head now. Or maybe it had simply evaporated into thin air—kind of like what used to be her orderly life. Or maybe she was just too tired to think.

She shoved a mound of winter coats aside—noticing how some of them dated back to Zinnia and Jake's childhood—and collapsed onto the big leather sectional sofa, willing her brain to work. The day hadn't even begun and she was totally worn out. What was wrong with her? What happened to all that drive and enthusiasm she'd had just a week ago? What about that speech she'd made on Monday when some of her coworkers treated her to lunch—encouraging them to consider making changes in their own lives. Stupidly parroting her "less is more" mantra. She felt like a hypocrite as she stared at her mounds and mounds of *more*. She really did want less. But how?

She was tempted to turn on the TV and play an episode of *Teeny, Tiny Home* for some inspiration, but she had no idea where the remote was buried. She stared blankly at what had once been a fairly attractive great room, but now resembled a badly organized thrift store, and let out a long sigh. Those TV people had made it look so easy in their thirty-minute episodes. No one had mentioned the difficulty of getting rid of stuff. But surely they'd struggled with it too. It had probably been edited out.

Surrounded by her fortress of cardboard boxes as well as a lot of mixed feelings, Kate wondered, once again, if it was too late to turn back. Could she put the brakes on selling her house? Beg Marion to get her job back? Perhaps she could plead insanity. Insanity by way of home improvement TV. And then she thought about Hank's lovely peaceful farm—her light at the end of this horrendous tunnel. Besides that, Rose and Seth were on their way. Superheroes to save the day.

Hearing the *bing-bing-bing* of her coffee maker, Kate returned to the kitchen to search for a coffee mug. Finally settling for a French jelly glass instead, she stood in front of the kitchen window, slowly sipping hot black coffee, trying to regain some sense of composure, normalcy. She didn't really think she'd lost her mind. Although she'd heard the crazy person was usually the last one to know. No, she *could* do this. She just needed to pace herself, give herself time, finish her coffee. As her wise old grandmother used to say, "Rome wasn't built in a day." Plus, Superwoman was coming.

Kate felt a flicker of hope as the sun began to rise. Life always did look better in the light of day. Perhaps she really could do this. She just needed to put one foot in front of the other—like she'd told Leota the other day. Just take it slow and steady, breathe deeply. She was just about to do that when she heard the phone jangling next to her. Most people, other than an occasional telemarketer, didn't call on her landline. But it wasn't even 7 a.m. yet. Curious, she answered.

"Oh, Kate, I'm so glad I reached you. I tried your cell phone a couple times, but you didn't answer." Jennifer sounded slightly urgent.

"Sorry. I'm not even sure where my cell is right now." Kate glanced around the chaotic kitchen, wondering what it was buried beneath.

"I'm sorry to call so early," she continued. "But I knew you'd be up for Rose. Anyway, I had a text from our buyers. They want to come to your house this morning to do some measuring and check out paint samples. I told them you wouldn't mind."

"Oh?" Kate looked at her crazy house. "Don't they understand I'm trying to move? That I'm packing? You saw the place last night. How can—"

"I explained all that. And they said not to worry. They'd overlook the chaos."

"Right." Kate let out a long weary sigh.

"So if you don't mind, I'll bring them over this morning. After you've gone to work, of course. So don't even think about it, okay? We'll just be in and out. No biggie."

"Hopefully they won't sue me if they trip and get injured."

Jennifer's laugh sounded forced. "Don't worry, I'll watch out for them. Besides that, Rose and her assistant will be fast at work by then. Maybe it won't be so bad."

"Or maybe the buyers will want to rethink buying my house." Kate felt a flicker of confused hope.

"Good grief, I hope not." In a brisk tone, Jennifer told Kate to have a good day then hung up.

"Have a good day?" Kate groaned as she set the landline phone on a pile of old *Sunset* magazines that she'd been saving . . . for what? Then, ignoring her coffee, she thought about the buyers' faces when they saw this place and immediately threw herself into high gear, desperately tossing items left and right into various boxes and not particularly caring where they landed. Maybe it didn't matter where this junk all wound up. The storage unit, the thrift store, or even the trash bin. The goal was to simply get it out of the way and out of here—*fast*.

By the time Rose and Seth arrived, Kate was in something of a frenzy, as if something in her had snapped. She no longer cared about any of these things. Not Grandma's chipped candy dish, not Kenneth's favorite pair of slippers, not even the big rubber plant she'd had for fourteen years.

"Just have at it," she told Rose, after explaining her various holding areas for household goods that would hopefully find their way to the right destinations. "I trust you."

Rose looked surprised then smiled. "That's what I like to hear."

They all worked together for about an hour, and Rose wasn't nearly as ruthless as Kate had expected. In fact, she insisted Kate hold onto a few things she'd been ready to toss. Like Kenneth's college letterman jacket and a box of old photos that nearly got lost in the shuffle.

"This is why you have a storage unit," Rose said as Kate was getting ready to leave for work. "Anything we're unsure about will go there."

As Kate drove to work, she felt a bit encouraged and totally exhausted. But at least the house seemed a little more cleared out. And hopefully it would be even better by the time she got home from work. And, sure, some things might get lost along the way, but really—did it even matter? What if a hurricane or flood or fire had ravaged her house? Surely, Rose and Seth couldn't do any more damage than that.

Chapter 8

Kate honestly didn't know how it all got done, or where it all went, but by Saturday afternoon, her house was completely empty. With Rose and Seth's supervision, a truckload of items had been picked up by Salvation Army, another truckload of furnishings and packed boxes had been taken and placed into the storage unit, and a fairly full dumpster was waiting to be picked up on Monday. And right now, cleaners (hired by Jennifer) were going through the house.

"I can't believe we're actually done," Kate told Jennifer as the two of them carried the last two boxes out to the U-Haul truck parked in the driveway. "All that's left is to get this stuff over to my tiny house now."

"It's been pretty amazing." Jennifer slid the box into the back of the truck. "But like I promised, it was all doable. Just one step at a time."

"I couldn't have done it without you. You and Superwoman, that is." Kate's smile was weary but relieved. "And thanks for helping me with this today. I appreciate you bringing this truck over and returning it."

"I needed to come for the keys and to check on the housecleaners. Plus it gave me an excuse to see your tiny home before it's hauled off to Pine Ridge."

"You'll have to visit me there," Kate reminded her.

"Absolutely. But I'll wait until you get that development going. I want to see that in action." Jennifer pointed to the small sofa that Kate had saved from the den to go into her tiny home. "Is that really going to fit?"

"I measured it." Kate frowned. "But I agree it does seem a little large for a tiny home. I guess I can always change my mind. But it's such a comfy sofa, really good for napping. I hope it fits."

"And that queen-sized mattress?" Jennifer looked doubtful. "You sure that's going to fit? I mean what kind of tiny home is this?"

"The salesman assured me my sleeping loft can handle a queen mattress. Of course, it'll be on the floor. There's not enough headroom to stand up in the loft."

"And this table and the lamps and all this other stuff? You measured for these things too?"

"I didn't measure for everything. But there's a lot of storage in a tiny home. You'd be surprised."

"I hope so. For your sake."

Kate slid the door down and sighed. Then, turning to take one last look at her house, she felt a lump growing in her throat. As relieved as she felt to be done with all the work, she also felt sad.

The end of an era . . . bittersweet. "I can't believe this is it." She let out a little sob as she dug her keys out of her jeans pocket and handed them to Jennifer.

"I know it's hard saying good-bye." Jennifer put an arm around Kate's shoulders, giving her a squeeze. "But if it's any consolation, your buyers are so thrilled to move in today. They absolutely love the house. Even when they walked through and it was such chaos, they were excited over how big it was. After a month of being squeezed into a hotel room with three lively kids, it probably felt like a mansion. But really, Kate, it's like you've given them a lovely gift."

Kate wiped a tear and nodded. "I hope so. I do want them to be happy. We were happy here. Well, until Kenneth got sick. But mostly we were happy."

"What did your kids say about it?"

"My kids." Kate took in a deep breath. "Actually, I haven't told them yet."

Jennifer's brows arched. "Seriously?"

"Everything happened so fast. Their opinions would only complicate things. Besides, they have their own lives. Jake's job keeps him so busy, he hardly ever comes to visit. And after graduation next month, Zinnia's doing an internship in Seattle, so it's not like she was coming home this summer. I'm sure they won't like hearing my news, at first, but I'll assure them that all their stuff, so *much* stuff, is safely in storage. I'll send them both a key, not that I expect they'll go looking for anything. And, of course, they can come visit me in my tiny home whenever they like." She chuckled. "Although that might be pretty snug. Jake could sleep on the sofa and Zinnia up in the loft with me. We'll make it work."

"What about holidays? Christmas?" Jennifer opened the driver's side door to the truck.

"Christmas?" Kate frowned. "To be honest, I've been so busy with everything, I didn't really give it much thought."

"You could do what my sister does. Her kids are grown, and she lives in a condo. She reserves cool spots at winter resorts every year. Her kids love it."

Kate slowly nodded. "I'll keep that in mind." But as she got into her car to lead Jennifer to the tiny house lot, she wondered, how would Jake and Zinnia react to having no place to go home to for the holidays? Oh, well, she'd have to think about that later. Perhaps have something in mind before she called Jake and Zinnia with the news. She had been planning to call them later today. Maybe after her tiny home was settled next to Hank's barn. Or maybe tomorrow. These were not conversations she looked forward to.

Kate spotted her tiny new home from the street even before pulling into the sales lot. Painted olive green with russet shutters and door, it was—to her—perfect! But small—very small. She'd almost forgotten how tiny a tiny home really was. It looked like a playhouse sitting out there in front. And it had wheels beneath it, all ready to be hauled away after she loaded her things inside. The salesman, Kirk, had already assured her his crew would help her pack it snug and tight so that nothing got too messed up during the transport to Pine Ridge. The transporters would be there around three to start getting it ready for the road. It was all very exciting.

She'd spoken to Hank shortly after closing the sale of her house yesterday, and he knew to expect them around six o'clock tonight. And, to her relief, he still seemed pleased to have her as his neighbor, and excited about their plans for the tiny house development. In fact, he'd shared some good news. His lawyer had already drafted a business agreement for them to look at. And the city, eager to annex some urban growth boundary into the city limits, planned to be very accommodating to their tiny home development. Not only were they top priority for utilities and such, due to the city's desperate need for real estate, they'd been offered incentive discounts because their development was considered "affordable housing."

"This is adorable," Jennifer said as they stood in front of the tiny house. "Like a dollhouse."

"Well, a little bigger than that," Kate said defensively as they went onto the little front porch.

"Hey, look, you've already got a flowerpot. Pretty!" Jennifer bent down. "There's a card here." She handed it to Kate.

"It's from Leota at work." Kate read the note out loud. " 'Something to make you feel more at home in your Home Sweet Tiny Home!' "

"How thoughtful."

"Leota's a doll." Kate opened the Dutch door, waving Jennifer inside. "Voilà!"

"Very nice." Jennifer stepped in, carefully checking it all out. "Appliances and a bathroom and everything. Just like a real house."

"It is a *real* house." Kate explained how the bathroom was fully waterproof and built to be a shower stall as well. "So you clean your bathroom while you bathe, and the water drains out here." She pointed to the drain in the center of the tiled floor.

"Clever." Jennifer went up the stairs to the loft, looking around. "This is roomier than I expected, and you even have a skylight! Plus you can look out these little windows. It's perfect. I can actually imagine it being pretty sweet." She came back down the stairs. "In fact, it's got me worried."

"Worried?" Kate took the box from one of the young guys helping to unload the U-Haul.

"Yeah. If these tiny houses really catch on, it could be bad news for realtors."

Kate laughed. "I doubt you need to be too concerned. Not everyone can appreciate a tiny home."

"Well, let's get your stuff unloaded so I can get the truck back to U-Haul."

With the help of the young guys, it didn't take long to unload, but now Kate's tiny house resembled an overstuffed storage unit. Would she really be able to find places for everything she'd brought? Or would she be back to sorting and sifting and pruning again? Not to mention she'd packed a lot of clothes and things in the back of her SUV.

"Well, I have to go," Jennifer said. "I promised to meet the new homeowners at three." She hugged Kate. "Good luck."

"Yeah." Kate, mesmerized by how packed her tiny new house had become, nervously smiled as she thanked Jennifer, once again, for all her help.

The U-Haul had barely left when a big semi-truck pulled into the lot, backing up so that it could connect to the tiny house. The salesman introduced Kate to the driver, and she watched as Tony and his partner hooked things up. How would her tiny house fare at highway speeds? Going sixty miles an hour produced a lot of wind. What if the shingles blew off? Or a rock hit one of the windows? Had everyone thought of that?

"You're still okay being our pilot car?" Kirk asked Kate.

"Yes, of course."

"Tony already has your cell phone number, but here's his. Just in case something happens."

"Something happens?"

"Oh, you know, someone gets a flat tire or separated or lost. I doubt that will happen, but you never know."

"Right." She wondered how it would be possible to lose a tiny home.

"And don't go over the speed limit." Kirk attached a set of magnetized yellow lights to her SUV's roof. The sign on it proclaimed OVERSIZED LOAD.

She smiled. "That seems like an oxymoron. A tiny house is an oversized load?"

"Compared to most traffic. Also, you need to take it easy on corners. About ten miles an hour below the limit."

She felt uneasy again. "But it's okay to go the speed limit otherwise?"

"As much as possible. Otherwise you'll aggravate other drivers. You don't want to encounter any road rage while transporting a tiny house."

"No, of course not." She grimaced. Maybe she shouldn't be the lead car after all. What if she messed up and they all wound up in a ditch, or worse?

"Don't worry." Kirk patted her back. "You'll

do fine. Just take it easy. The transporters know what they're doing. Just be sure to check your rearview mirror from time to time." He shook her hand. "And congratulations for being the proud owner of a really great tiny home. I hope you enjoy it."

She thanked him. "And I'll be sure to send others your way. In fact, we're trying to start up a tiny new home development in Pine Ridge. We might have lots of customers for you."

Kirk's eyes lit up as he reached into his shirt pocket. "Here, take some business cards. You send anyone our way and we'll give you a small commission."

"Wow, thanks." She slid the cards into her purse just as Tony hollered they were ready to roll.

"Be safe out there," Kirk called as she got into her car. "And take it easy."

"Take it easy," she said to herself as she got into place in front of the semi. "And keep an eye on the rearview mirror. And slow down for corners. You can do this."

Waiting for a good opening in the traffic, she pulled out onto the street, watching to be sure the semi pulling her home sweet tiny home was following. No problem, they were out there. She proceeded slowly down the four-lane road. Possibly too slowly because Tony gave a quick honk on his horn. She glanced in her rearview mirror to see him holding his thumb in the air, as if to say, *Speed up, Granny!*

So she went a little faster, finally up to the speed limit. But she took her time to change lanes, making sure the path behind her was clear. It felt good to be piloting what would soon become her home. And yet, at the same time, it was all rather surreal. The past week had been long and stressful and, more than anything, Kate was ready for a break. And the image of her darling tiny home stuffed to the gills with all that junk, resembling a mobile storage unit . . . well, that was not comforting.

But instead of obsessing over that, she kept herself focused on her driving and the semi behind her. It wasn't long before they left the city traffic behind, traveling a bit more comfortably on the back highway to Pine Ridge. Her grip on the steering wheel loosened some, and she started to relax. The road was familiar, and she knew it had a few sharp curves along the river. She would make sure to slow down before them. Really, she was the perfect person to pilot her tiny house home. *Home,* she thought. She was going home!

Chapter 9

By the time the semi was backing her tiny home into place next to Hank's red barn, Kate was a nervous wreck. The drive down the curving country road hadn't been as peaceful as she'd hoped. Maybe because it was a warm Saturday afternoon and people were out enjoying the warm weather. But it had felt like everyone and their great-aunt Martha had gone out for a drive. And, unlike Kate and the tiny home trailing behind her, these cars were driving fast and, in her opinion, recklessly. There had been a number of moments when she'd felt certain that someone—like the yellow convertible that had come sailing around a curve and over the center line—was going to wind up in the river. It was all rather unnerving.

"That's one good looking tiny home," Hank told her as the transport guys began unhitching it. "And even bigger than I expected."

"It's kind of a midsized model." She took in a slow deep breath, trying to calm her frazzled nerves and lower her blood pressure. Then seeing Chester looking eagerly up at her, she knelt down to pet him, and that helped to calm her.

"How was the drive over?"

"Ugh. Don't ask." She stood back up.

"Really?" His brows arched.

"It wasn't that bad. Just a lot of crazy drivers out on the road today."

"With summer round the corner, things are picking up. Pine Ridge was busier than ever today. Never saw lines at George's Groceries that long before in my life. Guess this town is growing even faster than I thought."

She smiled to imagine Hank waiting in a line with his shopping cart. It was a sweet image. "I suppose that's something I'll have to get used to, just one grocery store in this town."

"Actually, we have a new natural foods store too. Marco's—over on Fifth and Pine. It's a little limited, but I like to go there for produce and a few things."

"Good to know."

Tony was waving her over to the tiny home. He took a moment to explain how the wheels and jacks and things worked. "In case you want to relocate it later."

"Yes," Kate said eagerly. "We will definitely be moving it. On down the line."

"We went ahead and hooked you up to the electric and water." He walked her over to show where he'd connected the water hose and extension cord up. "But you'll have to figure out your holding tanks for sewage later."

Kate cringed. "Sewage?"

"You've got holding tanks underneath. Just like

a regular RV. But they only hold so much. Didn't Kirk explain all that to you?"

"I guess he did, I probably wasn't paying close enough attention."

"You've got that panel of gauges inside. You know, in the kitchen area."

"Oh, yeah, I do remember that."

"You'll have to check them regularly to make sure everything's working right. It's all there in the owner's manual. You've got that, right?"

"Yes." She nodded, wondering if she'd ever find it.

Tony waited for her signature then handed her a receipt for hauling the tiny house, a bill she'd already paid through Kirk and the tiny home company. He thanked her for her business as he walked over to the cab of his truck.

"And we might be sending more business your way," she said as he got into his truck. "We hope to have more tiny homes out here."

"Great!" He grinned. "I'm happy to haul 'em for ya." He waved as he started the loud diesel engine then slowly chugged on down the driveway.

"Looks like you're all set." Hank nodded toward her tiny house with a curious expression. "Bet you can't wait to get in there and set up housekeeping."

"Yes, for sure." She didn't want to admit that it probably looked frightening inside, or that she had no intention of inviting him in for an open house. Not yet anyway.

"I, uh, I got a few things for dinner." He looked down at his cowboy boots, as if uneasy. "I thought you might not be ready to start cooking and all that in your little house. My nephew Zeb would be joining us too. I mean, if you'd like to come on over for dinner, I'm grilling steaks."

"That sounds perfect," she exclaimed. "In fact, I didn't even bring much food with me. Just some non-perishables and, to be honest, I'm not even sure where to find them at the moment."

He smiled. "Great. We'll eat on the porch." He checked his watch. "Seven-thirty sound okay?"

"Perfect! I'm already hungry." She didn't mention that she'd skipped lunch.

"Then you're at the right place. I got steaks and green salad and potato salad. And berries and ice cream for dessert."

"Sounds fabulous." She beamed at him.

"In the meantime, feel free to park your car closer to your little house. And just make yourself at home. I'm sure you're excited about getting all set up. Can't wait to see more of it."

She forced a smile. He'd have to wait. She had no intention of letting anyone in there until it was somewhat sorted out. If that was even possible. Determined to at least make a path through the piles inside her tiny home, she parked her car nearby but didn't bother to empty anything from the back. She had enough to keep her busy.

But before going inside, she gave Leota a quick call, thanking her for the thoughtful flowerpot. "It's just beautiful," she said. "My favorite kinds of flowers. Pansies and lavender and alyssum. Thank you."

"I'm glad you like it. I thought it would be pretty against your olive green siding. I took it out there this morning, hoping to see you. At least I got to see the final paint job. It looks fabulous. You must be thrilled."

"I am." She explained about the task ahead—unpacking and sorting. "Hopefully it won't take too long."

"How about I come over there tomorrow and help."

"You'd really want to spend your Sunday doing that?"

"I'd love to. And then I can see where you're at and Pine Ridge and everything."

"Great!"

"Is ten o'clock too soon?"

"Sounds good to me."

"See ya then."

After Kate pocketed her phone, she questioned whether she really needed Leota's help. But as soon as she stepped inside her tiny home, she knew she did. And the tasks ahead didn't require too much decision making. Simply organizing,

105

putting things away, and straightening up. Leota was smart and energetic—she'd be good help.

"Need a hand with anything?" a male voice called from the doorway of Kate's tiny house.

"Huh?" She stuck her head around a pile of boxes to see a lanky young man peering inside with a puzzled expression.

"I'm Zeb. Hank, he's my uncle, he asked me to bring you these camp chairs." He held up a pair of dusty canvas chairs. "Can ya use 'em?"

"Sure. That'd be great. Go ahead and set them on the porch." She pushed hair out of her eyes. "I'm Kate."

"Nice to meet ya, Kate. And nice flowerpot ya got out here." Zeb leaned against the doorway, glancing inside with a furrowed brow.

"Pretty crowded in here, isn't it?" She forced a sheepish smile.

"I was just thinking that." He let out a low whistle. "Where ya gonna put all this stuff?"

"Good question." She made her way through the aisle she'd created between boxes and piles. "My tiny house has a lot of storage, but I might've overestimated it."

"Do you need a hand with anything?" His frown suggested he was just trying to be polite.

"If you could pass a couple of things up to me in the loft, I'd really appreciate it." She pointed to a large box marked bedding and another one marked books. "And that lamp there too." She picked up a duffle bag that was stuffed with some of her clothes and went up the stairs.

"I used to live in a camp trailer." He hoisted the box of bedding up to the loft. "It was even smaller than this. But not so crowded."

"I'm hoping it won't be this crowded once I get things put away. And anything that won't fit will just have to leave."

He picked up the box of books and started to hoist it then changed his mind and came up the steps. "Hey, this is pretty cool up here."

She took the heavy box from him, setting it next to the built-in bookshelves by the bed. "Cozy but nice."

"Good spot to read. I'll get that lamp for you now." He went back down.

Kate opened the big box of bedding, dumping the contents onto the mattress. The rest of her home might be in total disarray, but at least she'd be sleeping comfortably tonight. "Look out below," she yelled as she dropped the empty box.

"I'll toss it outside," Zeb called up. "Make a little more room." She was just making the bed as he carried up the reading lamp. "This looks better already." He set the lamp down. "Want me to empty any of those boxes downstairs? I could put the stuff sort of where it goes then toss the boxes outside. Might help make more space."

She smiled at him. "That would be lovely, Zeb.

Thank you so much." He quietly whistled as he rustled about down below. She guessed he was about the same age as her son, but she couldn't imagine Jake being this congenial or helpful under the same circumstances. Jake was a good boy, but a bit too bossy. Especially after his dad passed. Jake liked to tell Kate what to do and how to do it, as if being widowed had somehow robbed her of half of her brain. She tolerated his patronization because she knew it was motivated by love, but she didn't like it. She could just imagine him telling her where and how to put things away. More than likely he would tell her she'd lost her mind to do what she'd done, which was one reason she hadn't told him yet.

As she slid books onto the shelf, she thought Zinnia would probably be more supportive of this whole thing. After all, she was the one who encouraged Kate to watch the tiny house episodes. But, like Jake, she'd probably be worried about Kate's sanity—or lack of it. And more than likely, she'd call her brother and they'd both be on Kate's case. No, it was best to wait until the last of the dust settled before she told her children about this new adventure she had embarked on.

With her sleeping loft looking surprisingly sweet and cozy, she decided she better get downstairs to see how Zeb was doing. "Hey, it looks like progress down here."

"I set your dishes and kitchen stuff on the

counter so you could figure out where to put it." He threw another empty box out the door. "And those three boxes marked clothes, I just stacked them in that narrow closet there. You know, to get them out of the way for now."

"Perfect." She smiled. "You're pretty good at this."

"I worked at a big box store for a while. Stocking shelves and moving stuff. Not a great job, but best I could find while I was still using." He set a stack of pans on the last empty spot of countertop space.

"Using?" She tried not to sound surprised.

"Uncle Hank didn't tell you?"

She shrugged. "No, but it's no big deal."

"Well, it's kind of a big deal. I'm an addict. Admission and acceptance is one of the first steps to recovery. And thank God, I am a recovering addict. Almost two years clean now. Thanks mostly to Uncle Hank." He opened a box of bath linens.

"Just set that one on the stairs," she told him. "I'll use the drawers underneath for the towels."

"Want me to do that?" he offered.

"Sure. Thanks." She started to put dishes in the kitchen cupboard.

"You have really nice things, Kate."

"Thanks. It was hard deciding what to bring with me. I used to have this really big house. So I had to scale down. A lot." She paused to look at a hand thrown pottery plate. She and Kenneth had picked these out early on in their marriage because they wanted something special—substantial enough for the long haul. She still had the dinnerware, but no Kenneth.

"My parents have a big house too. They keep saying they're gonna downsize, but I don't think they ever will. At least not like you're doing. My mom's an antique fanatic. That woman won't let go of anything." He chuckled. "Not even her kids."

"What about you? You're not living with your parents." Kate tossed a wad of packing paper into an empty box.

"Oh, they were glad to get rid of me. I meant my two younger brothers. Cal and BJ are in their mid-twenties and still living at home. But that's probably my fault too."

"Your fault?" She closed the cupboard door, satisfied that so many dishes had fit into the small space.

"Because of the drugs, you know? My mom freaked that they would get hooked too. That's what she calls it. Hooked." He laughed. "Like some pirate with a hook for a hand swooped out and caught me by the shirt collar. Aye, Matey, I got ya!"

"So how *did* you get hooked?" She instantly wondered if she was being too nosy. But she was curious. She used to worry about Jake and

Zinnia, but as far as she knew they never dabbled in any of that. Thank God!

"Oh, it's the usual story. I smoked a little weed in high school, a little more in college. No big deal. Then start of my junior year, a friend introduced me to something stronger—something that was supposed to help me keep up with my class load, which was pretty heavy. Consequently, I never finished my junior year. All I could think about was where I was going to get my next fix. My mind was a total *meth*." He chuckled. "Sorry, that was pretty lame. But meth did become my drug of choice. Unfortunately."

"That's too bad."

"Yep." He closed the last drawer then carried the empty box to the door, tossing it out with the others. "But like Uncle Hank likes to say, live and learn."

"And he helped you get clean?"

"Yeah. He really came to my rescue. It wasn't long after Aunt Elizabeth died too. Man, was that a sad time. She was such a cool lady. At first I thought Hank was just using me as a distraction—you know, like a goodwill project to help him get over losing his wife. Like that's even possible. After a while, I realized he really did love me. He was willing to go the distance with me. I sometimes feel like he loves me more than my own dad. Maybe it's because Uncle

Hank never had kids of his own. But, man, I do appreciate him."

"I bet you do. I'm curious what he did—how he helped you to get clean. I've heard it's really hard to do."

"It *was* hard. He started by getting me into rehab. Twenty-eight days at a really good place. And it's not like I didn't want to get clean. I did. But drugs are tough to quit. Uncle Hank really believed in me, that I could do it. And that helped. But it was ultimately my decision. A daily decision."

"I've heard it's like that." She tossed the dishware box out the door, dusting off her hands.

"After rehab, he let me come here to live. I was pretty depressed. I mean here I was twenty-six years old, no college degree, no car, no girlfriend, nothing. A total loser. At first I was going to stay here for just six months. You know, so I could get more solid in my recovery. And he made me go to church and to AA meetings. They didn't have NA in Pine Ridge then. They do now." He opened a box of non-perishable foods.

"Those can go over there." She pointed to a tall narrow pantry between the bathroom and kitchen.

"Uncle Hank really put me to work out here on the farm. He had me digging fence post holes, driving a tractor, weeding, and painting. All kinds of stuff. I complained at first, but it turned out

112

to be really good medicine. The harder I worked, the better I slept at night. After six months, I didn't even want to leave."

"And Hank probably didn't want you to?"

"He said I could stay as long as I liked. As long as I stayed clean."

"And you've done that." She picked a wall clock from the top of a "miscellaneous" box. "Oh, it's almost dinnertime. We better stop." She looked around with surprise. "Thanks so much! I never could've gotten this far without you."

"No problem."

"And thanks for sharing your story with me." She cleared things out of the sink so she could wash her hands. "It's a really good one."

"I guess it depends on how you look at it. My parents sure wouldn't call it that."

"I'm sure they're thankful you're recovering. My kids are just a little younger than you. I can't imagine how grateful I'd be if someone helped them in a similar situation." She dried her hands on a potholder next to the stove.

He shrugged. "I guess so. But at the same time, I know they're kind of ashamed of me. And just as glad not to have me around."

She put a hand on his shoulder, looking into his eyes. "I think they should be very proud of you for beating drugs, Zeb. That's no small thing."

He smiled. "Thanks."

As they walked to the house, she thought about

her own kids. Did Jake and Zinnia know she was proud of them? Did she say that enough? Maybe when she called to tell them about everything, she would begin the conversation by letting them know.

Chapter 10

Kate caught a whiff of something good wafting from the barbecue as they approached the house. "Smells delicious."

"Uncle Hank's good on the grill," Zeb said as Chester rushed across the porch to greet them, tail eagerly wagging. "Looks like he's pulled out all the stops tonight."

"What do you mean?"

"He put a tablecloth on the table." Zeb chuckled. "I'm gonna go wash up."

Kate patted Chester then went over to where the picnic table was set with three places, all neatly laid out on a red and white checked tablecloth. Very homey and inviting. On the table was a big green salad that looked surprisingly good and what she guessed was store-bought potato salad and a basket of sliced bread.

"Oh, good, you're here." Hank came around the corner of the wraparound porch carrying a platter of steaks and some grilled ears of corn. "I was about to ring the dinner bell."

"You have a dinner bell?"

He pointed to a bronze bell on a corner of the porch. "Elizabeth put that up when we first moved out here. She used to think we'd have a bunch of kids running around the place and she'd use it to call them for meals and stuff." His eyes got sad again. "You can hear it clear on the other side of the property."

Kate looked at the platter he was setting down. "Wow, that looks really good."

"Where's Zeb?" Hank glanced around.

"I'm right here." Zeb came out of the house. "Just scrubbing up for dinner."

"Zeb helped me unpack." Kate sat in the chair Hank indicated for her. "Very much appreciated too."

"She's got some pretty cool stuff." Zeb sat down across from her. "And her tiny home is super cool."

"Besides good help, it gave us a chance to get acquainted," Kate told Hank as he sat down.

"That's nice." He glanced at Zeb then back to Kate. "Mind if we say a blessing?"

"Not at all." She smiled. "I'd love that."

Hank nodded to Zeb. "Your turn, buddy."

Zeb bowed his head. "Dear Father God, thanks for another good day and for helping me stay clean. Thanks for Uncle Hank and this farm. And thanks for bringing Kate here. And, mostly, thanks for this great looking meal. Amen."

Hank chuckled. "We usually keep our prayers short and sweet."

"I'm sure God doesn't mind." Kate unfolded her napkin. "Everything looks delicious. Thanks so much for having me."

As they ate, they talked about the tiny house development. Hank filled her in a bit more about the city's involvement. "They've already started the annexation process of thirty acres that border the city. The surveyor was out here yesterday."

"Things are sure moving fast."

"Like I said, the city is highly motivated. Partly for more taxable lots, but more because of the affordable housing."

"I told Hank I might want to get a tiny house." Zeb smeared butter onto his corn. "I've been saving up."

"That reminds me." Hank reached for the salad. "Aileen Marten—I think you met her in town—is very interested in a tiny house. Right now she's living with my nephew Ryan and his wife Jessie."

"They're the ones who gave me your name and number." Kate nodded. "Aileen did mention an interest in tiny homes."

"I suggested she come out and have a look at yours," Hank said. "I told her you could give her a call when you're all set up."

"Absolutely. So is Ryan your brother, Zeb?"

"No. He's my cousin."

"My older brother Gordon is Ryan's dad," Hank explained. "He and his wife live just outside of Portland."

"My dad's the youngest Branson brother," Zeb told Kate.

"We were the three Branson boys." Hank chuckled. "And, man, did we get into some trouble growing up. Nothing serious, but we did have a reputation."

"Interesting." Kate smiled as she broke a piece of bread in half.

"You mentioned grown kids," Zeb said to her. "How many?"

"Just two. Jake's the oldest. He's twenty-seven and works for a software company in Seattle. And Zinnia will be twenty-three in August. She's finishing college and going straight into an internship program with an online magazine in Seattle."

"That might be nice for them to live in the same city."

"I guess so." Kate wondered if they'd ever spend time together in Seattle. Zinnia and Jake had never been particularly close. She attributed that to the four year gap in their ages—plus their differing interests. Jake had been what Zinnia called a computer nerd. And Jake had considered his baby sister to be a superficial fashionista. Oh, well. At least they hadn't gotten into drugs.

"So what do your kids think about your tiny home?" Zeb asked.

Kate sighed. "To be honest, I haven't told them yet. My son tends to be a bit overprotective of me. I didn't want to worry him until it was all said and done."

118

"Would he have tried to talk you out of it?" Hank asked.

"Possibly. Ever since his dad died, Jake seems to assume that I need him to protect me or something. Sweet but aggravating. I thought if I had everything all squared away it would sort of prove to him that I can handle it."

"Sounds like me with my parents." Zeb grinned. "Only the other way around. I keep trying to prove to them that I can handle it."

"You are handling it." Hank reached over to clasp his shoulder. "And doing a good job of it too."

"Uncle Hank is gonna let me do a lot of the excavation and groundwork for the development," Zeb told Kate. "I've gotten pretty good with the tractor, if I do say so myself. I think it'll be fun."

They continued to talk and plan for the development. Zeb wanted to make a small dock for the pond in case anyone wanted to go swimming or just sit and hang their feet into the water. Hank hoped to plant a few more trees before summer. And Kate shared some of her own ideas for landscaping around the lots.

After dinner they went inside to go over Hank's most recent drafts for the new development. Seated around the well-lit dining room table, Kate studied his drawings. He'd put in access roads, water and sewer lines, electric and cable lines. The lots were actually drawn out according to scale, just like he'd originally suggested, in pie shapes surrounding the pond. But not too close.

"I've left four access paths—north, south, east, and west." He pointed to trails that led directly to the pond. "For maintenance vehicles and whatnot. As well as the public area all around the lake where the trees are growing." He pointed to the wide circular swath, which included a path. "And this is wide enough for a pickup."

"Or a golf cart."

"That reminds me, I haven't been out to Glen's development on the lake yet." He looked slightly uneasy. "But it might be good to glean ideas. Both of what we'd like to do as well as what we don't want to do. We sure don't want our place to be too much like his."

"I wish I'd taken notes when I was out there," Kate said.

"To be honest, I'm starting to think Glen might not welcome me out there now," Hank admitted. "I thought he'd be okay with this, but word's already gotten out about our development and from what I've heard, Glen's not a big fan. If he catches me snooping around, he might not appreciate it."

"How about if I pay them another visit? I never met Glen, so he wouldn't even know me. I can always just tell them that I'm on their waiting list but have made other plans. And while I'm there check it out better."

"Perfect." Hank nodded.

"These plans look great. I'm impressed. But then you are, after all, an architect. I guess I should've known you'd do it right."

"I was trying to wow the city." Hank started to roll them up.

"You must've done it too," Zeb said. "Since they waived a lot of your permit fees."

"Which reminds me." Hank reached for a large manila envelope. "This is the lawyer's first draft for our agreement. Read over it and make any changes you feel are necessary. I made an appointment for next Wednesday in the hopes we could both go in and go over it with him."

"Sounds great." Kate let out a sleepy yawn.

"I can tell you're tired." Hank pushed back his chair. "I'm sure you've had a busy time of it."

"That's putting it mildly." She stood. "I'm just glad that it's over."

"You're all set up in your tiny home?"

"I'm getting there, and Zeb was really helpful. Anyway, I have a place to sleep. And right now that's sounding pretty good." She stretched her neck. "It's been a long day. Really, it's been a long week."

"Let us know if you need anything." Hank held up his phone. "You've got my number."

"I'll give you mine too." Zeb told her the

numbers, and she plugged them into her phone. "And I'm happy to help you out more tomorrow." He glanced at Hank. "After church, that is. We usually leave here around 10:15—if ya wanna come."

"Yes, I meant to invite you." Hank nodded.

"I'd love to come." She pocketed her phone. "What a great way to start meeting people." She frowned down at her jeans, wondering how long it would take her to unpack her clothes, organize her closet, and find something nicer to wear. "Does your church have a dress code of sorts?"

Zeb laughed. "Yeah, like jeans and T-shirts and cowboy boots. We meet in a barn."

"A barn?"

"Last summer the congregation decided to sell the church building since maintenance and repairs were really taking a toll on the budget. Now we have more money to send to orphanages and missions and the homeless shelter." Hank opened the front door, leading them out to the porch. "My buddy Garret, a few miles down the road, offered his barn. It's a lot bigger than mine. Anyway, it's been working out okay."

"It's actually pretty cool," Zeb told her. "You can sit on a hay bale."

"There are folding chairs too," Hank pointed out. "And the music is good."

"It all sounds very intriguing. Like a downsized church." She slapped her forehead. "Oh, I just remembered my friend Leota is supposed to be here at ten tomorrow morning."

"Just bring her along," Zeb said.

"Sure, if she wants to come, just bring her," Hank echoed.

Kate agreed that was a good idea, and they all said good night on the front porch. Even though the sun was well down, it was easy to see as Kate walked toward the barn. The sky above was a deep sapphire blue, and the lights on the porch and a big one over the barn glowed cheerfully.

And the quiet! Sounds of crickets and frogs, and the sweet pungent smell of green things growing . . . It was amazing. Kate could hardly believe she got to live here. It felt magical.

That is, until she got over to her tiny house. All around her little porch was starting to resemble a dumpsite from all the cardboard boxes and packing paper that they'd tossed out. Still, she knew she could straighten that up in the morning. Right now, all she wanted was a shower and a good night's rest.

It felt strange to turn the lights on in her tiny house. She'd never been in it at nighttime before, but she could imagine it feeling sweet and homey—once she got everything sorted out and put away. She and Zeb had made a good dent on it, but there were still a lot of boxes and clutter spewed about. Part of her wanted to turn into Superwoman and put it all away. But it was a very small part, and the rest of her was way too tired to even care.

She went to the postage stamp bathroom and flipped on the light. It was definitely snug in here, but not impossible. And she knew the water worked since she'd washed her hands earlier. It was a little cramped getting ready to take a shower, which she desperately needed, but finally she was ready. She closed the door and turned on the water, trying not to screech when it came out full blast and icy cold.

She cranked it to hot, cowering against the sink and shivering while she waited for the water to warm up, but nothing happened. Finally, she couldn't stand another second. She turned the water off and, shaking from the cold, reached out the door for her towel. What on earth was wrong with the hot water heater? As she dried herself off she suddenly remembered how Kirk had told her to turn the hot water heater on when she got there. And to do that, she needed to turn the propane tank on first. Well, she had no intention of doing any of that tonight.

Still chilled to the bone, she got into her pajamas and went upstairs. Of course, once she was up there, she realized she hadn't turned off the overhead light downstairs. She was tempted to ignore it, except she knew she got her best sleep in a very dark room and this light was glaring right into her loft. So she went back down and, navigating through the boxes, turned it off. But on her way back to the staircase she stubbed her little toe—hard—against the small end table she planned to set next to her sofa. This time she did let out a shriek.

She hobbled back up the stairs, hoping her toe wasn't broken. The way it throbbed, she wasn't sure. Finally in bed, she was relieved to discover that the pillow-top queen mattress, spared from her old guest room, was actually quite comfortable. And the bed linens smelled fresh and clean. And above her, through the skylight just a few feet overhead, was a dark sky full of shimmering stars. What could be better?

"Thank you, Lord," she whispered. "You got me safely here. And now the adventure is really about to begin. Please, continue to lead our paths. And, oh yeah, can you do something about this toe? Amen." And she closed her eyes and fell instantly to sleep.

Chapter 11

Kate felt surprisingly refreshed the next morning. And clearheaded enough to turn on both the propane tank and the hot water heater. Now if she could only find her coffee maker and grinder and beans. She dug around a bit, unpacking a few things as she went and even unearthing a box of granola and a protein bar, which sufficed as breakfast—her evasive caffeine elements seemed to be AWOL. Finally, realizing she had about an hour to get ready for church, she decided to try her shower again. To her relief, the water was nice and hot today.

As she dressed, she wondered about Leota. She'd sent her a quick text invite to go with them to "barn church" early this morning but hadn't heard back. Hopefully Leota had gotten it by now and would want to come along. Kate checked her phone to see that Leota had texted back a big "YIPPEE-YI-YAY!" which Kate interpreted as an enthusiastic *yes*. Then hearing a voice calling out, Kate went out to her front porch to see Leota was already here.

"You found me," Kate exclaimed, hurrying out to embrace her friend.

"Yep. And all ready for barn church too." Leota

stuck out a foot, which was shod in a stylish cow-boy boot.

"Cute!" Kate nodded. "I might have to get some of those myself."

"Especially since you're living on a farm now." Leota looked around. "Wow, is this place cool or what?"

Kate checked her watch. "Want to see where we plan to put the tiny home development? I think we've got plenty of time."

"I'd love to."

Kate told Leota a bit about Hank's late wife Elizabeth and her dreams for creating a special place by the pond. "From all I've heard, she was a very special woman."

"This is a beautiful spot. And these trees must help keep it nice and shady on a hot day."

"Elizabeth planted all these aspens."

"Must've been a while ago, they're pretty big."

"I think Hank said it was more than twenty years ago."

"How long has she been gone?" Leota sat down on the old bench.

"About three years."

"So you guys are both widowed." Leota's brows arched with suspicion. "Any chance for romance?"

"Oh, I don't think so." Kate looked toward the pond, trying to keep her real feelings hidden. "I don't think Hank is ready to go there. I'm pretty sure he hasn't gotten over losing Elizabeth yet. He's still grieving."

"Maybe you can help him with that." Leota's dark eyes twinkled.

Kate checked her watch again. "We better get back. The guys will probably be ready to go soon."

"Guys? How many are there?"

"Hank's nephew Zeb lives with him." As they walked back, Kate told Leota about Zeb.

"He's a meth addict?" Leota sounded alarmed.

"He's a *recovering* addict," Kate clarified. "Two years clean. And he's the sweetest boy."

"Boy? Just how old is he?"

"I think he said late twenties."

"Uh-huh. So not exactly a boy then."

"He's a little older than Jake. But I think of Jake as a boy."

"Speaking of Jake. Did you tell your kids yet?"

Kate grimaced. "Not yet. I plan to call them tonight."

"Right." Leota slowly shook her head. Kate had already confided in her that she was postponing what she suspected would be a difficult conversation.

"Hey there." Hank waved to them from the front porch. Today he had on a less worn pair of jeans, a pale blue western style shirt, and a tan cowboy hat—not fancy, but as handsome as ever. "You gals ready to go to cowboy church?"

"Cowboy church?" Kate echoed. "Do I need a hat?"

Hank smiled. "That's what some folks in town call it."

Now Zeb came out. Like Hank, he had on jeans and a cowboy hat, but he sported a vintage rocker shirt with a slight tear on the shoulder. Kate introduced them both to Leota. "And, as you can see, Leota came dressed appropriately."

"Cool boots," Zeb told Leota. And unless Kate was mistaken, Zeb approved of Leota as much as he approved of her boots. And why shouldn't he? With her smooth coppery skin, expressive dark brown eyes, and espresso-colored hair pulled back in a ponytail today, she was gorgeous. In fact, Kate didn't know why Leota was still unattached. With her brains, personality, and looks, she would be quite a catch. Well, unless it was her family holding her back. It seemed that every time Leota started a relationship, one of her siblings would show up and unravel everything.

"You gals want to follow my pickup?" Hank asked. "The cab's too small for four people. And it's just a little ways down the road."

"I'll drive," Leota offered.

As Leota drove, Kate asked how things had gone with her sister Clarissa. "I know you kept thinking she was going to be on her way. Did she finally head out?"

130

Leota groaned. "I told her that today was her last day in my apartment. My lease won't allow her to stay more than two weeks. I even gave her bus money and a schedule. I kissed her good-bye, and I hope and pray she'll be gone when I get home."

Kate wondered how likely that was. And even if Clarissa did leave, who would show up next at Leota's door? "You should consider moving somewhere with no forwarding address," Kate teased.

"Like you just did? At least as far as your kids go."

Kate chuckled. "I guess that's sort of true, although I am having my mail forwarded. I called the Pine Ridge Post Office last week and got myself a PO box in town."

"Can you imagine if your kids decided to pop into your house? What would they think to find a whole new family living there?"

Kate cringed. "That would not be good. But seeing how they didn't even call me on Mother's Day, I'm not overly worried."

"They didn't call you on Mother's Day? I didn't know that. I'm sorry, Kate."

"They both have busy lives. Zinnia's probably cramming for finals week. And Jake, well, he's always buried in work. So, really, it's no big deal."

"If I'd known, I would've done something."

Leota smiled. "I know you're not my mom, but sometimes you treat me like your kid."

"Like I've told you, I'd happily adopt you—any day of the week."

"That would make me the middle child." Leota laughed. "I'm not sure Jake and Zinnia would appreciate that."

"They both like you, Leota. Although you could be right. It might make them jealous. But maybe that would be good—might make them appreciate their poor old mom a bit more. Anyway, I do plan to call them before the day is done."

"I can't wait to hear their reaction." Leota turned down a driveway behind Hank's green pickup. "Looks like we're here." She followed him into a stubble field where a lot of other vehicles were already parked. "This looks like fun. Thanks for letting me tag along."

"I'm glad you came." They got out and went over to join Hank and Zeb and were introduced to some of their friends—a neighbor family from a farm a few miles out of town and an elderly couple who'd recently relocated to Pine Ridge. They all walked into the barn together to see it was quickly filling up.

"The young folks like to sit on the hay bales," Hank told Kate. "But I prefer a chair."

"I think I would too."

"I'm happy to sit on a bale," Leota offered.

"Great." Zeb grabbed her hand. "Come with me."

Kate tried not to act surprised by Zeb's friendliness toward Leota and smiled as he led her to an unoccupied bale near the front. "Zeb's so sweet and friendly," she told Hank as they sat down near the back of the barn.

"Maybe so, but I think he likes her," Hank said quietly.

"Really? I mean likes her likes her?" She suddenly felt like she was in junior high.

He grinned. "I think so. Zeb is not usually that outgoing around girls his age. At least not with ones he's barely met. But on the way over here, he mentioned how attractive she was."

"Interesting." Kate smiled. "Leota's a lot more than just a pretty face."

The music up front was starting to play—a quartet of guitar, fiddle, banjo, and bass. And they sounded pretty good. Before long, people began to stand, starting to sing. The woman playing guitar seemed to be leading them and, fortunately, they were playing songs Kate was familiar with. Just in a countrified sort of way. It was fun.

After a few minutes of singing, a tall, lanky guy with a gray beard went up front, introducing himself as Pastor Rick, and welcoming any newcomers. Kate was grateful he didn't ask them to stand up. Then he told a couple of jokes and shared a short but meaningful sermon about loving your neighbor. Simple but powerful.

Afterward, people gathered outside where tables with lemonade and water and cookies were set up. "This is nice," Kate told Hank as he handed her a lemonade. "I feel like I've gone back in time, or maybe to a different country."

"I've never enjoyed church more than I have here in the barn." He waved to a couple of blonde women coming their way. Both had on sundresses, boots, and cowboy hats. Not matching exactly, but very similar. Hank took a moment to introduce Kate. "This is Molly and Abby," he said. "They're sisters . . . and they were Elizabeth's best friends. Really supportive of her during her illness. I owe them a lot."

"Elizabeth always gave us back way more than we could give her," Molly said sadly.

"That's right," Abby added. "Even when Elizabeth was in pain, she'd share happiness. I always left feeling better than when I came."

For a moment no one said anything, but Kate could see the sadness in Hank's eyes. Wanting to do something to alleviate it, she turned to Molly and Abby. "I thought you two looked alike. You're not twins, are you?"

They both grinned. "My mom says we're Irish twins," Abby told Kate. "We're only thirteen months apart in age. And we do tend to dress alike sometimes. Not on purpose, mind you."

"It's just that we have similar taste," Molly explained. "And then, of course, Abby likes to shop at my store."

"That's because Molly owns the best clothing store in town. Molly's Mercantile," Abby told Kate. "You've probably seen it on Main Street."

Kate nodded. "But I've never been inside. Not yet anyway."

"Kate just moved here." Hank told the women about the tiny house development they were working on together.

"I heard someone was doing that. I didn't realize it was you, Hank." Abby's eyes lit up.

"Abby works for the city," Hank told Kate.

"Everyone down there is real excited about this new development," Abby said. "We need places like that in Pine Ridge."

"Hopefully they'll stay excited and keep oiling the machinery to get this done," Hank said.

Zeb and Leota came over to join them. Zeb politely introduced Leota and all of them visited congenially for a while. Then noticing how the parking area was thinning out, Kate remembered everything she hoped to get done today. "Maybe we should get going," she quietly told Leota.

"Ready when you are." Leota smiled at the others. "I came here to help Kate put her tiny home together."

"You have a tiny home?" Abby's eyes grew wide.

"I just got it." Kate explained how she'd just spent her first night in it. "I still have lots to put away. Hopefully, with Leota's help, we'll get it wrapped up today."

"I'd love to see it," Abby told her. "Right now I'm living at Molly's house, but I really want a place of my own. I'm on the waiting list at Pine Ridge Lake Estates, but who knows how long that'll take. Maybe you guys will have your development done by then."

"Once I get myself all sorted out, I'll have you over to see my house," Kate promised.

"Sounds like you might become our model home," Hank said lightly. "Everyone seems to want to see your place."

"That's fine. I promised the tiny house company that I'd send business their way." She quickly described how they had lots of different models to choose from. "And Kirk is great to work with. Plus, I know the guys who do the hauling. It's really not terribly complicated."

"Wow, you sound like a tiny house expert," Molly said.

Kate shrugged. "I wouldn't go that far. But I'm learning." She confessed about her bone-chilling shower last night. "I won't make that mistake again." They all laughed and then she and Leota said good-bye and headed out.

"What nice people—and such a fun church,"

Leota said as they drove back to Hank's farm. "You're lucky to be here, Kate."

"Lucky maybe, but it feels more like I've been blessed."

"Yeah. Blessed. I'm trying not to be envious. But it's like you've suddenly carved out this whole new life for yourself. It actually seems nothing short of miraculous. I'm happy for you, and I know I should be inspired, but at the same time I feel seriously jealous."

"Instead of being jealous, you should just consider moving here. You could get a tiny home too. Even if you don't have the cash on hand, I'm sure you could easily finance one. Kirk said they carry loans. I'm sure the payments would probably be a fraction of what you're now paying for rent."

"I'm sure you're right. And it would be an investment. But what would I do for income in this small town?"

"I don't know. But Pine Ridge is growing so fast, I'll bet the job market is as strong as the real estate market."

"It is an interesting idea. I could imagine loving it here."

"And it would give you a little more distance from your family."

"That's for sure." Leota brightened. "I do have some other skills. I worked in retail to put myself through college."

"If I had my florist shop going, I'd hire you in a heartbeat." Kate sighed. "But that's going to take me a while. Right now I need to focus on the tiny home development. And, after glancing over the lawyer's papers, I have a feeling I'll be investing a lot of capital there."

"Is that going to be risky for you?"

"I don't know." Kate pursed her lips. "I mean, an investment is always risky, right? But the idea feels solid. We've got people interested in locating there and we haven't even broken ground. The agreement Hank's lawyer drafted seems fair. But I'll go over it more carefully. I won't go all in unless I feel like it's relatively safe."

At least, that's what she'd been telling herself. But sometimes, like last night, when she was with Hank, she thought she could easily just throw caution to the wind. Which was so unlike her. Really, what would her children say? Did she even want to know?

Chapter 12

A little before one o'clock, Kate carried the last box from her car into her tiny house. She and Leota had made a remarkable difference in just a short time. Or perhaps it hadn't been as bad off as she'd imagined.

"Wow, it's amazing. You can really walk through here now. Without risking life and limb. Last night I didn't want to get out of bed in the dark for fear I'd trip over something and kill myself." Kate looked around in satisfaction. "But this looks great."

"I love how it all came together. Your pale gray sofa and colorful cushions are just perfect. And the lamps and bright rugs and everything. It's just really homey—and yet classy too." Leota paused to straighten the large oil painting they'd just hung behind the sofa. Kate had painted it herself about twenty years ago. She'd used a photo she'd taken of Jake and Zinnia when they were small. They'd been on a picnic when the kids had taken off running through a field of wildflowers. One of those picture-perfect sort of days.

"Well, this is the last box." Kate set it on the sofa.

Leota frowned. "Do you honestly have room

for anything else? I could swear every single closet and cupboard and shelf is full now."

"These are to go on the walls." Kate opened the box and removed a large family photo taken at Christmas. The year before Kenneth got sick.

"You still have lots of wall space. Oh, and that reminds me. I have something else for you. A tiny housewarming gift."

"You already gave me that gorgeous pot of flowers."

"I know, but this is something small. I'll be right back."

While Leota was outside, taking longer than seemed necessary to get something "small," Kate went around putting up paintings and photos here and there. She was nearly done when Leota came back in.

"Last one." Kate hammered a small nail into the narrow wall space next to the bathroom, hanging up a needlework of birds that her grandmother had given her a long time ago. "Perfect."

"It is perfect." Leota slowly shook her head. "You're ready for an open house."

"So where's that small thing you went out for?" Kate set the hammer in the drawer beneath the stairs that she'd designated for tools.

"I left it on the porch. The reason I took so long is that Zeb was out there."

"Zeb?" Kate's brows arched. "Uh-huh?"

Leota gave her an innocent look. "What's that supposed to mean?"

"I guess you haven't noticed that Zeb seems to be enchanted with you." Kate smiled. "It's sweet."

"He's a nice guy. But we were just chatting, and he invited us for burgers on the porch. Seems he and Hank are fixing us lunch."

"How nice." Kate's stomach growled as if in agreement.

"How about you get that hammer and another nail and we'll go outside to relax a bit until lunch is ready."

"Okay." Kate did as told and met Leota on her tiny porch. Leota had set up the camp chairs, which barely fit, and the flowerpot. She handed Kate a plaque.

"I thought this would look nice out here, but you can obviously do whatever you like with it. Or put it in the give-away pile." She nodded to the two boxes near the porch, filled with the castoffs that just wouldn't work in the tiny house.

Kate took the plaque in her hands, reading the words out loud. *"The place to be happy is here. The time to be happy is now."* She smiled at Leota. "That's so lovely!" She set the plaque down then hammered a nail into one of the posts and hung the plaque. "That's absolutely perfect." She sat down on a camp chair with a weary but pleased sigh. "I am happy here."

"How could you not be?" Leota sat next to her. "It feels like heaven."

"I agree. But I also know there's lots of hard work ahead."

"It's not like you're going to be involved in the actual construction of the development, are you?"

"I don't know. I mean, I doubt I'll be digging ditches or anything like that. But I do want to get flowers planted. Maybe get a greenhouse in. Things that will help me get my florist business off the ground once I'm ready for it."

"Planting flowers sounds more like fun than work to me." Leota leaned back, breathing in deeply. "Oh, man, I could get used to this fresh country air."

"Well, the place to be happy is here, and the time to be happy is now." Kate made a contented sigh. "It sure feels good to relax." But she'd barely leaned back when a bell began to clang so loudly they both nearly jumped out of their chairs.

"Where's the fire?" Leota looked around with wide eyes.

"That must be the dinner bell. I'm guessing our burgers are ready."

Leota laughed. "Well, let's not keep them waiting. I'm starved!"

"Me too."

Lunch was pleasant and the food, though not fancy, was good. Both Kate and Leota were appreciative. And unless Kate was imagining things, not only was Zeb falling for Leota, but she also seemed to be flirting, ever so slightly, with him.

"Can we help clean up?" Kate offered as they were finishing.

"Nope. I'm on KP today," Zeb told her.

"Well, next time you better let me help." Kate stood, taking a moment to thank Hank for his hospitality. "And since you guys don't seem to need our assistance, I'd really like to show Leota some of the town. As well as get some groceries."

"Good idea." Leota poked Kate in the arm. "That new fridge of yours is looking pretty sad and lonely. Not even a jar of pickles in it."

"I'd planned to pack a cooler at my house," Kate confessed. "But everything got so wild and crazy at the end. The clock was ticking, and the new buyers were coming. We wound up tossing everything in the fridge. Fortunately there wasn't much. It was hard to see those condiments in the trash."

"This will be a fresh start," Hank told her.

"You should see the place," she said. "It's all together now."

"I'd like to see it."

"Tell you what. This evening, after I get groceries and everything, I'll have you guys over for a tiny open house. Just appetizers and drinks. You know, keeping it tiny."

"It's a deal." Hank nodded as he picked up a stack of dishes.

"Will, uh, Leota still be here?" Zeb quietly directed to Kate.

"No," Leota answered slowly. "I have to get back home. It's a two-hour drive. And I have work in the morning. I want to be on the road by four at the latest."

"Oh." Zeb nodded with a somber expression. "Well, it's been great getting to know you. Maybe you'll be back to visit Kate again."

"I'm trying to talk Leota into relocating," Kate blurted out. "I want her to have a tiny house and live in Pine Ridge too."

"I don't know if that's—"

"That's a great idea." Zeb's eyes lit up. "You should do it, Leota."

"I'd love to . . . if I could. But for starters, I'd need a job."

"What kind of job?" he asked eagerly.

"I wouldn't be too picky. I doubt there's a design firm in town."

"Not yet," Hank said. "But you never know. Town's growing fast."

"I put myself through college working at Banana Republic," she told them.

"There's a lot of shops in town," Zeb said. "I bet you could get a job in one of them. Hey, what about Molly—you met her at church today. After you guys left, she mentioned she

144

was shorthanded at her clothing store. Right, Hank?"

"She had to go in to work today because one of her girls didn't show. And she wasn't too happy about it."

"You should stop in and see her when you're in town," Zeb told Leota. "Ya never know."

Leota smiled. "That's true. You never know."

They both drove to town so that Leota could go directly from there and Kate could stop by George's and get groceries. But while Kate showed Leota around—AKA showing off the adorable town—they did stop at Molly's Mercantile. It was a nice store with lots of pretty things, and Kate, trying to give them room, pretended to shop. But she couldn't help but overhear them talking, and Molly sounded quite impressed with Leota's work background and even asked her to send a résumé.

"Leota worked under me at the design firm," Kate told Molly as they were about to leave. "I can vouch for her strong work ethic. If I had a shop, I'd hire her in a heartbeat."

"That's great to know. And we'll get even busier than this with summer coming on. So I can use help right away," Molly told Leota. "Please, get back to me ASAP."

Leota promised to do so and, as soon as they were outside, Kate nudged her with an elbow.

145

"Looks like doors are opening up for you, girl-friend."

"One door, maybe. But there are lots of other factors to consider."

"I know. Just keep considering them."

As they strolled through town, which was busier than Kate had ever seen it, Leota seemed to become even more enchanted. "I thought places like this only existed in romance novels or Hallmark movies," she finally said when it was time for her to head home. "I absolutely love it here."

"Enough to make the big move?"

"I'm thinking about it." Leota looked longingly down the charming street. With its old-fashioned lampposts, flowerboxes, cobblestone sidewalks, striped awnings . . . it really was picturesque.

"You could give your two weeks' notice," Kate suggested.

"Then what? Where would I live?"

"A tiny house?"

"Even if I could somehow manage to get a loan for one, where would I put it? Your development hasn't even been started yet."

"That's a good question. Maybe Hank would let you put your house near me, by the barn."

"You really think Hank wants to start lining up tiny houses next to his beautiful log home? Seriously?"

"He might." Kate considered Zeb's interest in

146

Leota and thought it might help motivate Hank. Not that she planned to say as much—to anyone. "At the very least, you can be praying about it. I will too. If it's meant to be, God can open the door. I mean think about it, you practically got offered a job today."

"At a clothing store."

"Yes, it's not exactly like climbing the corporate ladder." Kate felt guilty for enticing this young woman to consider giving up her career. "I'm sorry, Leota. I shouldn't be pushing you like this. You obviously know what's best for you. That's all I'd want for you—whatever is best." She hugged her. "Forgive me for trying to lure you to Pine Ridge."

"Pine Ridge is luring me too." Leota looked across the street at the ice cream parlor that they'd just gotten treats from.

"Remember, you can always come for visits." Kate forced a smile.

"Now you're saying you don't want me to live here?" Leota frowned.

"Not at all. I'd love it. But I meant what I said. I want what's best for you. As much as I love you and would love you living here, it might not be the best."

"Right." She nodded somberly as she opened her car door. "I will be praying about it. All the way home, I'll be praying about it."

"Good." Kate controlled herself from pointing

out other reasons Leota should consider moving here. The fact that her family would be a bit more removed, or the fact that her job was too demanding, or that investing in a tiny home was better than paying rent—those were things Leota could figure out for herself. Instead, she just smiled and waved as Leota drove away.

As Kate pulled into George's Groceries, she knew that God would direct Leota's path. And hopefully he'd direct her here. As she went inside, she could see the grocery store was busy, but not as busy as the store that Kate normally shopped in back home. But it wasn't "back home" anymore, was it? She got her cart then paused by the buckets of flowers. She could never resist a pretty bloom. She gathered up packs of purple irises, orange sunflowers, and a few other things she would arrange in her favorite vase at home. And someday, she would be growing her own flowers and not have to buy them at a grocery store. In the meantime, she'd enjoy these.

Kate felt unusually blissful as she guided her cart through the produce department. Was it her imagination or perhaps even the lighting—or did the fruit and vegetables in here look much better than at the big chain store she normally frequented? She picked out a number of things and then continued down the next aisle. For a small town store, the selection at George's seemed pretty decent. Oh, maybe the prices were higher here. Kate had never been great at keeping track of food costs. Not like some people did. But perhaps she would have to learn to tighten her belt. She'd be willing to clip coupons if it allowed her to live in Pine Ridge.

She got a few special items for her tiny open house. Probably too many things, but nothing extravagant. She suspected Hank and Zeb wouldn't care for anything too fancy. For that matter, she didn't either. And, seeing how much she piled in her cart, she knew she'd probably have leftovers.

At the checkout stand, Kate realized she'd brought no shopping bags, but it was a good excuse to buy new ones. With the store's logo above a lovely scene of pine trees and snow-capped mountains, they weren't just sturdy, they were pretty. She felt like a real local as she carried them through the parking lot. Completely satisfied that George's was a great place to shop, Kate was happy to become a regular. And the people were friendly.

As she drove home—and this really was her home now—she felt genuinely happy, which reminded her of the plaque Leota had given her earlier today.

The place to be happy is here. The time to be happy is now. Maybe she would make that her new motto.

Chapter13

It was fun putting appetizers together in her tiny new kitchen. First she made some spinach-artichoke spread, surrounded by rounds of toasted baguette slices. Next she laid out an attractive cheese and meat plate. Then she arranged a fruit and veggie platter. It wasn't fancy, but it did look nice on her quartz countertop. For beverages, she made a pitcher of iced tea. Then she texted Hank, letting him know that her house was open whenever they wanted to come.

She already had some soft jazz playing on the sound system and, because it was a moderate temperature, she'd left the windows open. On the little table in front of her sofa was her flower arrangement. Everything looked perfect. Perfect and tiny. But she loved it.

"Hello in the house," Hank called over the opened top half of the Dutch door. "Wow, this place is really swanky."

She laughed as she opened the bottom half. "Welcome to my tiny palace."

"See, I told you it was nice," Zeb said as they both came inside. "And it's even better than the last time I was here." He pointed to the flower arrangement. "Nice touch."

"I brought this to help celebrate." Hank held

up a bottle of champagne. "It's been chilling all afternoon."

"How festive." She backed up so they could come into the kitchen area. "My champagne flutes are in storage—along with a million other things I'll probably never need again. But I do have wine glasses." She got three out and set them on the counter.

"But first I want the whole grand tour," Hank said.

"I can give it to you," Zeb offered.

"He probably knows this place almost as well as I do." She laughed as she sat on the sofa. "Go ahead, check it all out. Every nook and cranny if you like."

It didn't take long to see everything, then Hank popped the champagne open and after it bubbled up, he filled their glasses. "Here's to Kate's new tiny home and becoming a citizen of Pine Ridge."

They all clinked glasses and took a sip. "I feel like I should pinch myself," she said as she offered them plates to fill. "A citizen of Pine Ridge? It's amazing. Everything has happened so fast."

"Sometimes that's how life goes. Life races along . . . and then it doesn't." Hank's eyes grew sad, and she suspected he was thinking of Elizabeth again.

"I know what you mean." As Kate watched the

two men load their plates with appetizers, she wondered if she should've prepared them a full meal. Maybe some other evening. "Go ahead and sit on the sofa," she instructed. "It's more comfortable than it looks." After they got situated, she filled her plate and opened up a wooden folding chair to sit across the little coffee table from them. "I'm still figuring out the best uses of my small spaces in here. I'm sure it'll take some time."

"For three of us in here, it's not all that crowded." Hank looked around. "But I doubt you could have a big dinner party. Not that you're planning on entertaining." His brow creased. "You're not, are you?"

She laughed. "No worries there. Besides knowing hardly anyone in this town, I've never been one for hosting big crazy parties."

"Even so, I think we'll need a community building for our tiny house development. It'll give people a place for larger celebrations. I envision it as being a year-round building with an outdoorsy feel. A big stone fireplace in the center with glass garage doors that can open up in the summertime to feel like a giant gazebo."

"That sounds perfect. And I love the idea of not feeling like I'd have to clean house, not only before but after, a social gathering. It's a very freeing thought. Might even make me want to entertain more."

"Elizabeth was great at entertaining." Hank sighed. "That was one reason for the big house. She knew how to decorate it and cook and, well, everything."

"I remember the year you guys had that huge Christmas party," Zeb said. "Elizabeth had those luminarias lining the walk all the way up to the house and all around the porch. I was just a kid, but I was pretty blown away by it. And it was a really cool party too."

"Probably the best gathering we ever had here. That was before Elizabeth got sick." Hank's mouth twisted to one side, as if he didn't want to talk about this. The room grew quiet, and Kate fidgeted with her napkin, trying to think of a happier topic.

"So, did Leota get off okay?" Zeb asked. Probably trying to fill the dead air space.

"Yes." Now to help fill up more space, she told them about how they'd gone to town and to Molly's Mercantile, and how Leota practically got a job offer.

"Do you think she'd really move here?" Zeb looked hopeful.

"Anything's possible. And I can assure you, she's in love with Pine Ridge."

"She seems like a real nice gal." Hank took a sip of champagne. "I liked her."

"I did too," Zeb said.

Hank chuckled. "We noticed."

Zeb looked slightly embarrassed but said nothing.

"Leota is a treasure," Kate declared. "And I'd love to have her here. But like I told her today, I want her to discover what's best for her. Not just do something because other people pressure her." She explained a bit about Leota's somewhat dysfunctional family and how they regularly sponged off of Leota and liked to push her around. "Just because she's so nice."

"Maybe they'd quit taking advantage if Leota lived in Pine Ridge," Zeb suggested. "Not so convenient for her relatives."

"I had similar thoughts." Kate popped a grape tomato in her mouth. "I even suggested she give notice at her job. Then I took it back. It wasn't right for me to push her like that. But I do know she'd love to have her own tiny house."

"To bring here?" Zeb's eyes lit up.

"Why not?" Kate broke a cracker in half.

"Makes me wish we were further along with our development." Hank set his glass down. "But things should start moving fast this week. Just need final approval on some of the permits. Abby assured me, after you and Leota left, that will likely happen this week. She even offered to run herd on everything for us. To make sure it keeps going through the right channels and across the right desks."

"That's great to hear." Kate nodded.

"So back to Leota," Zeb said eagerly. "What if she did give notice on her job? How long do you think it'd take her to relocate here?"

"If her experience was anything like my whirlwind, it could be just a couple of weeks. That would make Molly happy. She said she needs help ASAP." Kate glanced at Hank. "Problem is, even if it all worked out for Leota, and if she got a tiny home as quickly as I did, which might not even be possible since I got a closed-out model that they were trying to get rid of—"

"Someone wanted to get rid of this little gem?" Hank looked around her tiny home. "Why?"

"Younger people are the stronger tiny house market right now. And they prefer a more contemporary style."

"Oh, they want sleek lines, low roofs, minimalist design, mid-century modern." Hank nodded knowingly.

"It's all the rage in tiny homes."

"Not for me," Zeb said. "If I had a tiny home, I'd want it to look like a log cabin."

Hank grinned. "Man after my own heart."

"I saw a really cute log cabin tiny home on that TV series," Kate told them.

"But back to Leota." Zeb leaned forward with an urgent expression. "What exactly would it take to get her here?"

Kate couldn't help but chuckle. "Well, praying might help."

"I can do that." He grinned.

"But even if Leota decided it was right for her, and even if everything went as quickly for her as it did for me, where would she place her tiny home? The development won't be ready that quickly."

"That's true." Hank rubbed his chin. "Maybe we could create a sort of holding area. You know, a section where tiny homes could camp while waiting for our development to be done. Probably needs to be by the barn so we could run water and electric. And I could probably run a line from the barn's septic tank. In fact, I was thinking I should do that for you, Kate."

"The barn has its own septic tank?" Zeb asked.

"Connects to the bathroom in the barn. It was originally Elizabeth's idea. Not for the barn bathroom, but because Elizabeth wanted to create a mother-in-law suite above the barn. I had the plans all drawn and we even ran rough plumbing up there for it. Of course, that, like so many other dreams, never materialized." Hank looked away, his gaze settling on the Christmas photo of Kate's family. "Nice looking kids you got there, Kate. Have you told them about your new digs yet?"

She sighed. "Not yet."

"So back to what you just said." Zeb looked at Hank. "You think it's okay for Leota to park her tiny home here by the barn too?"

"Sure, why not?"

"You'd really do that?" Kate felt doubtful. "Make a holding area for tiny homes?"

"It's my property, I can do what I want," he declared. "Within reason. I realize there are county codes to abide by out here. Like I've said, tiny homes aren't considered permanent structures, so having a few temporarily parked here and there, while we're developing, shouldn't be a problem."

"But you don't want your farm looking like a trailer court." She felt guilty concern for his lovely log home and well-maintained property.

"No, of course not." He seemed to consider this. "But maybe we could take in just one more tiny home. If it was for Leota."

"Yeah!" Zeb eagerly agreed. "We could make room for Leota."

It warmed Kate's heart that they'd welcome Leota and her tiny home here. Even if Leota decided it wasn't for her, it was still very generous of Hank.

"I'm sure things will work out right for Leota. One way or another, in God's timing." Kate sipped her champagne. "Like it did for me."

It was around seven-thirty when Kate finally worked up the nerve to call her children. She wasn't sure why this felt so difficult. Well, besides the fact that they probably wouldn't approve. She wasn't sure who to call first. Zinnia

158

would be easier, but Jake was the oldest. And so she started with him. But the connection was bad, plus it sounded like Jake was distracted by something. After she made it clear that she was okay and nothing was wrong, he abruptly told her he was in the midst of an online gaming tournament. "Can I call you back later, Mom?"

"Yes, of course." She was actually glad to hang up. Next she called Zinnia.

"Hi, Mom. What's up?"

"Quite a bit actually."

"Is something wrong with your phone?"

"I'm afraid the connection isn't too strong." Kate already knew that the metal roof on the barn played havoc with her signal.

"Why don't you call me back on the landline?"

"Well, that would be difficult." She hurried outside, going to the one spot where she got a good signal. "I'm not home." Now that wasn't quite true. She was home. But she needed to break this news gently.

"Where are you?"

"I'm in Pine Ridge."

"Oh, fun. But it's kind of late. Shouldn't you be heading for home by now? Don't you have work tomorrow?"

"I'm not working tomorrow, honey."

"Taking some vacation time? Cool."

"Not exactly. I'm actually living here."

"Living where?"

"In Pine Ridge."

"What?" Her voice was so loud, Kate had to hold the phone away from her ear. "Did you say you're living in Pine Ridge?"

"Remember that tiny house show you wanted me to record?" Kate quickly relayed how inspired she was by it. "So I got a tiny house and moved it to Pine Ridge. And, well, here I am."

"You're kidding me, aren't you?"

"Not at all. I'm living in a tiny house and—"

"How is that even possible? When did this all happen?"

"Well, to be honest, it sort of started on Mother's Day." Kate gave a nervous laugh. "Just a coincidence really."

"Is that what this is about? You're pulling my leg because I totally forgot you on Mother's Day. Here's the deal—I went with Alyssa to the beach that weekend. We rented this yurt with no phone service. Nada, nothing. I meant to call you on Monday, but I had early classes and—"

"I know you kids are busy with your own lives. And, really, that's how it should be. In fact, I've been meaning to tell you and your brother how proud I am of both of you. You're both doing so well. It's really wonderful, and I hope you realize how much that means to me, Zinnia."

"Mom? Are you okay?"

"Of course, I'm okay. I'm perfectly fine."

"You're not dying or anything?"

Kate laughed. "No, honey, I'm in great health."

"But this tiny house biz—is that for real?"

"Yes. I got a tiny house. I'll send you some pictures tomorrow."

"In Pine Ridge?"

"That's right."

"I, uh, I just don't know what to say. This is so totally weird. It's not like you to do something like this. And behind our backs."

"Behind your backs?"

"We're a family. You and me and Jake. Then you go and get a tiny house and move to some Podunk town without telling us? It's just really bizarre."

"I needed a change."

"What about your job?"

"I quit my job."

"You quit? You're too young to retire. What are you going to—"

"I'm going to run a florist shop."

"A florist shop?" Zinnia's shocked tone sounded like she thought her mother planned to operate a mortuary.

"There isn't one in Pine Ridge yet."

"Mom? Seriously, are you okay? I don't mean physically. But are you mentally stable? Because you sound like a real wack-a-doodle. Have you been drinking?"

"Well, I did have a glass of champagne, but—"

"Why are you drinking champagne?"

"To celebrate my tiny new home. I had a little open house this evening." Her tiny house looked so charming in the dusky light, with the window glowing cheerfully from the light inside. She wanted to take a photo. "Oh, you should see the place. It's called the—"

"It's called total lunacy," Zinnia declared. "I honestly think you must be losing it. Does Alzheimer's or dementia run in your side of the family? Because it's like you totally forgot you're a mother with two children."

"Two grown children," Kate said firmly. "That I have put through college. Children who are living their lives—beautifully, I might add. And, yes, I am a mother. I will always be a mother. But that doesn't mean I can't have a life of my own. And that's exactly what I'm doing. I'm sorry if that upsets you, Zinnia. But I think if you give this some time and some careful consideration, you'll come to understand that—"

"What about our house?" she demanded. "Did you just abandon it?"

"No. I sold it."

"You what? You cannot be serious!"

Kate held the phone away from her ear again. "I am serious."

"You sold our house? What about my stuff? I have stuff in my room that I still want. Where am I supposed to put that?"

162

"It's already in a storage unit."

"In a storage unit? Seriously? How could you do this to us? Besides the fact that this whole thing sounds totally nuts, how could you have done all this in such a short amount of time? I mean Mother's Day was—what, like two or three weeks ago?"

"I admit it all happened very quickly. But that just seemed to confirm that it was right."

"Something happens fast so that makes it right? Like a train wreck is right?"

"I'm sorry this is so hard on you."

"You bet it's hard. It's certifiable. So, if what you're saying is really true—you quit your job, sold our house, and you're living in a tiny house in Pine Ridge—how do you plan to support yourself?"

"I already told you, I want to open a florist shop. But not right away. First I plan to help with a tiny house development. It's on this pretty little farm."

"Like a funny farm?"

"Don't be silly, Zinnia. We're making a partnership. It's all drawn out by a lawyer. And then we'll create what will be a very nice community around the irrigation pond. We already have people who want to join us. Once that's done, I'll open my florist shop."

"My head is exploding. I can't take this all in. I'm not trying to be mean, but I seriously think you're losing it. None of this makes any sense. Did you tell Jake yet?"

"He's busy playing some online game."

"Man, I can't wait to hear his response. He'll probably want to have you put away."

"Oh, Zinnia."

"You're really not just making this all up, are you? I mean, to get back at me for missing Mother's Day? Because that would actually be pretty funny."

"Everything I told you is absolutely true." Kate's phone beeped. "I think my phone is about to die. And I'm not sure where my charger cord is at the moment. So maybe I should say good-bye."

Zinnia glumly said good-bye and hung up. As Kate turned off her phone, she experienced a strange mix of emotions. Part of her felt relieved for getting it out there and she had no doubt that Zinnia would call Jake at first opportunity. She also felt sad that Zinnia had seemed genuinely hurt by being left out of the loop. On top of all that, she felt angry. Zinnia's tone and accusations hadn't been respectful. Kate wondered, as she went back inside, hadn't she taught her children better than that? Maybe not, but time would tell.

Chapter 14

Kate wasn't too surprised when Jake called her the next morning. At least she'd found her phone charger last night and after scurrying outside, still in her pajamas, she could actually hear him.

"According to Zinnia, you are off your rocker, Mom."

"She definitely seemed to think so last night. But I assure you, I'm perfectly sane. And how are you? Did you win your internet game?"

"Never mind that. Is it true? Did you quit your job, sell our house, and join a commune?"

"Join a commune?" She couldn't help but laugh. "Seriously?"

"That's what Zinnia said."

"It's true that I quit my job and sold the house. But I have not joined a commune."

"Zinnia said something about tiny houses on a farm—and that it's a commune."

"Part of that's true. I do live in a tiny home now. And we plan to make a community for tiny homes, but we are most certainly not a commune."

"Who are *we?*"

"What do you mean?"

"It sounds like there's a group. Who are the others?"

"My partner in this development is Hank Branson. He owns a very nice farm just outside of town. We are developing a tiny house community—not a commune. Right here on his lovely farm."

"What do you mean by partner? You're not putting your own money into this crazy scheme, are you?"

"First of all, it's not a crazy scheme. And—"

"A tiny house community? Seriously, that's not crazy? Who does that?"

"Pine Ridge is growing fast, and there's a lack of real estate. In fact, there's a thriving tiny house community at Pine Ridge Lake right now. With a waiting list. And we plan to put a similar development right here on Hank's property."

"How did you meet this Hank?"

"I met his niece-in-law and her mother at breakfast a while back, and they gave me Hank's number."

"This really does sound insane, Mom. Are you sure you're okay?"

"I am fine. In fact, I haven't been this happy since before your dad died."

"And you're not, uh, smoking anything?"

"Don't be ridiculous."

"I'm trying to wrap my head around it, but I gotta say it sounds like you're losing it. Normal people just don't quit their jobs, sell their houses, and move away like that. Zinnia said it's because you're mad at us because we both forgot you on Mother's Day. I meant to send you flowers, but it's been super busy at work."

"Mother's Day had nothing to do with my decisions." But she wondered if that was totally true. "I realize you and your sister have your own lives. And, like I told her last night, I'm very proud of both of you. Really, Jake, you're doing so well up in Seattle. I couldn't be more pleased. But I need to have my own life. And that house was just way too big. And my job hasn't been fulfilling for a while now. I've always dreamed of having a florist shop."

"A florist shop? Where did that come into the picture?"

"I want to open a florist shop here in town. That's part of my plan. But first I need to grow some flowers. Maybe make a greenhouse."

"Oh, Mom, you sound crazier by the minute." He let out a loud exasperated sigh. "But I gotta go. I'm at work and have a meeting in five minutes."

"Thanks for calling." She didn't really feel grateful. "And have a good day." She hung up and just shook her head. Kids!

"Good morning."

She turned to see Hank, with Chester at his heels, strolling over to her. Realizing she still had on her *I Love Lucy* pajamas, she felt her cheeks grow warm. And it wasn't that she was indecent or anything like that, but she did feel embarrassed. "Uh, good morning." She knelt down to scratch Chester's head. "Good boy."

"Looks like a beautiful day."

As she slowly stood, she felt him peer curiously at her. "I was, uh, on my phone." She held it up. "Had to come outside because the connection's better out here."

"The metal barn roof messes with it."

"My son called, but I had to take it." She looked down at her bare feet. "Even though I was still in my pajamas."

"I noticed." He grinned. "So you told your kids then?"

She nodded grimly.

"Didn't go so well?" He frowned.

"Not at all." She folded her arms in front of her. "I didn't expect them to be happy about it, but I never dreamed they'd take it quite so badly. They both seem to think I've lost my ever-loving mind."

"Really?"

"Yes. And they weren't very nice about it either."

"Maybe they just need time to process it."

She slowly nodded. "That's what I told both of them. And if they don't call me for a while, it'll be just fine with me." She let out a frustrated sigh. "Kids."

"Sorry to hear that. But here's an idea to

distract you. How about going under cover over at Pine Ridge Lake Estates today? I want to finalize my plans, and I'm curious as to whether we've overlooked anything. Care to play spy?"

"I'd love to. Should I take photos or anything like that?"

"No, let's keep it low-key. Just nose around and see if there's anything you think we should add to our plans. I promised the city I'd have the final site plan to them by noon."

She made a mock salute. "I'm on it, sir."

He laughed. "You might want to change your uniform first."

She rolled her eyes. "Yes, I plan on it."

"Oh, another thing, Kate. Did you have a chance to read the agreement the lawyer drafted?"

She nodded. "It actually looks pretty good to me. Although I'm no legal expert."

"Do you have your own attorney? Someone to look at it for you?"

She remembered Gerald Rothwell, the attorney who'd handled Kenneth's will. "Yes, I guess so."

"Can you get him to go over it? If you want, I can fax it to him. Or have my attorney send an e-copy."

"That'd be great. How about if I text you my attorney's number?"

"Perfect."

"And then I will go under cover over at Pine Ridge Estates." She grinned. "Should be interesting." As she went inside, she decided to step up her game a bit. Not only would she dress a bit more carefully than the jeans and T-shirt she'd planned to wear today, but she'd also do something about her hair and even put on a bit of makeup. If she wanted to be taken as a serious prospective customer, she should look the part. Besides, next time she crossed paths with Hank again, she'd like him to forget the image of her bedhead hair, pillowcase-creased face, and those silly *I Love Lucy* pajamas. Good grief.

Chapter 15

Kate convinced herself that she wasn't really spying at Pine Ridge Lake Estates. She was simply a fellow businessperson looking for a few pointers. Besides, she wanted to remove her name from their ever-growing waiting list. She parked in the visitors' lot and got out and just looked around. This development felt more like a resort than a housing development. But that was partly due to the beautiful lake. And the tall lodge with its wide open porches looked inviting. She knew there was a community room with a big stone fireplace inside because she'd studied the brochure. It also had laundry facilities, a small general store, and a coffee shop.

"Can I help you?" A man dressed in khakis and a polo shirt approached her as she stood out in front of the handsome lodge building.

"Maybe." She tipped her sunglasses to see him better in the shadows of the towering pine trees. He appeared to be about her age or perhaps older. She'd never been good at guessing ages. His hair was dark with gray at the temples, and he wasn't unattractive. Although only a bit taller than her, he had a somewhat imposing stature. Maybe he was just that sure of himself.

"I'm Glen Stryker." He extended his hand with

a wide smile. "Welcome to Pine Ridge Lake Estates."

"Kate Burrows." She smiled back. "This isn't my first time here."

"Well, that's a good sign. Are you here to visit a friend? Or looking for a fun place to live?"

She explained about her last visit. "Although I was disappointed to hear that you only lease lots, I put myself on your wait list."

"I see." He pursed his lips, as if pondering. Did he suspect she was a spy?

"I assume you're the owner." She felt a bit uneasy now. "I've heard your name before."

"Owner and developer. So, you want to own your own lot?"

"That's right." She nodded.

"I've been thinking about developing some of my land for people to purchase. Of course, it wouldn't be lake front property, but it would be bigger lots." He seemed to be studying her closely.

"The woman helping me the other day, I think her name was Kerry, never mentioned anything about that."

"Kerry's my daughter. I told her to keep this idea under her hat for the time being. Don't want it getting around quite yet."

"But you're telling me about it?" Kate grew suspicious.

"Well, you could be a potential customer."

She smiled again. "That's true. You see, I already have my own tiny home. I just got it. And I had been looking for somewhere to place it."

"Want to see the land I'm talking about?" he offered.

It felt deceptive to agree, especially considering she had zero interest in relocating here. "Oh, I don't want to waste your time." She glanced around nervously. "I really just came out here to let Kerry, or someone, know that they can, uh, remove me from the wait list."

"Come on, Kate. Let me show you the property I'm talking about. You might be just the incentive I need to start developing it."

"But I—"

"There's my Jeep. Come on, let's take a ride." He actually grabbed her hand, leading her toward a white Wrangler with the top down. "This'll be fun."

Not knowing how to explain her way out of this, she allowed him to lead her over to the Jeep and, feeling guilty as he opened the passenger door, she turned to him. "I really don't want to waste your time. I'm pretty sure I won't be interested in those lots. I really wanted something on the water and—"

"Some of the land is elevated." He helped her into the Jeep. "And if a few trees were removed, there'd be a nice lake view to boot."

"I wouldn't want to be on a hillside." But he'd already gotten into the driver's seat.

He continued to talk—like a salesman—as he turned onto an unpaved road. Before long they were going on what seemed more like a trail, straight up a rugged looking hill.

Kate hoped the Jeep wasn't going to roll over. As they bumped along a very rough road, she clung tightly to the seat, trying to listen to Glen's explanation of how he'd attained this property.

"I got this inheritance from my grandfather when I was in my twenties. Naturally, my buddies wanted me to go live it up. I almost bought a forty-two foot sailboat. But then my mom told me about this land, convincing me it was a good investment. My buddies thought I was crazy." He laughed as he pulled over next to a fairly steep ridge. "But they don't think so anymore." He opened his door. "Well, this is it. Want to take a peek?"

Kate really didn't want to take a peek, but still feeling guilty for leading him on like this, she knew she had to play along. She carefully got out, watching her footing for fear she might tumble down the rugged hillside. And perhaps she would deserve it.

"I'll admit it's beautiful up here." She looked around, inhaling deeply of the pine mountain air. "But I would much rather place my tiny home on flat ground."

"Come over here." He called to her. "You can see the lake through the trees in this spot. Might give you an idea of how nice it could be, cleared out some."

She went over to stand by him, looking out the direction he was pointing toward. "It could be a pretty view," she agreed. "But it doesn't seem very accessible to me."

"You have to imagine a paved road and leveled lots." He used his hands to explain. "Everything's possible."

"Maybe so. But I want a lot where I can grow flowers." She nervously explained her ideas for a florist shop in town, hoping this would convince him she was not his best customer.

"Good for you, Kate." He smiled. "This town could sure use a good florist."

"I do appreciate you showing me this, but I really can't imagine putting my tiny house up here. Although I'm sure plenty of people would love it."

"And you're sure you don't want to be the first?" He sounded disappointed.

"No, thank you."

He frowned. "So you're saying I really can't talk you into putting your tiny house up here? Not even with the lot all nicely flattened out, some trees removed, and the beautiful lake view? You can honestly say no to all this? What if the price was right?"

"I'm sorry, but I still don't think it would work for me." She firmly shook her head.

He sighed loudly as he opened the Jeep door for her. "You can't blame a guy for trying."

"I'm sure you'll have no trouble finding people who'll be very interested." She frowned as she got inside. Hopefully she hadn't inspired him to develop even more lots and create more competition for what she and Hank hoped to do. If so, maybe they deserved it for sending her up here to spy like this.

"I really feel bad for wasting your time," she said.

"No worries. I love an excuse to come up here," he assured her. "In fact, I might have the first tiny home up here. I already have a house. A nice big house. But I wouldn't mind having a little getaway place."

She wondered what he needed to get away from. She'd assumed he was married at first but had later noticed an absence of a wedding ring. Still, you never knew. Not that she cared one way or another. "Do you think it could be precarious to get up here in the wintertime?" she asked as they bounced down the hill with a little too much speed. "What if there was snow or ice?"

"We'd just deal with it."

"Uh-huh." She let out a little shriek as a wheel on his side went over a big rock, tipping them precariously toward her side of the trail. Were they about to flip?

"When I first bought this property, I had this old army Jeep that I could take clear to the top of that hill. Now, that was exciting." He turned onto the graveled road that led to the lodge.

She was glad to be back on the solid ground of the asphalt parking lot as Glen helped her out of the Jeep. "Thanks again for showing me that." She sighed. "I guess I'm more of a flatlander." She peered out over the lake. "A lot with water access. Now that would be tempting."

"You like being on the water?" he asked.

"I know those lots are all taken or spoken for," she said quickly. Hopefully they really were. What would she say if he offered her one?

"How do you feel about boats?"

"Boats?" She blinked. "Are you selling boats too?"

"No." He laughed. "But I wanted to take mine out this morning. Care to come along? I could show you even more of the lake from out there."

The idea of a boat ride was appealing, but Kate knew she needed to get out of here. She'd already gotten in over her head. She was trying to think of an excuse to bow out, but once again, he grabbed her hand. "Come on, Kate, we're wasting time."

"But I—"

"Don't worry, I'm not trying to sell you anything. This is just for fun."

"For fun?" she echoed as he led her over to a dock where several boats were tied. "Okay then. If it's just for fun. As long as you understand I'm not interested in purchasing anything up here."

He waved his hand. "No problem." He led her to the end of the dock where a large, sleek looking boat was gently bobbing. "There she is, the *Bloody Mary*."

"*Bloody Mary?*" Kate frowned.

He laughed as he helped her onto the boat. "For my mom. It was her nickname. Her name was Mary, and she loved serving her friends Bloody Marys on Sunday mornings. Kind of corny, I know. But Mom passed away a few years ago."

"Oh. Well, that's nice. I mean that you named it for her. I'm sorry for your loss."

He was untying ropes and things, tossing them into the boat, and then he jumped onto it himself. Before long they were racing across the lake. "There's a speed limit out here," he called out over the noise of the engine. "But if I don't see any sheriff boats around, I like to kick it up. Helps to blow the carbon out of the motor."

Again, Kate was holding on tightly, wondering if Glen was always such a speedster. "Do you race cars too?" she asked.

He laughed. "Nope. But I wouldn't mind trying

it." He slowed it down now. "Sorry, was I making you uncomfortable?"

She relaxed a bit. "Maybe a little. But I'm sure I deserve it."

"Why's that?" He glanced at her with a puzzled expression.

"I have a confession to make."

"A confession?" He slowed the boat down even more, turning to look at her.

She quickly poured out the story of how she and Hank were going to make a tiny home development on his farm. "I honestly didn't know anything about it when I first came out here. At that time I really did want to put my tiny home here. But Kerry made it clear I couldn't do that. Then I met Hank. And now my tiny home is parked at his farm and we're trying to make a place—a more affordable place—for tiny homes." She paused to catch her breath. "I came out here today to spy on our competition."

He looked totally shocked and then he started to laugh. Loudly.

"So you're not offended?"

"Offended?" He shook his head. "No, I'm flattered. I think it's a nice compliment."

"Of course, our development won't be anything like yours," she assured him. "I mean it's on a farm for starters. Not nearly as beautiful as what you've got out here. No one can compete against that. And our residents will lease the lots but own their tiny homes. And our lots will be a little bigger."

"I heard that someone in town was going to start a tiny house development, but I didn't know it was Hank. That's interesting."

"So you're not mad about me spying?"

He chuckled. "If someone sends out a beautiful spy, who am I to complain?"

Kate felt her cheeks grow warm. "Thank you . . . I guess."

"And now that I have captured my spy—out here on the lake with no place to run—I think I'll interrogate you. I want to know what brings you to Pine Ridge, and where you're from, and why you're so interested in tiny homes." He turned the motor off then led her back to a lounging area. "Sit down and relax while I get us something to drink." He grinned. "How do you feel about a Bloody Mary?"

She waved a hand. "No thanks. But water would be fine."

"Sparkling water?"

"Even better." She smiled, feeling relieved as she sat down. He really didn't seem the least bit disturbed by her failed attempt at espionage.

He went down below, and she looked around the lake. Their boat was floating in a quiet cove a little bit east of Pine Ridge Estates. And from here the tiny houses looked even more charming. On the opposite side of the lake was the state park

where she and Kenneth used to take the kids . . .
a lifetime ago. Naturally, this reminded her of the
conversations she'd had with Zinnia and Jake.

"Something troubling you?" He set two glasses
of sparkling soda, complete with lime wedges, on
the low table then sat down across from her.

"I was just thinking of my kids." She nodded
to the park. "My late husband and I used to take
them there sometimes."

"You're widowed?"

"Yes. Five years." She took a sip. "I think
you'd make a better spy than I did."

He chuckled. "For the record, I'm divorced.
Eight years."

"Oh." She nodded and then answered his earlier
questions about where she was from and why she
was here. "And the real reason I looked unhappy
just now was because my kids, who are normally
well adjusted adults, are both furious at me for
moving here."

"That's too bad."

"Hopefully, they'll get over it."

"And how did you meet Hank?" he asked.

She explained about meeting his niece-in-law
and her mother.

"Aileen and Jessie."

"You know them?"

"It's a small town. It doesn't take long to know
everyone. At least it used to be like that. Pine
Ridge has been growing fast these last few years.

I used to go to George's for a gallon of milk and it would turn into a happy reunion. I'd see all my old friends and we'd visit for an hour. Sometimes I go now and don't see a single person I know. It's weird, and sad."

"Thanks to outsiders like me moving here."

"Some outsiders are welcome." He lifted his glass like a toast. "Here's to more like you, Kate."

"Even though I was a spy?" she teased.

"A most beautiful spy." He winked. "But back to Hank. I haven't seen him in a while. I know he lost his wife. Very sad. I hear he's had a hard time getting over it and that he lives like a hermit. Is that still true?"

"I really don't know him that well. We only just met," she admitted. "But I do think he's still grieving. And yet I think he's trying to move on."

"Maybe you're helping him to move on?"

She didn't know what to say, and so she started to question Glen the same way he'd questioned her. Besides being divorced, he had three grown kids. One son in the Air Force. A daughter on the east coast with a husband and child. And Kerry, his youngest and right-hand gal.

Kate asked him some questions about Pine Ridge Lake Estates and actually learned quite a bit about his development. Now she understood why his lots were so small and so very expensive. His development fees, especially for sewer and water, thanks to the proximity of the lake, had been very costly.

"It would've been ten times that much if I hadn't started when I did," he finally said. "Environmental laws keep changing. Fortunately, I was grandfathered in on a number of things."

"Hopefully Hank's property won't be as complicated."

"I'm sure it won't. Still, the EPA could throw a wrench in the works. You never know." He smiled slyly. "But if things don't work out for you there, I'll still make you a good deal on one of my hillside lots. Maybe I'll start developing it this summer. Could be ready by fall."

"Don't do anything on my account." She set her empty glass down. "Now, if you're finished with my interrogation, I really should be getting back to town. I have a number of errands to run today."

"And I have an appointment at eleven." He checked his watch. "Yikes, looks like I'm already late. Hopefully Kerry is holding down the fort." He started the engine. "Hold on to your hat, Katie." And like a shot, he took off.

Kate grabbed the glasses to keep them from tumbling to the deck then braced herself against the back of the seat as he zipped over the water. The man definitely had a need for speed. And sure, maybe Glen was their competition, but he was okay. She was even somewhat flattered by his unconcealed interest in her. And under different circumstances, she might've even returned that interest.

With Glen hurrying off to his meeting in the lodge, Kate enjoyed the liberty of snooping around for a bit. She didn't really discover anything that she and Hank hadn't already considered for their own development. In fact, by the time she was leaving the estates, she realized that some of their ideas might actually be better than what Glen had going on here. Of course, they wouldn't have the scenic lake. But hopefully, the pond would help make up for that. Plus the larger lots that allowed tenants to not only place their own tiny homes, but have a fenced yard and pets if they so chose. Really, in Kate's mind, their tiny house development would be better.

Chapter 16

Once Kate was in town, she texted Hank about her espionage at Pine Ridge Lake Estates. Without going into details over the special treatment she'd received from Glen, she assured him that she didn't think they'd missed anything in their plans and wished him good luck with the city. Hopefully it would go well.

After a trip to the hardware store for a few items to make tiny home life more comfortable, followed by a quick bite of lunch, Kate headed back to the farm. She wasn't too surprised to see that Hank's pickup was gone, and Zeb was nowhere to be seen. Although it did give her a feeling of being somewhat isolated out here. Of course, she knew they both had lives to lead and chores to do. She couldn't expect them to sit out here and hold her hand.

And, actually, she decided she was grateful for an undisturbed afternoon of peace and quiet. When had she last experienced that? Maybe this was something she should get used to. Kate carried her bag from the hardware store into her tiny house and looked around with satisfaction. It felt good to be home. She laid out the things she'd gotten earlier. Hooks to go on doors for jackets and hats and whatnot. Cup hooks to make more shelf room in the kitchen cupboards. A paper towel holder, toilet paper roll holder, and a towel bar for the bathroom. Along with a few other necessities to make her abode even more comfortable. She got out her toolbox and was all set to go to work. But first she put on some music.

It was fun to putter around, taking her time to fix and tweak her compact new home. It reminded her of when she was a little girl. A neighbor friend had the most delightful play-house in her backyard. Kate instantly loved it. Probably more than she loved her neighbor friend Julie. Looking back, Kate understood that Julie had been spoiled. Probably because she was an only child and her parents doted on her. Anyway, Julie's dad built the playhouse for her birthday, but Julie didn't seem to appreciate the small structure nearly as much as Kate did. Even when Kate made curtains, from flowery pillowcases she'd snuck from her mom's linen closet, Julie had acted uninterested. Kate had brought over a number of other pilfered things to make Julie's playhouse homier. A teapot and vase with flowers from her mom's garden. She even donated a braided rug that her grandma had made. But in the end, Julie couldn't care less. The door to the playhouse was eventually locked. And Kate quit going over there.

But this playhouse was Kate's. And having the

afternoon all to herself with her new playhouse was truly fun. She hung hooks and arranged and rearranged, making everything just right. And then she took a nap on her sofa with soft music playing. It was heavenly. Just the vacation she'd been needing.

It was around five when she took an iced tea out to her little front porch and sat down. The camp chairs were okay, but Kate liked the idea of rocking chairs. It looked like enough room to squeeze in a pair. Hopefully she could find some old-fashioned wooden ones. She realized as she sat out there, she still had flowerboxes to fill. How had she managed to overlook that? And what about some wind chimes? Shouldn't a tiny home have wind chimes? And maybe a little table to set out here.

She made herself another list, planning to go to town again tomorrow. And then, seeing that neither Zeb nor Hank appeared to be around, she went inside and began fixing herself a light dinner. As she sat down to eat, she noticed that Hank's pickup was back. Parked in front of his house. And Zeb was home now, sweeping the front porch. She wondered what they were having for dinner. But she felt glad they didn't feel compelled to include her. It would be awkward to assume they were making her part of their family. She certainly didn't expect that.

After she finished her dinner, she washed her

dishes, which turned out to be another tiny house delight. When had she last washed dishes by hand? It was surprisingly soothing. And a good way to get her fingernails really clean. With everything clean and dry and put away, she made herself a cup of herbal tea. She would take it outside and watch the sunset.

Fortunately, her tiny house was situated so that she could sit on her front porch out of sight of Hank's house. Although she could sneak a peek through the lattice on the side opening of her porch and get a partial view—if she wanted to. Not that she planned to do that. Of course, she was a little curious, but it wasn't like she wanted to be a voyeur. Or a nuisance. She really did not want to be a nuisance.

But when she heard a door closing, she couldn't help but take a peek. With no lights on in her tiny house yet, she felt sufficiently hidden enough not to be observed. She peeked through the lattice in time to see Hank pacing back and forth on his porch. She felt guilty for watching. Except that she couldn't seem to stop herself.

It looked like he was talking to himself. Pacing and talking. Or maybe he was on the phone. She couldn't really tell from here. But it went on for a bit. Then he sank down into one of his porch chairs, leaning over with his head in his hands—like he was crying. She turned away quickly, catching her breath. This was not something she wanted to see. Or to be seen watching.

Almost afraid to move or make a sound, she remained frozen in the camp chair, waiting for Hank to leave. Her half-drunk tea grew cold in the mug as she sat there. Finally, hearing the front door solidly close, she snuck a quick look. He seemed to be gone.

Feeling guilty, nosy, and intrusive, she slipped back into her house. But instead of turning on the lights, she just sat down in the darkness, wondering. What had that been all about? Her best guess was that Hank was still working out his grief. She remembered her own moments like that. Times when she would shake her fist at God and the universe, crying out that it was unfair, demanding to know why she'd been left alone.

Fortunately, that had only lasted for the first year. Oh, maybe a time or two after that. But eventually, she'd come to grips with God. Certainly, she didn't understand his ways, but she trusted that his ways were higher than hers. After two years, she was able to be grateful for all the years she'd had with Kenneth. And by the third year, she'd pretty much moved on. Well, mostly. But Hank had three years behind him, and yet he was still this deep in grief?

As she got ready for bed, still in darkness because for some reason she didn't want to turn on lights and draw attention to her intrusive presence over here by Hank's barn, she wondered, would he ever get over the loss of his wife? Elizabeth, Kate knew from what she'd heard from all who knew her, had been a very special woman. A dreamer and a doer who had fought cancer and lost. She wouldn't be easy to get over.

Kate had noticed a portrait of what she knew had to be Elizabeth hanging above the fireplace in Hank's home. She'd spotted it on the night they went into the dining room to go over the plans for their tiny home development. With just a glance, Kate had taken in the golden hair, sparkling blue eyes, creamy complexion—Elizabeth had been a natural beauty. Probably just one more reason Hank wasn't over her. And maybe never would be. Kate knew enough from her grief counseling and reading books to respect that some people never recovered. Some people mated for life—and never moved on from the loss of a loved one. At least not enough to love again. Maybe that was Hank.

Chapter 17

Once again, by the time Kate took her cup of coffee out to her front porch the next morning, Hank's pickup was gone. By now she knew that although Hank did some work from home, he also had an office in town where he met with clients to go over building plans. Plus he was still meeting with city officials in an effort to keep their tiny house development moving along.

"Good morning," Zeb called out as he strolled toward the barn.

"Morning," she called back. "Beautiful day."

"Yep." He nodded. "I get to start work on the development today."

"Really?" She set down her coffee and went over to talk to him while he fiddled with a big tractor. "What are you going to do?"

"Uncle Hank said I can start grading the access roads. He and the surveyor got 'em all marked out yesterday afternoon."

"Maybe I'll walk over there and take a look."

"It'll be a dusty mess while I'm running the tractor. You should probably wait until the end of the day, you know, to let the dust sort of settle. Plus you'll be able to actually see where the roads go by then."

"Good point."

"Oh, Hank said to ask if you'd heard back from your lawyer yet." He got up into the tractor seat.

"No, but I'll check on that today."

"Sounds like everything is going nice and smooth down at City Hall."

"I'm sure it must be keeping Hank pretty busy."

"That and this client who keeps making changes to her house plans. Driving him crazy."

"That must be a pain."

"She's got too much money and too much time on her hands. At least, that's what Uncle Hank says. She can't make up her mind about anything." Zeb laughed as he turned on the tractor. "Or else she's just trying to keep Uncle Hank around for the fun of it." He spoke loudly to be heard over the engine.

Kate smiled. She could sort of understand that.

"Well, I better get going. Burning daylight here."

"Have fun." She waved then returned to her coffee. So Hank had a wealthy female client that liked having him around. Well, that wasn't too surprising. She got her phone to check in with her attorney via email, but was surprised to see he'd already sent her a message, along with a bill for his time. His post stated that he'd read over the contract, since Hank's attorney had said it was urgent, and found it to be sound and well written. Although he couldn't do anything more to legally protect her capital interests, since this was an investment venture, it seemed like a solid idea with the potential to pay off nicely. And he wished her good luck.

Without giving it too much more thought, Kate pulled out the contract Hank had given to her and signed it. Then, eager to get it back into his hands, she decided to take it over to the house. At first she was going to just set it on the little porch table by the front door, but then she decided, if the door wasn't locked, it might be safer to just put it inside. The door, not surprisingly, was unlocked. And so, feeling a bit like an interloper, she went inside and started to place the envelope on a big oak table in the foyer. Chester came tearing around the corner but, after letting out a half-hearted bark, recognized her. Wagging his tail, he came over, eager to be petted. She knelt down to give his ears a good scratch.

From there, she could see the fireplace, with the portrait of Elizabeth hanging above it. And, even though she felt even more intrusive now, she stood up and, with Chester following her, went closer. She wanted a really good look at this amazing and beautiful woman. Of course, the more she looked, the worse she felt. Not only for the loss of what she knew was a really fine person, but because Kate felt certain she could not hold a candle—whatever that really meant—to someone like Elizabeth. She felt she understood even better now how difficult it would be for someone like Hank to get over her.

"What are you doing in here?"

Shocked to hear his voice, Kate turned to see Hank at the foot of the stairway, staring at her. "Oh!" She sheepishly held up the envelope. "I, uh, I brought the signed contract in here for you. The door was unlocked and I, uh, I was looking for someplace to set it."

He walked over to take it from her. "Thank you."

"I thought you were gone. Your pickup wasn't—"

"It's over in the garage. I was adding some brake fluid." He set the envelope on the foyer table.

"I'm sorry." She headed for the door. "I shouldn't have just walked in."

"It's okay." He sighed. "It's just that you took me by surprise."

"That portrait of Elizabeth, it's so beautiful. She was so beautiful." Tears were filling Kate's eyes now. She wasn't even sure why. "I, uh, I can see why it was so—so hard to lose her." Her voice cracked with emotion. "Please, excuse me." And then she dashed out the door. Feeling awkward and foolish, she hurried to her tiny house, grabbed up her purse then jumped in her car and drove away.

It wasn't until she was in town that she was able to calm down. But it took her a moment to remember why she had wanted to come to town today. Had she made a list? Then seeing a hanging flower basket, she remembered. She wanted to get plants for her flowerboxes. And she wanted rocking chairs. And wind chimes. But where to find these things? She decided to start with the hardware store.

To her delight, the hardware store not only had a decent selection of flowers in their garden section, including some red geraniums that she knew would look lovely in the flowerboxes, they also had wind chimes. She was just purchasing these items when she felt a tap on her shoulder. She turned to see Glen Stryker standing behind her in line.

"We meet again." He grinned with a twinkle in his eye.

She smiled. "So we do." She finished paying and picked up the box of blooms and wind chimes, letting him step up to the cash register to make his purchase of just one item.

She was balancing the box and trying to open the rear of her SUV when Glen showed up and offered to help. "Wouldn't want you to spill your pretty blooms all over the street." He waited for the back to rise then slid the box into place. "Looks like you've got work to do now."

She told him about the window boxes as she closed the back. "For my tiny home." She brushed dirt from her hands. "Now I need to find some rocking chairs."

"Rocking chairs?" He grinned. "Maybe I can be of help."

"How's that?"

"I know a guy on the edge of town. I get my rocking chairs from him."

"Really?"

He nodded eagerly. "If you want to follow me, I can show you where his shop is located."

"Sure. Where's your Jeep parked?"

"No Jeep today." He pointed to a shiny white pickup parked right across the street. "Had to run some errands and pick up a few things so I brought my truck."

She wondered how many vehicles and boats and toys this guy had but said nothing as she got into her SUV. After a short drive, they were both standing in front of an old-fashioned house with a dozen shaker style rockers sitting in the front yard.

"See." Glen looked pleased with himself. "What'd I tell you?"

"These are perfect," she exclaimed. "Just what I wanted."

"What color?"

She pointed to a pair of white ones. "I think those will do nicely."

Now Glen was introducing her to an old gentleman named Harvey and even negotiating for a special price on the two rockers. Harvey shook her hand, and she paid for them. Glen gave her a sly look. "How you going to fit those into your SUV?"

"Good question." She frowned.

"I'll be happy to deliver them for you," Glen told her, "on one condition."

"What's that?"

"You have lunch with me."

"Lunch?"

"You do eat, don't you? And it's nearly eleven now. We'll get these to your place then come back to town for lunch. Deal?"

She shrugged. "Okay. Deal."

"Your enthusiasm is overwhelming." He laughed.

"Sorry." She smiled. "I'm actually pretty hungry. Haven't had breakfast yet."

"Then let's get going. I know where Hank's place is, so I'll meet you there."

"Knowing how fast you like to go, you'll probably get there first." Just the same, she hurried to her car, hoping to get a head start while he and Harvey loaded up the chairs. She wasn't sure what Hank would think to see Glen driving onto his property, but hopefully she'd get there first. And maybe Hank was gone by now.

She didn't exactly speed back to the farm, but she didn't dillydally either. And she made it there before Glen. She had already unloaded her plants, setting them in the shade, before Glen roared up the driveway. She walked out to meet him, casting a quick glance over to the garage, but unable to see if Hank's pickup was there or not.

"Let's get these unloaded and back to town for lunch," she said as he opened his tailgate. "I'm starved."

Surprisingly agile, Glen hopped into the back of his pickup and slid a chair toward her, helping her to ease it to the ground. And then the next one. They were just carrying it across the driveway when Hank came out the front door with a curious expression.

"Hey, Hank." Glen set the chair down to wave. "How ya doing, buddy?"

As Hank greeted them, he strolled over to investigate. "What's up?"

Kate awkwardly explained about meeting Glen in town and his help in acquiring the rockers. "Wasn't that nice of him?" She forced a smile.

"Yeah. Nice." Hank still looked confused.

"But my help was conditional," Glen said. "Kate has to go to lunch with me now."

She made an uneasy shrug then continued to lug her rocker toward her tiny house. Meanwhile, Glen remained behind, chatting with Hank like Mr. Congeniality. Oh, well. Hopefully she could explain the situation better to Hank . . . later. She stopped by her front porch, and since the fellows were still visiting, she removed the camp chairs and folded them neatly, leaned them against the house. Then she put the first rocker in place and stepped back to admire it. Perfect!

She was just going back for the second one when she noticed a silver convertible coming up the driveway. This place was starting to look like Grand Central. Kate paused, watching the vehicle more closely. It was a Corvette being driven by an attractive blonde, who was now getting out and waving to the men. But Chester didn't seem pleased about her arrival. Barking wildly, he had to be called back.

"Quiet, Chester," Hank commanded. "Sit, boy."

"Hey there, Natalie." Glen smiled brightly as he went forward to shake the woman's hand. "What brings you out here?"

She pointed to Hank. "This man. I've been calling you all morning, Hank. Don't you ever check your phone?"

"I was working on my truck."

"Well, that's okay." She beamed at him. "I just needed an excuse to come out here. You promised to show me your house, but you never seem to get around to it."

"Guess this is your lucky day." He jerked his thumb toward his house. "Go ahead and look around."

"But I want *you* to give me the grand tour." She linked her arm in his.

Kate felt like an outsider as she approached

them, but soon Hank was introducing her, explaining that Natalie was his client. "Kate is living in that tiny house right there," he told Natalie.

"You gotta be kidding?" Natalie's eyes grew large. "You can't actually live in something that small. Or is this just for a short visit?"

"It's my permanent home." Kate stood taller.

"How can you stand it? Isn't it claustrophobic?"

"Not for me."

"Lots of people like tiny homes, Natalie." Glen's smile faded.

"So you say." She turned back to Kate. "Of course, you must be a friend of Glen's. You know, he tried to talk me into coming out to Pine Ridge Lake Estates to live." She actually snickered. "I can't imagine living in one of those little wood boxes." She poked Glen in the chest. "And I happen to know you don't live in a tiny house either, Glen."

"I never claimed it was for everyone." He looked slightly irritated.

Kate reached for the other rocker. "I'll just go put this away."

"Let me," he offered.

"Thanks." She led him over to her tiny house.

"Don't mind her," Glen said as he set the rocker on Kate's porch. "I like your tiny house. It's a nice design."

"Thanks."

"You sure you don't want to put it on my hill? It would look nice up there."

She couldn't help but smile. "You never give up, do you?"

He chuckled. "Can't blame me for trying. Okay, you said you were starving a minute ago. How about we blow this joint?"

Kate looked at her SUV, which was blocked by Natalie's Corvette. But seeing that Natalie and Hank were already headed toward his house, she just rolled her eyes.

"Don't worry. I'll drive." He reached for her hand. "I promise not to speed. Not too fast, anyway."

As she got into his pickup cab, she wasn't even sure she cared how fast he went. She just wanted to get away from that awful woman. "Who is Natalie anyway?" she asked Glen as he turned onto the main road.

"Natalie? We went to school with her."

"We?"

"Hank and me. Natalie was a couple years younger. Popular girl. Cheerleader and all that. But a poor family. Anyway, ol' Nat left town right after high school and about ten years later, showed up here with her much older and very wealthy husband, Allan Spalding. They bought a vacation home here." Glen laughed. "A million-dollar vacation home. They got divorced about a year ago. Natalie got the vacation house and a boatload of money. And now she likes to make sure that everyone in town knows it."

"I see." Kate sighed. "And Hank is designing a new house for her."

"That's what she was saying. But sounds like she's dragging the process out. Hank was just trying to pin her down on some decisions and she couldn't seem to make up her mind."

"Maybe her mind's made up on Hank."

"You could be onto something." Glen's brows arched. "Except I don't think Hank's the marrying type. Maybe Nat's not aware of that yet."

"But everyone else in town is?"

"That's the scuttlebutt. That man got his heart broke when Elizabeth passed." He blew out a slow sigh. "Understandable too."

"I never knew her, but I've heard she was pretty amazing."

"One of the sweetest people you could ever meet. And what a trouper. Even with stage-four cancer, she would be out there helping others. Everyone thought she was going to beat it."

"But it beat her."

"Yep. Too bad. And too bad for Natalie. She's wasting her time on Hank." He chuckled. "All that talk about claustrophobic tiny houses. I bet the house she grew up in, with four other siblings, wasn't any bigger than your house."

"Maybe that explains why she dislikes them so much."

"You know, that could well be it."

He took her to the historic Pine Lodge Inn for lunch and, despite feeling gloomy on the drive there, she brightened after their food was served. "I always wanted to come here," she told him, explaining how it had been on her and Kenneth's bucket list. "We were waiting until the kids were grown. And then we just never got around to it."

"I'm glad I'm the one who got to bring you here. It's a pretty special place." He explained how his great-great uncle originally built the inn. "It was a busy stagecoach stop for the first few years, but apparently the trains took over and the business went under. The property sat vacant for years, until the town got bigger. Then it became a hotel. Later on a hotel and restaurant. Now it's just a restaurant."

"Is it still owned by your relatives?"

"They let it go a long time ago. But my dad used to tell us that story practically every time we came here to eat." He laughed.

By the time Glen was driving her back to the farm, Kate felt surprisingly comfortable around him. Oh, he wasn't really her type. Not in a romantic way. But he seemed like a good friend. The problem was that she suspected he hoped she would be something more. "Looks like Hank is already working on your tiny home development." Glen pulled over to watch Zeb driving the tractor, putting his window down to see better. "Didn't think things would be moving this fast over here."

"They're starting the access roads," Kate said quietly, hoping Glen wouldn't resent their new development.

A cloud of brown dust wafted toward them, and Glen put his window up. "Interesting location. Not very scenic." He turned to Kate with a frown. "Sure you don't want to reconsider my place?"

She smiled. "You're not seeing the place at its best today. And you can't even see the pond from here. But, thank you, I will keep your scenic hillside lots in mind. Just don't count on me moving there anytime soon." She knew she was simply being polite, but as he drove up the driveway and she noticed the silver Corvette parked there, she wondered. If Natalie got seriously involved with Hank—not that it seemed very likely, but if so—well, maybe Kate would consider another location for her tiny home. Or maybe she was just being juvenile.

Chapter 18

By five o'clock that same day, Kate was starting to feel trapped in her tiny home. Oh, she knew she was being silly, but she just didn't want to venture outside while Natalie's Corvette was still parked in the driveway, still blocking Kate's SUV. She hadn't even gone out to plant her flowerboxes, and that was something she'd really been looking forward to doing. At least the geraniums were still in a cool spot.

Even when Kate finally took a glass of iced tea out to her porch, hoping to hang her wind chimes and enjoy her new rocking chair, her stay was cut short. She couldn't stand to remain out there after hearing Natalie's shrill laughter drifting over from Hank's front porch. Apparently he was serving drinks out there. Whatever!

She'd just gone back inside, pacing the floor and feeling like a caged animal, when her phone rang. Knowing she'd have to go outside to get service, she checked to see who it was—hopefully not one of her kids calling to growl at her some more. But seeing it was Leota, she hurried outside, breathlessly saying hello in complete disregard to Hank's lady guest.

"I did it, Kate."

"Did what?"

"I gave my notice yesterday."

"Seriously? That didn't take long."

"And I'm so glad I did. Marion is retiring at the end of the month. Apparently she wanted to keep it secret. It almost slipped out when you quit. But someone heard about it over the weekend, and it was all over the office yesterday. And you'll never guess who's taking her place."

If Kate had still been there, it might've been her. Not that she'd wanted more stress with her job.

"Barrett," Leota declared.

"Barrett?" Kate was dumbfounded. Everyone hated Barrett.

"Can you believe it?"

"No. But it makes me glad I quit."

"I'm glad too. And guess where I am right now?"

"I have no idea."

"At the tiny house lot. Kirk is helping me."

"Seriously?"

"I know. It feels crazy, but here I am, following in your brave footsteps."

Kate grew nervous. What if Leota found out that Kate had just been considering leaving Hank's farm to live out at the lake? Oh, not seriously maybe, but considering it.

"Kirk showed me a model that's more of a modern design, but I really like it. It seems to suit me."

"That's great."

"And it's got a sleeping loft like yours. And a sliding front door that opens out onto a deck. So it's kind of indoor-outdoor living, you know?"

"That sounds nice."

"I'll send some photos to get your opinion. But I think I'm going to pull the trigger on it. Kirk says with my down-payment and good credit history, my payments will be super low. I can afford to work at a place like Molly's Mercantile and still have enough money for groceries and utility bills." She laughed. "But I'll be too broke to help anyone in my family."

"That's a good thing."

"And I'll be living in Pine Ridge."

"Yes." Kate looked toward Hank's house to see the porch was vacated. Apparently they'd gone inside since the Corvette was still here.

"I just wanted you to know. And, by the way, when will the development be ready? Kirk said that because I picked a popular model, it could be ready sooner. Because the factory is making a lot of them."

"I'll check with Hank." Kate told Leota about Hank's offer to let Leota park a tiny house here. "Just temporarily. Until the development is ready."

Leota let out a squeal of delight. "Perfect. I'll tell Kirk."

"By the way, Zeb will be thrilled to hear this. He really likes you."

"As a matter of fact, I'm rather fond of him. He was part of the reason I could make this decision. But don't tell him that. I'd rather just see where this goes."

"Absolutely. But I will let them know you're working your way to Pine Ridge. They'll be happy to hear it."

"You know, after spending Sunday with you, it almost felt like family there. And not a dysfunctional family either."

Kate wasn't so sure about that but didn't want to burst Leota's bubble. "Well, keep me informed. And send me those pics."

Leota promised she would and, as Kate hung up, she hurried back into her house. She didn't want to be caught standing out in the driveway when Hank and Natalie finally came out. Didn't want them to think she'd been spying on them. Or that she cared.

She was just going onto the porch when Zeb called out to her. "What'd you think of the access roads?"

She couldn't help but smile to see the young man coated with a fine covering of dirt. "It was hard to see much. There was so much dust flying around."

He smiled to reveal teeth nearly as brown as his face. "I warned you it would be a mess out there. But the roads are looking pretty good. Nice and flat."

"Nice work." She sat down in a rocker.

"You get a new car?" He pointed to the Corvette still blocking her SUV.

"Are you kidding? I couldn't afford something like that." She quietly explained about Natalie Spalding and his brows shot up.

"Seriously? She's here right now."

Kate solemnly nodded.

Zeb looked down at his dirty clothes. "I better not go in there looking like this. She has a hissy fit when Chester gets too close to her. And I'm way dirtier than him."

"Isn't there a back door?"

"Yeah, but it goes through the kitchen." He frowned. "They might be in there."

She held up a glass of tea. "Need a drink?"

His eyes lit up. "You bet." He came over and opened up a camp chair. "But I'll just stay down here so I don't get your porch all messy."

She thanked him then went to fill a big glass of tea. "Here you go." She reached over the railing to hand it to him.

"I like your new chairs." He pointed to the rockers. "Classy."

She smiled and sat. "Comfortable too."

He took a long sip then sighed. "Wow, thanks. I needed this."

"I have a bit of good news."

"I hope it doesn't have to do with Glen Stryker. I was kinda surprised to see you riding around with him today. Is that part of the spying plan?"

"No." She laughed. "In fact, when I had to confess to him that I was spying, he was very nice about it."

"So why were you with him today?" Zeb looked slightly suspicious.

"It was sort of accidental." She explained about bumping into him in town, how he helped her with the rocking chairs. But she didn't mention going to lunch with him. "But that's not my news." She told him about Leota, and he let out a loud whoop.

"Seriously? She quit her job? She's getting a tiny home and coming here?"

"Kind of looks that way."

"My prayers have been answered." He looked upward with a grateful expression.

"I'm happy about it too." She glanced nervously toward Hank's house.

"How long's she been here anyway?"

"Who?" Kate feigned oblivion.

"Natalie Spalding."

She shrugged. "Oh, I think it was a little before noon."

"You're kidding? All day? What are they doing in there?"

"I assume they're working on Ms. Spalding's house plans."

"For five hours?"

She shrugged again.

He drained the last of his tea then set it on her railing. "Thanks, Kate. But, dirt or no dirt, I think I better go in there now. And I'm going through the front door."

"All right." She nodded with pursed lips, thinking she'd like to see Natalie's expression when Zeb swooshed through the house in a cloud of dust. Kate didn't like feeling this way toward anyone, but for some reason she wasn't overly fond of Natalie Spalding. And it wasn't necessarily jealousy either. Natalie had spoken down to Kate and made fun of her tiny home. She'd been rude to Glen as well. But in all honesty, it probably was just plain old jealousy.

Still, as she fixed a light dinner, Kate asked herself why she should be jealous. According to almost everyone, Hank had no interest in romance. He was still in love with his dead wife. Natalie was obviously barking up the wrong tree. Well, unless she wasn't.

Kate had already gotten ready for bed when her phone rang. She was tempted to let it go to voicemail, but seeing it was Zinnia, she knew she had to take it. After all, it could be an emergency. She grabbed her sweatshirt and hurried outside into the darkness, relieved to see that Ms. Spalding's fancy car was no longer blocking her in. That was something.

"Zinnia?" she said breathlessly from the drive-way. "Can you hear me?"

"Of course, I can hear you. It's not like you moved to Antarctica. You didn't, did you?"

"No, of course, not."

"Jake and I are worried about you."

"You both made that abundantly clear."

"We wanted to know if it's too late for you to get out of whatever it is you've gotten yourself into."

"What exactly do you think I've gotten myself into?"

"You know that communal living thing with tiny homes. Are you really locked into it, or can you get out? Because Jake found this cool place in Seattle. It's a senior living center with an activity room and bus trips and all kinds of stuff. And he thinks he can get you into it—"

"A retirement home? He wants to put me in a retirement home?"

"It's a place for older people. I don't think they call it a retirement home."

"I don't care what it's called, I have no interest in something like that."

"But you'd be close to us. We could all get together."

"Really?" Kate felt skeptical. "We didn't live that far apart before, but I hardly ever saw you, Zinnia. You kids have busy lives. I get that."

"So you won't even consider the senior—"

"I like it here in Pine Ridge. And as a matter

of fact, I did sign a contractual agreement." She cringed to think of how she'd stupidly signed that document this morning. Maybe it wasn't too late to pull the plug.

"Jake's not going to like hearing this. He was all excited about this place. They have all these clubs and all sorts of things."

"Maybe Jake should live there."

Zinnia actually laughed. "Yeah, maybe."

"Look, honey, I know what I'm doing. And I'm not too old to want my own life. I need to chase some of my own dreams for a change."

"I sort of understand. Anyway, I'm trying. Why don't you send me some pictures of your new place? That might help."

"I'll do that."

"And I'll let Jake know it's no go on the old folks' home."

"So really—it's an old folks' home?" Kate grimaced at the idea of wrinkly old half-deaf people without their teeth playing canasta. "You want your mom in an old folks' home?"

"No, just pulling your leg. Sorry, I gotta go. Love ya!"

"Love you too, Zinnia." She hung up and pocketed her phone. Did Jake really think she was ready for an old folks' home? Really? She leaned her head back to look at the stars, surprised at how bright and close they seemed to be.

"Pretty, huh?"

Kate snapped her head back down and peered across the shadowy driveway to see Hank's silhouette barely visible up on the porch. "Oh! I didn't know anyone was there."

"Sorry, I wasn't trying to eavesdrop." He came down off the porch. "I just happened to be sitting here when you came running outside with your phone. I didn't want to distract you, so I just stayed put." He was standing in front of her now. "Your kids really want to put you in an old folks' home?"

She sighed. "I don't know. I don't think so, but I'm not totally sure."

"Kids." He shook his head. And for a moment, neither of them said anything. Finally, Hank broke the silence. "I was surprised to see you with Glen today."

"Yes, I could tell."

"You said you ran into him in town. But it seemed like you two were old friends. And then you took off with him. You seemed to have been gone for quite a while."

"It wasn't that long. Maybe a couple hours. He just took me to lunch."

"Uh-huh. Well, maybe I missed him bringing you back. I thought you spent the whole day with him."

"Looked like you spent the whole day with Natalie Spalding." She instantly regretted that. Not just the words, but the jealous tone.

He sighed loudly. "That woman is infuriating."

"Really?" Kate turned to look at him in the shadowy light. "You seemed to be getting along with her okay when I was here."

"She's my client. I have to get along with her. But the woman can't make up her mind."

"Maybe about some things."

"Huh? What's that mean?"

Kate just laughed. "You can't be that dense. Both Zeb and Glen seemed to have it all figured out. Natalie Spalding has set her sights on you."

He waved a hand. "She just likes attention."

"I hear she's loaded. She might make a good business partner for the tiny home development."

"I thought you were my partner."

"I signed the paperwork, Hank. But I'm starting to wonder if that was wise."

"You want to back out?"

"I don't know." Her emotions rose to the surface again.

"Because I won't hold you to that contract if you want out. I just felt like it was your idea. I wanted you to own a part of it. I thought you were all in and had a vision for it and—"

"I did. And I still do. But it's tricky." She wanted to be honest with him but was uncomfortable admitting what was really troubling her. "I mean, we should have a good business relationship. As well as a friendship. Right?"

"Absolutely."

"But then feelings come into play. And, well, I suppose I feel kind of confused." How was she supposed to say this without sounding like a middle-aged woman with a schoolgirl crush?

"What kind of feelings?" he asked quietly.

"Oh, I don't know. I guess I just care about you." She took in a quick breath. "Maybe too much. And I suspect that's not good for a business relationship."

For a long moment, he said nothing then blew out a deep breath. "Okay. I understand."

She didn't know what to say. Maybe he agreed it was time to pull the plug, that they'd jumped in too quickly, that feelings would get messy. Her feelings anyway. Because she doubted that he *really* understood. "But maybe we should talk about this later." All she wanted was to escape this awkwardly embarrassing conversation. Just cut her losses and leave. Maybe she would move her tiny house to Glen's development after all.

"Can I confess something to you, Kate?"

"Yes, of course." She braced herself.

"When I saw you with Glen today . . . I, uh, well, I got jealous."

She blinked. "You did?"

"It pretty much blindsided me. Kind of like a sucker punch."

"Oh." Maybe he really did have feelings too.

"To be honest, it didn't feel good. In fact, it felt pretty awful."

"Uh-huh." She didn't know what to say. Part of her was thrilled. Another part was uneasy. Despite her feelings for him, she didn't want things to get too deep, too fast.

"I could tell by the way Glen looked at you, the way he acted . . . well, he's putting the move on you. In case, you didn't notice."

"I guess I sort of noticed."

"So what I want to know, Kate, is how on earth did that happen?" His tone grew sharper. "Yesterday, you go out to Pine Ridge Lake just to snoop around. And today, you have Glen Stryker practically eating out of your hand."

She shrugged. "I honestly don't know. I did nothing to encourage it. Nothing. It just happened."

"Maybe it's a good sign that I'm so aggravated by this." He ran his fingers through his hair. "I'm sure that makes no sense to you."

Except that it did make sense. And it could be a good sign. Hank was trying to express that he had feelings for her. Of course, this didn't mean he was over Elizabeth yet. That might not ever happen. But at least he felt conflicted. She shivered in the chilly night air, pulling her sweatshirt more tightly around her.

"Well, it's late. I didn't mean to keep you out here. I can tell you're getting cold. Good night, Kate."

She told him good night then hurried into her

tiny house, still trying to wrap her head around all that had just transpired outside. Hank was obviously trying to tell her he cared about her. But did he care as much for her as she cared for him? She didn't think so. And even if he did, how would what surely would be an awkward romance impact their business relationship? Would it cloud things up and impair their decision making? Would it ruin everything? She'd feel terrible if a rocky relationship turned the whole development on its head. It was some consolation that Hank was willing to pull the plug, if she wanted to. Now she just needed to figure that out.

Chapter 19

Kate woke up early the next morning. Still trying to figure out what role she should play, if any, in the tiny house development, she decided to take a walk over to the pond and hopefully clear her head. The dust from yesterday's road grading had settled, but the land still looked a bit torn up and not as pretty as the first time she'd seen it. Also, she noticed some of the aspen trees had bright orange tape tied around their trunks. Did that mean they'd be cut down? And, if so, why?

She walked all the way around the pond, trying to imagine what it would feel like to have it encircled with tiny homes. She paused on the south side of the pond. From this point she could look across the pond and actually see the tops of the mountains in the distance. It would be a good location for a tiny home. She sat down on a large rock and wondered how it would feel to live here. At the moment it would feel rather lonely, but with other tiny homes, it could be nice. And the area behind her, which could become her backyard, would get lots of good sunshine for growing flowers. And she'd have quick access to the main road for getting into town—to manage her florist shop. All in all, it would be pretty sweet. But was this where she was meant to be?

She closed her eyes and asked for God to guide her steps.

She was just opening them when she heard voices. She looked across the pond to see Hank and Zeb measuring something. Standing up, she watched as Zeb held one end of the tape near the pond, and Hank moved away from him. Curious as to what they were doing, she walked over to investigate.

"Hey, Kate." Zeb smiled.

"Morning, Zeb. What's up?" She bent down to pat Chester, his tail wagging happily against her leg.

"We're just measuring lot length. You know, to see how it feels in person."

Hank called out a greeting. "Come on over here, Kate, tell me what you think."

She walked over to him, trying to act natural, as if they hadn't had that awkward conversation last night. "Will this be the back of the lot?" she asked, turning around to look from there back to the pond. "It's pretty big."

"Keep in mind how narrow the front of the lot will be. Having this extra room back here is supposed to make up for it. But maybe it's too big."

"Not for me. I'd love having this much room to grow flowers and maybe have a dog."

"And that's what our development has to offer," he reminded her. "Something Pine Ridge Lake Estates will never be able to do."

"Actually, they might."

"What?" He started to reel in the tape, and she explained Glen's plan to develop the hillside by the lake.

"But those won't be flat lots."

"No, but they'll be bigger lots. And he plans to sell them. Not lease."

"That's a good way to put more money in his pocket. Up front anyway. I've wondered if we should consider selling some of these lots. So we'd have more cash to put into our development."

"I wouldn't mind owning my own lot," she admitted.

"But then we'd have to make codes, covenants, and restrictions."

"Wouldn't you have CC&Rs for the leasing tenants anyway?"

"That's true." He put the tape measure in his jacket pocket as Zeb joined them.

"How'd that look?" Zeb asked Hank.

"Pretty good." Hank nodded at Kate. "She thought so too."

"Which lot do you want for your house?" Zeb asked Kate.

She pointed across the pond. "I'd like one over on the south side. See that one with the big boulder. That'd be nice."

Hank smiled. "Consider it done."

She wondered if this meant she really was going

to continue with their plan. By the light of day, it seemed just fine. Hank was acting perfectly natural, and she no longer felt so uncomfortable. Maybe she'd just overblown everything last night.

"I was doing some thinking, Kate." He began slowly. "I know you were feeling a little nervous about the contract my lawyer drew up for us. Maybe we need to do this differently."

"I don't know." Did he want her out of this? Because of what she'd said last night? "The contract seemed fair to me, Hank. And my lawyer thought so too."

"Right. But I'm realizing you might not want to be that tied into this thing. I'll admit it's a lot to take on. And I know it's making your kids nervous."

"Well, that's true."

"It's not that I want to cut you out of this, I just want to give you credit because the idea was partly yours."

"I appreciate that."

"And I know you need to have cash to invest in your florist shop."

"I've been thinking about that too."

"So maybe we should do this differently. I know of another way, probably a safer route, that way you could still be an investor."

"How's that?"

"What if you just purchased a bunch of the

lots? As many as you like. Just straight out buy them from me. And for a good pre-market price. Then that money could go directly into the development of the property. Then when the lots are finished you could sell yours. Probably make a nice profit."

"If you bought the lots next to yours, you could pick your neighbors," Zeb said. "Like Leota."

"Good point." She considered this idea. On one hand, she felt a bit sad to think she would no longer be an official partner in the development. On the other hand, it would feel good to be free from possible entanglements that could become messy. And the possibility of actually making a profit on down the line was appealing. She could invest that into her florist shop. "I think I like that idea." She smiled at Hank.

"Don't know why I didn't think of it in the first place. Anyway, I'll give you back your contract so you can tear it up."

Her smile faded. Was this his way of separating himself from her? Making it clear that they could never be partners? Not in business, or any other way.

"I'm still interested in any ideas you have for the development," Hank assured her. "Especially since you'll be a homeowner."

"Right."

"And a female perspective is probably helpful too," he added.

"That reminds me." She pointed to the trees wearing ribbons. "Why are those trees marked?"

"They'll have to be removed."

"Why?" She suddenly felt protective.

"Several reasons. Some just aren't safe. And some aren't healthy. A few of them are in the way. Don't worry, we'll still have plenty of trees. I want to plant some more. Not aspens though. Those things spread like weeds. I thought some evergreens might be nice in the wintertime. Add a little more variety and texture."

"I like that."

He checked his watch. "Well, I've got to get going. Lots to do today." He looked at Zeb. "You squared away on what you're doing today?"

"Trenching where it's been marked off."

Hank nodded. "We want to get ahead of the game. So when our permits are approved, which could be next week, we'll be all set to start laying pipes and wires." He pointed toward one of the access roads. "How about we go take a second look before you start trenching."

Kate excused herself. It wasn't that she wasn't interested, but she knew they didn't need her input for this. Probably didn't need her input for much of anything anymore. Sure, this new arrangement was more freeing for her, and probably more sensible, but she also felt left out.

As she walked back to her tiny house, she considered Hank's offer to let her purchase lots.

It actually did make sense. For the development and for her own investment purposes. She'd have to ask him what he considered a "fair pre-market price" to be and then decide on how many she could afford. And she liked Zeb's idea of getting the lots next to hers. Maybe she could purchase the entire south side. That might be fun.

By Wednesday, Kate struck a deal with Hank to purchase twelve lots, including her own. It temporarily drained most of her house sale money, but she knew it was only a matter of time until she started getting it back. Besides the dozen lots, Kate also purchased a three-acre strip of land between the main road and tiny house development that Hank thought would be perfect for her flower growing business and was already connected to his irrigation system. Plus it was adjacent to her own tiny home lot.

Hank, who seemed relieved to be free of their business partnership, had even offered to design and build her a greenhouse. Perhaps his way of making the breakup a bit less painful. But, as he pointed out, he probably couldn't start on it until their development was finished. Hopefully by summer's end, before the weather started to turn. Because of the higher elevation, Kate knew the winters would be harder here than what she'd been used to. She hoped raising flowers wouldn't be too much of a challenge.

So, despite her slight melancholy about dissolving their short-lived partnership, Kate told herself it was for the best. And now she had her own project to work on. Three acres of farmland to get ready for flowers. Most of it would be planted with perennials like lavender, phlox, asters, roses, peonies. But she also wanted annuals like sunflowers, zinnias, cosmos, larkspur, dahlias, and snapdragons. She wanted flowers that looked good in arrangements. And besides flowers, she hoped to grow a variety of herbs as well as pumpkins and gourds.

And if all went well, she hoped to have her business up and running by August. But first she needed to get the soil ready for growing flowers. That meant getting a load of organic compost delivered. Fortunately for her, Hank knew a horse breeder down the road who was happy to deliver aged horse manure—free of charge—on Thursday afternoon. And he offered to bring as much as she needed. Apparently it was piling up over there on the horse farm. But, according to Zeb, it would make her flowers grow like crazy.

By midmorning Friday, Zeb had finished his trenching and was eager to help her get her "fertilizer" mixed into the dirt. Although it was aged and dried, Zeb claimed it smelled some. So he ran the tractor over it so many times that the soil literally fell apart between her fingers. She rewarded him with a big homemade submarine sandwich for lunch. Then went out and began planting her seeds that she'd gotten from the hardware store.

It was around two when Glen called. It was the third time he'd called in as many days, but she'd missed his other calls and, despite his cheerful messages, she'd failed to call him back. Today, she decided to just get it over with. "Hey, Glen."

"Kate! You're really there. I was getting worried. About to drive over to Hank's farm to check on you. Everything okay?"

"Yes, of course. Everything is fine."

"So what are you up to that's keeping you too busy to answer your phone?"

"Right now, I'm up to my elbows in horse manure."

"What?"

She explained about her flower project. "Actually, I'm planting pumpkin seeds at the moment."

"For a florist shop?"

"I think it'd be fun to have gourds and pumpkins around the shop in the fall. Sort of festive and fun."

"I guess that makes sense. Anyway, I wanted to see if you were available for dinner tonight."

She considered her answer. "Thanks, Glen, but I really can't."

"Other plans?" He sounded disappointed.

She looked over her ripe and ready field of dirt. "Yeah. Other plans. I'm sorry." She didn't want to admit she planned to stay out here until it was too dark to see.

"But you do plan to be around for the holiday weekend, don't you?"

She pushed another seed into the ground then stood. "Holiday?"

"Haven't you noticed the signs in town? It's Founders' Day. Kinda corny, but fun. You should see town. I've never seen so many tourists crawling around."

"Oh, well, good reason to avoid town."

"I agree. That's why I wanted to invite you out to the lake. How does tomorrow sound?"

She gazed fondly over her vacant lot. "I actually have plans for tomorrow." She didn't want to admit those plans were simply going to a nursery in a nearby town to gather some perennial seedlings and getting them planted before the day was over.

"And Sunday?" he asked.

"Well, there's church. And, really, I don't know my schedule right now. I'm outside planting pumpkins. I'll check my calendar and let you know, okay?"

"You'll get back to me?"

"Absolutely." She would get back to him—and somehow she'd gently and tactfully let him know that she had no interest in dating him.

"I'll be expecting your call."

By that evening, Kate's back ached from

planting seeds, but it was a good ache. And as she took a glass of tea out to her front porch, she sighed happily. She was really starting to live out her dreams. Oh, sure, her flower farm would require a lot of work, but the payoff would be worth it. As she rocked back and forth in her rocker, gazing out at the twilight sky, a tired contentedness settled over her that she simply wanted to savor.

"Want any company?" Hank was strolling toward her front porch with a mug in his hand, Chester at his heels.

"Sure, come on up. Both of you."

"I was having coffee on my front porch and heard you come out over here." He sat down in the other rocker and Chester sat between them. "This is pretty comfortable."

"Yeah. And good for an achy back."

"You have an achy back too?"

She smiled. "Mine is from planting seeds all afternoon."

"And most of the evening too. Zeb said he saw you out there after seven-thirty. Going at it pretty hard, aren't you?"

"Maybe, but it's a good hard." She reached down to stroke Chester's smooth coat.

"I guess we're all going after it *good* hard." He gave her the updates on the development, but nothing Zeb hadn't already told her about. "Things seem to be falling into place."

"That's great." She leaned back, gazing up at the first stars appearing in the sky. "Beautiful night."

"Uh-huh." He leaned back to look too. "You've got a pretty good view of the sky over here."

"I never saw stars this bright and clear before. Living in the city."

"Don't know how folks can live in a city like that." He shook his head. "But to be honest, Pine Ridge is starting to remind me of a city."

"Glen said it was crazy busy today. But probably because of the holiday."

"So . . . you're still seeing Glen?"

She suddenly realized her mistake. "No, I didn't see him. But he called. Actually he's called a few times. I finally picked up."

"Uh-huh?"

For some reason this aggravated her. Did Hank think he had a right to know about her personal life? And, if so, why? But she decided not to go there. She just sat silently, allowing him to think whatever he liked.

"Sorry," he finally said. "It's none of my business."

"Well, we are friends, Hank. I guess it's okay for friends to discuss things going on in their lives. Glen was asking me out tonight, but I told him I was busy."

"Busy?"

"Planting pumpkins," she declared. "I was busy planting pumpkins, okay?"

Hank chuckled. "Yes, well, that was true."

"So he asked me out for tomorrow."

"And . . . ?"

She rolled her eyes. "And I told him I was busy."

"Planting more pumpkins?"

"No," she answered a bit sharply. "I want to go to Hartley's Nursery and get seedlings tomorrow. They just got in some good lavender and a few other things I want to get into the ground."

"And you plan to bring them back in your SUV?"

"That's my plan." Okay, it wasn't a great plan.

"You could probably get more plants in my pickup."

"Your pickup? Are you offering me your pickup?"

"Only if you let me drive it."

"You want to go to the nursery with me?"

"Sure. Sounds like fun."

"You can spare the time? I know you've been super busy."

"It's Saturday. Why not? It shouldn't take all day, will it? I don't have anything I have to get to until around two."

"I wanted to go first thing in the morning. Hopefully I'll have the rest of the day to get them planted."

"Then, unless you object, I'll take you in my pickup."

"It's a date." She grimaced. "I don't mean it's a *date* date. I mean, yes, that sounds good. Thanks."

"You can call it a date if you want."

Her phone rang before she could respond. "Excuse me a minute, it's my daughter."

"Want me to exit?"

"I doubt this will take long." She accepted the call. "Hi, Zinnia, what's up?"

"Hi, Mom. How's life on the commune?"

"I don't live on a commune, honey. Remember?"

"I know. Just teasing. Anyway, Jake just called me and he's driving down from Seattle tomorrow. He's going to pick me up and then we're heading your way for a little visit."

"A little visit?" Kate felt her blood pressure elevate.

"We want to see your new digs. Anything wrong with that?"

"No, of course not. I'd love to see you kids. But be warned it's a *tiny* house."

"Are you saying you don't have room for us? Because if that's the case, we can just—"

"I'm saying it'll be cozy, honey. Jake can sleep on the sofa—you know the one from the old den—and you can share my bed with me."

"Wow, that does sound cozy. Maybe we should bring our own tent and sleeping bags."

"If you like."

"Just kidding. So anyway, we should be there sometime late in the day. Probably in time for dinner. That okay?"

"Sure, it's okay." Kate sighed.

"Great. See ya then." Zinnia hung up.

Kate turned off her phone and looked at Hank. "My kids, they're coming to see me."

"Uh-huh. Is this a visit or an intervention?"

"Probably both." Kate slowly shook her head. "I hate to imagine how they'll react to staying in my tiny house. I can't even remember the last time they both came home at the same time, you know, when we had the big house. Probably Christmas, a couple years ago. They're usually so busy."

"But they're both coming at the same time tomorrow."

"I'm sure Jake plans to convince me I've made a mistake."

"Have you?"

She looked at him. "Are you suggesting you think I may have?"

"Not at all."

"You know, I was actually sitting out here tonight, feeling pretty good about my life. Even my achy back felt kind of good. Like I was accomplishing something. Chasing my dreams."

"That's great." He stood, preparing to leave. "So what about the nursery tomorrow? Still on for that?"

"Yes, of course. I'm not going to allow my kids to change my life." Even as she said this, she doubted her words. Since when hadn't she not only allowed kids to change her life, but encouraged them to take it over?

When they were small, she put her career on hold. And when they became more independent and she returned to the workforce because Kenneth needed her to—she'd worked part-time and catered to her kids the rest of the time. After Kenneth passed, she'd been forced to work full-time, but her kids had gotten all the rest of her time. She'd put them both through college. But they were launched. Or nearly. Zinnia wasn't completely on her own yet. But they were grown kids, living their own busy lives. And she was a grown woman who needed to be living her own life. Right?

Chapter 20

As Hank drove his pickup through town, Kate was surprised to see how crowded and busy the streets looked. "Pine Ridge is turning into a happening place."

"A bustling metropolis," he grumbled.

She chuckled. "You sound a bit like an old curmudgeon."

"I'm not a curmudgeon. I just get a little grumpy when I see Pine Ridge being overrun by out-of-towners."

"You mean like me?"

"You're not a tourist."

"I used to be."

"But you live here now. You're a resident." He stopped to let a family cross the street.

"I bet the shop owners appreciate the tourist traffic."

He continued slowly through town. "I guess I should be more tolerant. It's just that I've lived here my whole life, and maybe I don't like change much."

"What about the tiny home development? That's going to be a big change."

"I know." His expression looked somewhat grim.

"Are you having second thoughts?"

"No. Well, maybe I do sometimes." He shook his head. "Maybe I am an old curmudgeon after all."

"Have you really considered what it'll be like having all those tiny homes? So near you? They might be out of sight, but they'll be there. Are you sure you can handle it? I mean if you really hate change like you say you do?"

"I guess I need to get over it." He sighed. "Life is about change." He stopped for an elderly couple crossing the street. The old gentleman, with his hand beneath the lady's elbow, smiled up at the pickup.

Kate waved to them. "I bet that couple has seen plenty of change in their lifetime."

"You're probably right." He glanced at her. "And you've sure made a lot of changes to your life, Kate."

"But you know what's weird? I used to hate change too. I never wanted my kids to get older and leave home. I fell apart when Kenneth got sick. After he died, I was a real stick in the mud. I didn't want anything to change—ever again."

"And look at you now."

"That's because I got sick of my boring life." She laughed. "I wanted to shake it up."

"And you're still glad you did?"

"I have moments when I question myself," she confessed. "I'm sure I'll have even more doubts when Jake and Zinnia get here. Of course, that's because they'll be bringing it with them." She cringed to think of this evening.

"I was thinking about them last night. I have a big empty house. Why not let them stay with me while they're here?"

She turned to look at him. "That's really generous. And part of me wants to jump at the offer. But I think they need to stay with me. I need to prove to them that even a tiny house can be home."

"Well, if you change your mind, the offer stands."

"Even at midnight?" she teased. "If my kids run screaming from my tiny house and pound on your door, you'll let them in?"

He laughed. "Sure. I don't lock the door. They can make themselves at home."

"For a guy who doesn't like change, you can be quite accommodating."

"Yeah, go figure."

As they drove together in companionable silence, she decided that Hank was a bit of a dichotomy. Not an easy man to figure out, he liked simplicity, but he could be complicated. He could be generous or he could hold back. He could be independent or he could be needy. He was happy and he was sad. Yes, he was a dichotomy.

As it turned out, Hank was helpful to have at the nursery. Not only did he know more than she expected about plants, he had an artistic eye. Of course, he was both a farmer and an architect. So it probably made sense. And as they loaded flats of perennials in the back of the pickup, she realized he'd even brought some crates and extra boards to create two levels of plants. And then he secured everything with rope.

"Did you used to be a boy scout?" she asked after they were back in the cab.

He grinned. "Nope. But I had a dad who was better than a troop leader. He taught us boys how to fend for ourselves."

"Had a dad?"

"He passed away about a year after Elizabeth. But he was in his eighties."

"Oh, I'm sorry. How about your mother?"

"She died when I was a kid."

"Again, I'm sorry."

"Thanks. How about your parents?"

"They're both living in a retirement complex outside of Portland. Kind of like where Jake wants to send me. Although, the place he found is in Seattle, so I can be near them. Like they plan to come visit me every weekend. Not."

"Well, they're making the trek here. That should be interesting."

"Speaking of that. Would you mind stopping by the grocery store? I need to stock up on some things before they get here."

"No problem, I need a few supplies too. But

be warned, the place will probably be packed by now."

"The price we pay for living in this beautiful bustling metropolis?"

"Yeah, I guess."

Hank turned out to be right about the grocery store. By the time they left George's it was nearly noon. "I'd ask you to get some lunch," he said, backing out of the space, "but I bet all the restaurants are crawling with tourists."

"And I have perishables." She frowned at a busload of tourists unloading in the parking lot. "Weirdly enough, I'm starting to feel like an old curmudgeon too. Where do all these people come from?"

He laughed. "Sorry, I didn't mean to rub off on you like that."

"I'm just thankful we're going home."

"Yeah." He nodded with a smile. "Home."

By the time Hank pulled his pickup next to Kate's waiting field, it was getting pretty hot out. He helped her unload the plants then looked around. "If you're not getting these into the ground right away, along with some water, they might get stressed out here in this hot sun."

"I was just wondering about that. It's going to take a while to get them all planted."

"And I'm guessing your kids aren't coming here in order to help you with this. That probably wasn't the plan." His eyes twinkled like he thought this was humorous.

"You'd be guessing about right." She felt a mix of embarrassment and defensiveness. "We weren't the kind of parents who made our kids do a lot of chores. Maybe that was a mistake, but I felt like keeping up their studies was their job. And they both did really well in school."

"That's saying a lot." He nodded. "And they never got into drugs either."

"I'm grateful for that."

"How about if we set up a tarp to make sort of a lean-to tent, to give 'em some shade?"

"You wouldn't mind doing that?"

He checked his watch. "I'm running short on time, but I can get Zeb on it."

"That'd be great. Tell Zeb I'll pay him for his time."

"I'll tell him, but not sure he'll take it." Hank opened his pickup door. "You want a ride back?"

"No, I'm going to start planting." She went over to her wheelbarrow where her tools and things were stashed. She rolled up her sleeves then dug out a straw hat and pair of gloves that she'd gotten at the hardware store the other day.

"You're a real farm girl, Kate." He chuckled as he got into the cab. "I'll send Zeb right out."

Kate smiled as she carried a flat of lavender starts over to the edge of her field. Her plan was to use the lavender to border the other flowers since it was heartier and would eventually grow into a short hedge. Then, humming happily, she started to dig a hole. She was just finishing up the last plant in the flat by the time Zeb showed up with Hank's pickup filled with a tarp, poles, stakes, and ropes.

"Hear ya want a lean to for shade," he called out. "Over here by the plants?"

"Yes. That's a good spot."

While Zeb constructed her lean-to, she started on another flat of lavender. By the time she was done, Zeb pounded in the last stake. "How's that?" he called out.

She went over to examine it. "I thought Hank might've been a boy scout, but I'm certain you must've been too."

He chuckled. "I actually was a boy scout. Only a few years. I would've kept up with it, but my friends teased me, said it was geeky."

"Not the same friends that introduced you to weed?"

His brows shot up. "Come to think of it, you're right." He sadly shook his head. "Guess I should've stuck with scouting, huh?"

She patted his back. "Well, you're a good scout now. That's what counts, right?"

He grinned. "Want some help planting these?"

"Will you let me pay you for your time?"

"That kinda takes the fun out of it."

She considered this. "If you honestly want to

help me, I'd really appreciate it. I'm not even sure how long I'll last in this heat."

"What if I turn the irrigation on for a little bit?" he suggested. "That'd keep us cool."

"Why not? The plants could use a drink too."

So with the sprinklers sweeping back and forth, Kate and Zeb got sprinkled randomly as they planted a few more flats. And it felt good. Finally, realizing the ground was adequately soaked, Zeb turned the water off. Then they worked until Kate was too hot and tired to go on. "I'm calling it quits." She put her hat and gloves in the wheelbarrow then checked on her plants still waiting in the shade. "I think everything should be okay for the time being."

"Then I'll quit too." He dropped an empty flat in the pile they'd started.

As they walked back, she told him about her kids coming later on. "Driving from Seattle, but they should probably be here in a couple hours. I'll have enough time to get cleaned up and get things started for dinner."

"Cool. I'd like to meet your kids."

She glanced at him, wondering if he really meant that. Zeb was so different than Jake and Zinnia. So much more down to earth—literally. And, in his own laid back way, he was a pretty cool dude. In fact, that's what Leota had said about him. And it's not that he'd judge her kids, but he'd probably think Jake was a computer nerd and Zinnia, well, if she started talking about her passion for fashion, he might think she was an airhead. Oh, well.

At her tiny house, she thanked Zeb again. "I probably wouldn't have lasted half that long without you."

"The water helped too." He removed his cowboy hat, giving it a shake.

She was about to go inside, but Zeb was still standing there with a slightly perplexed expression on his face.

"Is something wrong?" she asked from her porch.

"Well, uh, you offered to pay me, Kate."

"Oh, yes, of course," she said eagerly. "I'd be happy to pay you. And not just for today either. You've been a lot of help on my little flower farm."

"Well, I wasn't thinking of cash exactly." He twisted his hat in his hand. "I know you got all the lots on the south side of the pond . . . and I was thinking I'd kinda like to buy one of those lots."

"Oh?" She nodded. "That's fine. And I'll give you the same deal that Hank gave me."

"You don't have to do that. I know you expect to make a profit and—"

"Not off of you, Zeb. If you want one of my lots, you'll have to pay the same price I paid Hank." She stuck out her chin.

He grinned. "Great. Thanks. So I thought maybe I could keep helping you with your flower garden project. You know when I have spare time."

"Do you have spare time?"

"Oh, sure. Sometimes we're waiting on something. Like the electrician or plumber or city inspector. There's time to help you."

"Then I'd happily deduct your help from the lot price. But only if you agree to the same price that I paid Hank. Otherwise I'll feel guilty. You're family, Zeb." She shrugged. "I mean Hank's family. Although I'd gladly adopt you."

"Thanks. And one more thing."

"Yeah?"

"Do you think it'd be okay if I got a lot next to Leota's? I mean do you think she'd mind?"

Kate didn't know what to say. "We don't know for absolute sure that Leota's coming yet."

"I know. But you were saving a lot for her just in case, right?"

"That's right."

"It's not like I plan to stalk her or anything. I promise I'd keep my distance and respect her space."

Kate still felt uncertain. "How about if I speak to Leota first. I'll let you know what she says."

"Thanks, Kate." He put his hat back on. "So how about church tomorrow? Do you want to go with us again?"

She considered this. "I guess I should check with my kids."

"I forgot they were coming. Hey, how about we do a barbecue tomorrow? Like after church? Would your kids be into that?"

"I don't know about them, but I would."

"Great. I'll talk to Hank." Zeb grinned. "He's the grill master. But I'll let you know."

As she went inside, she wondered what her kids would think of Zeb. Hopefully, Zinnia wouldn't treat him like a country hick. And Jake wouldn't ignore him because of his lack of interest in electronics. Anyway, if her kids were rude, well, she'd set them straight. In the meantime, she had lots to get done before her vigilante offspring arrived and the showdown started. Was she really ready for this?

Chapter 21

Because Kenneth had suffered allergies to shellfish, Kate had never prepared it for dinner until after he'd passed. About a year after his death, she made seafood fettuccine alfredo one night and her kids went nuts for it. That dish quickly became their family favorite, and that's what she was making tonight. Unsure of when her kids would arrive, she made a pretty green salad, set her little table, and got everything else ready to go. She would throw the entrée together when they arrived.

When it was past seven, and she was hungry, she tried both Zinnia's and Jake's phones. With no answer, she figured they were in the "dead" zone coming over the pass, which meant they'd be here in twenty to thirty minutes. So she decided to go ahead and start on the pasta and have it ready when they arrived.

But with the seafood fettuccine alfredo done—and looking lovely—still no sign of her kids. She tried their phones again. Still no answer. Had they gotten lost? She'd given Zinnia specific directions to the farm. Or perhaps it was something worse? Driving over the mountain could be treacherous at times. She checked the road report to be sure there'd been no wrecks. The highway appeared perfectly fine and so she went back inside and, extra ravenous from working hard and skipping lunch, she fixed herself a plate, thinking she'd just nibble. By eight o'clock, she'd finished her meal and put the rest of it in the fridge. *Where were her kids?*

It was nearly eight-thirty and getting dusky out when she saw Jake's car coming down the driveway. Trying to repress her irritation, she reminded herself they could've had car trouble, or a flat tire, and went out to meet them with hugs. "What took you so long?" she asked as they unloaded their bags from the car. "I've had dinner waiting for—"

"We ate in town," Zinnia told her as they went into the house. "Didn't Jake tell you?"

"I thought you told her," Jake said as he carried a large duffle inside, dropping it on the floor.

"We didn't want to trouble you." Zinnia dropped two more bags as well as an oversized purse, so that the floor was nearly covered in their luggage. "We figured it wouldn't be easy to cook in this tiny house."

"I made seafood fettuccine alfredo." She frowned. "And it was very good."

"We ate at this place called Pine Lodge Inn," Jake said. "And what a wait."

"It took almost an hour to get a table."

"And you didn't think to call me?" Kate heard the edge in her voice.

"We left our phones in the car." Zinnia exchanged glances with her brother.

Kate studied both of them. Since when did they go or do anything without their phones? She was tempted to ask them but decided to let it go. Really, what was the point? Clearly they wanted to have dinner by themselves with no regard for their mother. Well, fine. "I hope you enjoyed your dinner," she said crisply.

"It was okay." Jake was looking around her tiny house with a creased brow. "Man, Mom, how can you stand this?"

"What?"

"This tiny house. It feels like a coffin."

"I don't know." Zinnia sat down on the sofa. "I think it's kinda cute. Small, but cute."

"Thanks." Kate was determined to be the adult here, take the high road, not be offended. "How was the drive over?" She sat down next to Zinnia.

"The traffic was gnarly." Jake tested the folding wooden chair then sat. "But we made it."

"I was worried there could've been a wreck." Kate stared at their bags still piled on the floor, wondering why on earth they brought so much stuff for just a night or two. Of course, Zinnia never traveled light. But Jake? Maybe this was intentional, their way of showing her that her house was too small.

"Do you have a bathroom?" Zinnia popped up and looked around. "I heard some tiny homes don't." She wrinkled her nose. "Please, tell me you don't have a camping toilet outside."

Kate pointed to the door. "Right there. Water and plumbing and everything."

"That's a relief." She went into the bathroom then let out a tiny shriek. "You've gotta be kidding! How can you possibly do anything in here?"

"It works for me," Kate called back.

Jake stood and went up the stairs, taking a peek at her sleeping loft. "Don't you hit your head on the ceiling when you stand up?"

"I don't stand up," she calmly told him. "I usually lie down when I'm in bed."

"But when you get up. Don't you stand up and whack your head?"

"Nope." Okay, she almost did once early on, but then she got used to it.

"I still think this is totally nuts." He came down the stairs with a scowl. "It's not like you're broke or anything. You aren't, are you?"

"Not broke." She took in a slow breath. "But I've had to tighten my belt after I invested most of my money in the tiny house development."

He groaned and rolled his eyes. "Seriously, Mom? You put all the house sale money into that commune?"

"It's not a commune, it's a community. And it's a good investment. When the lots begin to sell, I get my money back and then some."

Zinnia emerged from the bathroom with a curious expression. "Why is there a showerhead in the middle of the ceiling in there?"

"Because the whole bathroom becomes a shower. It's watertight."

"Eew."

"It's very efficient. You clean your bathroom while you shower."

"Double eew!"

Kate stood up, folding her arms in front of her. "Okay, it's clear that you two do not approve of my new home. And while you're entitled to your opinions, you're not entitled to rudeness. I did not raise my children to be rude."

"Sorry, Mom." Zinnia came over to hug her. "It's just that we care about you."

"And we're worried about you." Jake peered curiously at her. "We think you could be losing it."

"Thank you very much, but I'm perfectly fine. In fact, I haven't felt this good in years. Not since before your dad got sick." She told them about planting flowers all afternoon. And the pumpkin seeds from yesterday. "I plan to start looking for a small piece of business property soon. Something I can lease for my flower shop. I'd like to be set up by August, if not sooner."

"I thought you were out of money," Jake pointed out.

"I didn't say that. I just said I need to tighten my belt." She sat back down.

"Does that mean I don't get my allowance this summer?" Zinnia asked with wide eyes.

"I thought you had a job."

"It's more like an internship. It pays practically nothing. And, trust me, it won't be cheap living in Seattle."

"I thought you were going to live with Jake."

Of course, this started up an argument of a completely different kind. But finally, Kate just held up her hands. "I guess you two will have to sort that out between yourselves. And, Zinnia, I can keep giving you your allowance throughout the summer. But after that, you're on your own."

Zinnia unzipped her bag, tugging out a sweater. "It gets kinda cool up here in the mountains, doesn't it?"

"I like it." Kate smiled and stood up. "I usually sit on my front porch this time of evening with a cup of tea." She turned on the element below her teakettle. "You guys want some tea?"

Zinnia said yes, but Jake was opening her fridge. "I'd rather have something cold." He pulled out a sparkling soda and popped it open. "Pretty tight fridge, Mom. Can't see you having us here for Thanksgiving this year."

"You guys didn't come for Thanksgiving last year," she pointed out.

"Is that what this is about?" Jake demanded. "We miss a holiday or two, we forget to call you on Mother's Day, and you sell the family home right out from under us?"

She stared at him. "Right out from under you?"

"You never told us. That house was ours too, you know."

"It was yours when you were kids, growing up. But it was legally my house, Jake. Both your father and I were purchasing it. And your father left it to me."

"That's not what he means, Mom." Zinnia came over to the counter. "He means that it was emotionally our house. You got rid of it without bothering to tell us. And we don't really like that." She looked at her brother. "Right, Jake?"

He just nodded.

"Well, you guys have obviously discussed this." Kate measured loose tea into her teapot then turned to face them. "And I'm sorry I didn't tell you sooner. But honestly, everything happened so fast." She explained about Jennifer having a buyer. How she gave notice on her job. "And the pieces just kept falling into place." She waved a hand. "And suddenly I was here. And I couldn't be happier." Well, she could be happier. If only her kids would let her.

"But what about us?" Jake pointed to the sofa. "You really expect me to sleep there every time I visit?"

"You really expect to visit a lot?" She locked eyes. "You've been pretty busy with your own life. And your work." She put a hand on his shoulder. "And like I said the other day, I'm proud of you for that, son. You're doing great."

Zinnia picked up her bag. "Do you have a closet? A place for our stuff?"

"Not really." The teakettle whistled and she busied herself with that. "But it seems you guys brought a lot of stuff. Maybe you can leave it in the car. Just take out what you need for the night and—"

"Like we're camping?" Jake said. "Guess I should've brought my backpacking tent and sleeping bag."

She shrugged as she poured a cup of tea, handing it to Zinnia. "Maybe so." She filled the second one for herself then opened her front door. "It's awfully nice out. You kids want to join me on the porch?"

"Is there even room?" Jake complained.

She pointed to the camp chairs that she'd set up down below. "We have up or down seating here. Take your pick." He chose a camp chair and Zinnia joined Kate on the porch.

"I'm sorry this is so hard on you two," Kate said carefully. "I never dreamed you'd take it like this. Oh, I figured you wouldn't like it, but I didn't think you'd turn against me. I love both of you and I'm so happy to see you following your dreams and living your lives. I just figured you'd be like that for me."

"But you're the mom," Jake declared. "You're supposed to be like the anchor that holds our family together."

Kate felt more like he wanted to tie an anchor around her neck, but didn't say so.

"Yeah, Mom," Zinnia chimed in. "What happens when we get married and have kids?"

"Oh?" Kate turned to her. "Something I should know about?"

"No. But someday. I always dreamed of coming down the stairs in my wedding gown . . . at our house when I got married."

"Really? You'd want to get married in our house? Most of your friends seem to pick more interesting venues. Like Josie's wedding in the vineyard. I seem to recall you saying you dreamed of doing something like that."

"Well, I don't know. But as a little girl I dreamed of coming down our stairs."

"So, I should've put my life on hold, lived in a house that was too big, and kept working a job I didn't really like in order for you to come down those stairs?"

Zinnia shrugged. "It was more than just the stairs, Mom."

"Yeah," Jake jumped in. "Like I'm missing my old room with my own bath and my old bed. Tonight I'm forced to sleep on a sofa and share a pint-sized bathroom with two women. Nice."

"I'm sorry, Jake. But I'm not forcing you."

"Good point." He reached for his phone. "Maybe I'll see if there's a hotel in town."

"Good luck." She remembered how busy town had been earlier.

"Good luck? I can't even get a signal here." He shook his phone.

"Go over there." She pointed to the front of the barn. "That works. But, seriously, I don't think you'll find a room. It's a holiday weekend and town was packed today."

"Great. So I'm stuck on a sofa with no phone service. Does it get any better than this?"

She suddenly remembered Hank's offer. "As a matter of fact, it does. My friend Hank owns that house over there. And he offered you guys rooms, if you want."

Zinnia jumped up. "We want, we want."

"Count me in." Jake was already heading into the house for his bag.

"Let me go check with him. I'll be right back." She hurried over to his house, relieved to see there were still lights on inside. She knocked on the door and was greeted with a wide smile.

"Good evening." He looked amused as he stepped out onto the porch, turning the light on. "I saw your houseguests arrived. Anything I can help you with?"

She sighed. "You were right. They're not thrilled with my accommodations. When I mentioned your house, they practically bolted over here. I just wanted to be sure you were still okay with it."

"Perfectly okay." He smiled. "Are they giving you a hard time?"

She couldn't help but roll her eyes. "I had no idea I raised such selfish, rude children, but apparently I did."

"Want me to knock them around a little for you?" He chuckled.

"Probably too late for that." She nodded to where her kids were already headed their way, bags in hand. Zeb came out to the porch and Kate introduced everyone, and Jake and Zinnia made some tiny house jokes then thanked Hank for his hospitality. At least they were nice to him.

Glad to escape her somewhat entitled children, Kate forced a smile as she told everyone good night. And when she got back to her little house, she couldn't believe how roomy it felt with her kids gone. Yes, they were right about one thing— her house really wasn't big enough for her and her two full-grown kids. But maybe that was a good thing.

Chapter 22

Kate wasn't surprised that Jake opted to sleep in the next morning, but she was taken slightly aback to see Zinnia up and dressed—and ready for church. Oh, it wasn't that her children were heathens. She and Kenneth had taken them to church as children, but when the teen years hit, Jake pulled back, finally refusing to go. And Zinnia, well, she vacillated back and forth on church attendance, depending on her friends. But like she reassured Kate from time to time, she was still a believer.

"Did you hear that church is in a barn?" Kate asked her daughter as she washed up the breakfast dishes.

"Zeb said it's pretty cool."

"So, you don't feel, uh, overdressed?"

"You know me well enough to know I dress however I want to dress. I'm unconventional. And today, I wanted to look feminine."

"Well, you look pretty." Kate smiled.

"Is that what you're wearing?" Zinnia frowned at Kate's jeans, plain white shirt, and leather loafers.

Kate shrugged. "I dress how I want to dress too." She paused by the mirror. "I might add a bandana."

"A bandana?"

"You know, since it's cowboy church." Kate shook out a blue bandana she'd used to tie her hair back the other day then tied it loosely around her neck. "How's that?"

Zinnia's expression was enough of an answer. She obviously didn't approve. But when had she last appreciated her mother's fashion sensibilities? Ten or more years ago?

"What I really need are some cowboy boots." Kate slipped in some hoop earrings, hoping that might appease her daughter some.

"Boots would be a nice touch." Zinnia nodded. "As long as you get good ones."

"Good ones?" Kate picked up her purse. "I actually want sturdy ones. You know, to walk around in the dirt. Like the guys wear. They seem practical."

"Zeb had on some nice looking boots this morning." Zinnia's eyes twinkled. "He's awfully cute. Do you know if he's available?"

Kate blinked. Her fashionista daughter was interested in Zeb?

"I mean, it's not like I want to date him or anything. But I'm just curious." She unzipped her cosmetics bag, removing a mirror to check her face.

"He's not taken. But I happen to know he's interested in someone." Kate had no intention of letting out anything about Leota. It was too soon.

"Oh? Will this person be at church?"

"I doubt it. She doesn't live here."

"A long-distance relationship . . . ?" Zinnia touched up her lips and smiled. "Then there's still hope I could turn his head."

"You just want to turn his head?" Kate frowned. "Just for the fun of it?"

"Oh, Mom." Zinnia gave her the look. "Don't be such a buzzkill."

"Excuse me, Zinnia, but Zeb is a really nice guy. And I consider him a good friend. I'd hate for you to do anything to hurt him."

"Why would I want to hurt him? I think he's adorable. And did it occur to you we both have Z names?"

Hiding her exasperation, Kate led the way outside. "That's how you measure your men? By the letters in their name? Z for a Z? Seriously?"

"No, of course, not. I just thought it was a fun coincidence."

Kate waved to Hank and Zeb standing next to the old green pickup. "Meet you there," she called out.

"Can't we ride with Hank and Zeb?"

"That pickup only has one narrow seat. We'd be like sardines."

"But it's such a cool truck. Care if I ride with them?"

Kate shrugged. "Guess that's up to you—and them." She watched as Zinnia skipped over to the pickup, probably complimenting Hank on how "cool" his truck was, then begging for a ride. Kate didn't really care as she got into her SUV. In fact, it was kind of sweet to see at least one of her children eager to mix in. Although she wasn't too sure about Zinnia's sudden interest in Zeb. But if Kate could get Zinnia to see her side, it would be easier to deal with Jake.

Kate was just starting to back up when the passenger door opened. She braked then turned, expecting to see a disappointed Zinnia. But it was Hank.

"Can I hitch a ride with you?" he asked.

"Of course."

"I let Zeb drive my truck. Kind of crowded in there with three."

She laughed. "Exactly what I told Zinnia."

"Your daughter seems to have taken a fancy to Zeb."

Kate nodded grimly. "Didn't you notice they both have names that start with a Z? Apparently that's meaningful to my daughter."

Hank laughed.

"She even asked me if Zeb was involved. I hinted that he might like someone but didn't mention names."

"Does Zinnia know Leota?"

"Sure. Considering how different their personalities are, they get along surprisingly well." She glanced at Hank. "So did my kids behave themselves last night? No temper tantrums, hissy fits, or late-night pillow fights?"

"They were fine. I think they must've used up all their angst on you."

"How nice of them."

"In fact, Jake and I had a pretty good talk after the others turned in. He's a good boy, Kate."

"Oh, I'm fully aware of that. I just don't like that he thinks he knows better than his old mom. I'd appreciate a little respect."

"It's just that he thinks he's supposed to watch out for you. Apparently it was something his dad told him. He asked Jake to take care of you and his sister. And he seems to take it somewhat seriously."

"Oh, dear, that's a lot to put on a young man."

"That's what I told him."

"I really don't want him to feel responsible for Zinnia or me." She bit her lip as she followed a short string of cars into the farm that hosted church.

"He might need to hear that from you, Kate."

She nodded somberly. "Thanks. I'll make sure he does."

"Another thing you might find amusing . . ."

"What's that?"

"I got the impression he was interviewing me."

"Interviewing you? For what?"

"For you."

Kate felt her eyes grow wide as she parked her

car. "That's, uh, interesting." As they got out, she wanted to ask where her son got the idea that Hank and she were anything beyond mere business acquaintances. Even if she did have more than just a passing interest in Hank, it wasn't like she'd told anyone.

"Just thought you should know," Hank said quietly as they walked toward the barn. She thanked him, but still wondered . . . did Jake have any real reason to suspect she and Hank were involved? *Were they?*

After church, Hank invited Kate and her kids to join him and Zeb for a barbecue lunch. "I'll bring a salad," she offered. "And I have a loaf of rosemary bread. And I was going to make strawberry cheesecake today. I could bring that for dessert."

His eyes lit up. "Yum! We'll eat around one."

"While you're making cheesecake, I'd like to look around. I'd like to see where this tiny house commune is going to be." Zinnia glanced appealingly at Zeb. "Any chance I could get you to give me the tour while Mom's busy making her famous cheesecake?"

"Sure." He nodded. "But you might want to change. It's pretty dusty and dirty over there right now."

"Give me five minutes." Zinnia hurried into the house.

"Thanks, Zeb." Kate tried not to feel disappointed over the fact she wasn't the one showing the area by the pond. "I hoped my kids would want to see what's going on here."

"Hey, maybe Jake would like to go too." Zeb rolled up his shirt sleeves.

"Good idea." She smiled at Hank. "I'll see you at one."

Back in her little house, she began to set out ingredients for cheesecake. She had just enough time to get it done before lunch. Hopefully her toaster-convection oven would do the trick. She'd never used it for cheesecake before. She was just putting the cheesecake into the oven when Jake came in.

"Hey, Jake." She closed the door. "I thought you went exploring with Zeb and Zinnia."

"Nah. They were talking about swimming in the pond. Didn't sound good to me."

"Oh." She nodded. "Want something to drink?"

He helped himself to the fridge and a tall glass of orange juice before he sat down on the sofa. "Hank's house is nice."

"And big." She got herself a sparkling soda then sat across from him in the folding wooden chair.

"He doesn't seem to mind."

"Well, he's got Zeb living there too. But I do recall him saying that house was too big for him."

"Doesn't seem too big to me." He glanced

around her compact space. "You really like this? I mean better than our old house?"

"It's like apples and oranges. I liked our old house when we were all there. It served us well. But I like this house for what it is. It suits me."

"You don't even have a TV." He frowned.

"Yes, I do." She pointed to a canvas reproduction of Van Gogh's sunflowers hanging over a small flat-screen with a built in DVD player. "It's just hidden."

"Oh." He set down the empty glass. "Clever."

"I haven't even turned it on yet." She sighed happily. "Haven't even wanted to."

He leaned back and, folding his arms over his chest, really seemed to study her house. "I guess this place isn't so bad. It's actually not much smaller than my apartment."

She blinked. *Was Jake coming around?*

"If you're that comfortable here, well, I guess I'll just have to accept it."

She happily stood, then went over to hug her son. "Thanks, Jake. That means so much to me."

"I'm still a little irked at how you did it though."

"I apologize."

"If you make any more big life decisions, like you decide to relocate to China or something, it'd be nice to be in the loop."

"I have no plans to move to China."

"Or if you got involved in a relationship . . ."

He seemed to be eyeing her closely now. "And thought you might get married . . . it'd be nice to have a little head's up."

"No worries there either, Jake." She got up to check the temperature of the toaster oven.

"I wasn't so sure about that. But after talking with Hank last night, well, I guess that's nothing we need to worry about."

She turned to look at him. "What do you mean?"

"I guess I thought maybe you were interested in him. You know, romantically. But after talking with him, it's obvious he's not the remarrying type."

"Oh, that." She nodded. "Yes, I know."

"He's still in love with his wife. And, man, I saw that painting of Elizabeth. She was super beautiful. I get why he couldn't get over losing her."

"Uh-huh." She busied herself with the strawberries, carefully stemming and slicing them in preparation for topping the cheesecake later.

"Is that how it is for you? I mean with Dad. I know how much you missed him. Especially in the beginning. Do you still feel like that?"

Kate didn't know what to say. "Well, of course, I'll always miss him." She kept slicing. "But it's gotten better over the years. And part of my reason for making this change was to help me get over it. Sort of start life over, you know?"

She turned to look at him. His confused expression reminded her of when he was a little boy, trying to figure something out. "I guess it's complicated."

"Yeah." He sighed.

"Hank told me something, Jake." She set down the knife and, wiping her fingers on a dish towel, hoped she could do this right. "He mentioned something about what Dad told you, before he died. It had to do with you sort of taking care of me and Zinnia after he was gone."

He barely nodded.

"I never realized he said that. And I can understand why he did. He was such a good protector and provider. I'm sure he felt like he was abandoning us. Not that he could help it." She felt a tightness in her throat. "But I don't want you to feel a responsibility for me. I'm a grown woman. And I've gotten pretty independent these past few years, especially lately. So, please, don't worry about me. Not like that anyway."

Again, he barely nodded.

"As for Zinnia." She slowly shook her head. "I'm sure she thinks she doesn't need anyone to look after her, but she's still young. She could probably use a big brother's help or advice from time to time. Especially while she's settling into Seattle. Still, I don't like thinking of you carrying the weight and responsibility of your little sister. I don't want her to be a burden for you."

"I don't mind."

She smiled. "I know. You're a good man." Her eyes grew misty, but not because she was still grieving for Kenneth—because she was proud of her son right now. Sure, he could be overbearing and opinionated at times, but he really was a good man.

Chapter 23

With Jake's help, Kate carried over her contributions to lunch at a little before one. Hank told them to go inside while he tended the grill, but Kate had never been farther than the living room and dining room before. Jake, acting perfectly at home, led her straight into the kitchen. "Here you go."

"Wow." She looked around the modern kitchen. "This is nice."

"Pretty swanky, huh?" He opened the oversized fridge so she could put her strawberry cheesecake inside. "I guess his wife was quite a cook."

Kate looked at the state-of-the-art appliances and nodded. "But this wouldn't suit me," she said quietly.

"Too big, huh?"

"Well, there's that. But I don't like the way it's all by itself. If I'm cooking I like to be able to see others."

"Like our old house?"

"Yeah. It was a good design for a family." She looked over to where a small breakfast nook was nestled into a bay window. "But that's nice."

"Yeah, nice view too. You can see the mountains. But you can see them even better from the living room. And upstairs is good too. Hank designed this house and I gotta give it to him, it's pretty cool."

She just nodded, repressing the urge to go snooping about. But it seemed a bit unfair that her kids had seen more of this beautiful house than she had. Probably more than she ever would. She remembered what Jake had told her about how he thought Hank would never love anyone again. He was probably right.

As they went back out to the porch, she could hear voices. Assuming it was Zeb and Zinnia back from their adventures at the pond, she went out to see. But to her surprise, it was Glen Stryker.

"Hey, Kate." He grinned at her. "Hank said you were here."

"Oh, hi." She smiled nervously.

"You never returned any of my calls. The last message I left, I told you I was going to come check on you—to be sure you were okay." He glanced at Hank. "I thought maybe he had you locked up down in the cellar or something."

"Funny." Hank didn't look amused.

"My kids came for the weekend." Kate introduced Jake to Glen. "I was kind of distracted."

"Nice to meet you." Glen heartily shook Jake's hand. "I was trying to get your mom to come out to the lake."

"Lake?" Jake asked with interest.

"Glen has a tiny house development out there,"

Kate explained. "Not too far from the state park."

"And I have a boat," Glen told Jake. "I thought I'd get your mom to go on another boat ride with me. But she's not answering her phone," he teased. "Maybe you'd like to come out."

Jake's eyes lit up. "I'd love to go out to the lake."

"But we're about to have lunch," she said quickly.

"Glen can join us," Hank told her. "We have plenty of food."

"And something smells good." Glen glanced toward the grill. "But I hate to intrude."

"No intrusion." Hank smiled. "And Kate made strawberry cheesecake. I barely saw it go by, but it looked great."

Now Zeb and Zinnia were coming onto the porch and Kate introduced Glen to her daughter. The pair looked damp and cool and happy.

"I absolutely love your pond," Zinnia told Hank. "Zeb said you might put in a dock someday. I highly recommend it. Then we wouldn't have to get all muddy." She held up a grungy flip-flop. "I'm going to grab a shower before lunch."

"These steaks will be done in about ten minutes," Hank warned.

"I'll hurry." Still holding her dirty flip-flops, she hurried inside.

"How about I set the table?" Kate said.

"Thanks."

"Need help?" Glen offered.

"I think I've got this." And eager to escape the awkwardness of Glen showing up for lunch, Kate hurried inside. With an excuse to poke around the kitchen cabinets, which were impressively organized, she soon found the dishes and things Hank had used when she'd eaten there. She even found a drawer with tablecloths and, thinking this was a festive occasion, picked out a plaid one that looked good with the dishes. She carried it outside to where the table was in a nice shady section of the porch.

Taking her time to carefully set it up, she realized it could use some flowers. She hurried over to her tiny house, clipping several tall geranium blooms, a few other flowers, and a few greens. She arranged these in a mason jar and was just setting it in the center of the table when Hank came over. "Nice."

She smiled. "I wish I had a better selection of flowers. Someday."

Before long, all six of them were seated around the table. Today it was Hank's turn to ask a blessing. Glen looked a bit surprised but bowed his head. As they ate, the conversation flowed surprisingly well. And when it got quiet, Zinnia—the usual chatterbox—filled in the gaps. To Kate's relief, she'd become quite a fan of the farm and not totally opposed to tiny homes. She listened attentively to Glen explaining about his development.

"I have this friend, Garson," Zinnia said eagerly. "He's about to graduate in architecture and design—or something like that. He built this really cool off-grid tiny home for his final project. It turned out so good he was featured on that TV show *Teeny, Tiny Home*."

"That show was one of the reasons I'm here now," Kate confessed. "It's how I got hooked on tiny homes. Although I doubt I'd ever want to go off-grid."

"I think off-grid sounds pretty cool," Zeb said. "I wouldn't mind trying it. Kind of like being a pioneer."

"Not me." Zinnia shook her head. "I like my amenities." She turned to Glen. "Do you live in a tiny home?"

He laughed. "Nope. My house is about the same size as Hank's. Looks out over the lake."

"So you don't practice what you preach?" Zeb teased.

"Tiny homes aren't for everyone," Glen admitted. "Although I'm thinking about setting up a tiny house for a little getaway."

"Get away from what?" Jake challenged. "You live at the lake and have a boat." He poked Zinnia. "Glen offered to take me out on the lake after lunch."

"I want to go too," Zinnia declared.

"Of course." Glen smiled at Kate. "You can all come."

"How about you?" Zinnia nudged Zeb.

He shook his head. "I've got plans."

"What about Hank?" Zinnia asked.

"I've got plans too." Hank's smile was polite. "Some other time perhaps."

"Sure, just Kate and the kids." Glen nodded with what seemed a satisfied expression—like this was going exactly as planned.

"Anyone ready for strawberry cheesecake?" Kate stood, picking up her plate, eager to escape what felt awkward again. She didn't appreciate how Glen seemed so comfortable around her family, as if he planned to become part of it.

Barely in the kitchen, she was joined by Hank, carrying a load of dirty dishes. "Need help?"

"I guess." She set the cheesecake pan on the granite countertop. "I need a sharp knife, a pie server, and six small plates."

"Coming right up."

"That was very hospitable of you to invite Glen to join us," she said as she sliced through the cheesecake.

"You know what they say, keep your friends close and your enemies closer." Hank chuckled.

"You think Glen is your enemy?"

"No. I was kidding. But he is sort of the competition." He held out a plate for her to put a piece on. "I mean in the tiny home business.

I'm sure he sees us as competition for him too."

"With his waiting list?" She lifted out another piece.

"Yeah." He caught it on the plate. "You're probably right. I doubt he's worried about us at all. And really, I like Glen. I didn't mean to sound like that. He's a good guy, Kate."

She didn't know how to respond, but Hank had already put four pieces of cheesecake onto a small tray. "I'll get these out there if you can get the last two."

"Perfect." She used her finger to clean off the knife then licked it, instantly regretting her bad manners. But Hank simply looked amused.

After cheesecake, she insisted on helping with cleanup and Zeb offered to help. Glad to get away from Glen and his presumptuous ways, she was soon rinsing plates while Zeb loaded them into the dishwashers. Yes, there were two. One just for glasses and silverware, the other one for the rest.

"I know it's none of my business," Zeb said quietly, "but are you and Glen, well, you know. Are you guys dating or something?"

She nearly dropped the plate. "No, not at all."

"Oh." He gave her a sideways glance. "You sure about that?"

"Of course. I can't speak for Glen. But I know I'm not interested in him like that."

"I was just curious." He took the plate from her. "Hear anything from Leota lately?"

"No, but I haven't forgotten about the neighboring lot thing. I plan to call her after my kids leave."

"Uh-huh. And when are they leaving? Not that I'm trying to get rid of them. Just curious."

She shrugged. "Tomorrow, I guess."

"Seems like they like it here well enough."

"You should've seen them when they first got here." She shook her head. "They could've been carrying pitchforks."

"Nah, that'd never happen." Zeb laughed. "They don't look like farmers to me."

Now she laughed.

"Hey, I watered your seedlings while we were over by the pond. They looked a little thirsty."

"Thank you!" She shook her head. "I nearly forgot all about that."

"They'll probably need a little babying at first—you know, till they get established. And I got to thinking, we haven't had much deer through here lately, but they do jump that fence and get into the alfalfa sometimes. Spring and fall are the worst. But you never know."

"Meaning they might eat my flowers?"

"You can count on it. Without a fence to keep them out, they'll have a field day." He chuckled. "I guess that was kind of a pun. But these deer have been known to jump fences as high as six feet. The one around our property's only around five feet and the deer sail right over it."

"What can I do?"

He described how some people run a high wire that's made visible with sparkly streamers. "The stuff looks kind of like the tinsel you hang on a Christmas tree, but it seems to work."

"And my flowers would be safe?" She handed him the last dish to dry.

"Oh, sure. And I could do that for you. Run a wire fence with something like that across the top."

"I'd really appreciate it. And we'll take your time off of your lot price. I already started to tally up the time you've already given me."

"Cool. I'll get right on it."

"And just bill me for the materials."

"Sure. But we've got a lot of scrap fencing junk just sitting out behind the barn. I'm sure Hank would like to see me get rid of it."

"Thanks, Zeb." She looked intently at him. "I mean really, thanks."

"Huh?" He closed the dishwasher.

"What I'm saying is thanks for being you." She smiled.

"Same back at ya." He grinned. "And, hey, when you talk to Leota, will you tell her hey for me? And that it's okay if she doesn't want me for her neighbor. I understand. And tell her I'm praying everything works out that she'll get her tiny house and get over here. I know that's probably a selfish prayer, but I figure God can always say no."

Kate promised to relay all to Leota and then, trying to think of some acceptable excuse to get out of going to the lake with Glen and her kids, she went outside to discover that Glen and Jake and Zinnia had already left in his pickup.

"Glen said to just meet them down on the dock." Hank carried a few last pieces into the house.

"Really?" She held the door open for him.

"Your kids were pretty eager to get to the lake, and Glen was ready to go." Hank studied her. "He said you'd know his boat since you've been out with him before."

She grimaced at how confident Glen was acting. "Well, thanks for everything, Hank. That was a nice lunch."

"Hey, you provided more than half of it. Thank *you*."

"I better get going." She stifled fresh irritation. Mostly at Glen, but partly at Hank. He seemed to assume she was involved with Glen too. But, really, what was the point in trying to straighten him out? Oh, sure, he'd mentioned being jealous before. But it wasn't a serious kind of jealousy. Not the kind of jealousy she'd felt walking through his living room just moments ago. Jealous of a dead woman. Okay, Elizabeth wasn't dead to him. And for all Kate knew Elizabeth might be up in heaven dancing with Kenneth right now. And, despite her previous aggravations, she had to chuckle over the image of Elizabeth and Kenneth waltzing in heaven . . . that was amusing!

Chapter 24

Kate tried to be a good sport as Glen zipped her kids around the lake in his fancy boat, but she was not enjoying herself. Although it was amusing when Zinnia decided she wanted to try wakeboarding. And Jake laughed long and loud when she fell flat on her face. That was enough for Zinnia. And she'd had enough of the boat too. Relieved to be done with this, Kate was eager to go home. But before they were even off the boat, Glen was making plans to take them up to his house. And her kids seemed happy about it.

Glen's house was impressive, in a masculine steel and glass sort of way. And although the view of the lake was fabulous, the big house reminded Kate of an oversized bachelor pad. But because her kids seemed to be enjoying themselves, she continued trying to be a good sport. All the while keeping a safe and polite distance from Glen. Hopefully he would get the hint.

Finally, it was getting close to dinnertime and Kate hinted that it was time to go. But, of course, Glen had other plans. "Do you like trout?" he asked them. "I caught a nice bunch of browns yesterday." Of course, they all did like trout. And so they stayed for dinner. When they were finally on their way back to the farm, both Zinnia and Jake seemed to be impressed.

"I know we were hard on you at first, Mom," Jake said. "You know, about moving here. But seems like you landed in a pretty sweet spot."

"And your man friends are both nicely set up," Zinnia added. "Good job, Mom."

"They are not my man friends," Kate declared. "They are just friends. That's all."

"Whatever." Zinnia laughed. "Anyway, it gives us hope. You're not out here living in a commune with a bunch of losers."

Kate bristled at that. "When the tiny home development is up and running, you guys might have a different reaction. Not that the people living there will be losers as you put it, Zinnia. But they won't be wealthy. It's considered an affordable housing development. It's meant to help people—people like me—who don't have unlimited resources. People trying to start a new business, or a new life."

Neither of her kids responded. "I didn't mean to rain on your parade," she said quietly. "But just because Hank and Glen both seem pretty well set up as you say, doesn't mean anything to me. I like my life just as it is. I'm excited about my down-size, and growing flowers, and starting up a florist business. And I hope you both can respect that."

"Sure, Mom," Jake said in a flat tone.

"Whatever." Zinnia's tone was even flatter.

"There are a lot of good people in this town," Kate continued. "I've met a few through church. And I wasn't going to say anything, but Leota is probably moving here too. She wants a tiny home."

"Leota?" Jake sounded surprised.

"She wants a simpler life too."

"That's cool," Zinnia said.

Kate told them about some of the others who were interested in tiny home living, and the ones who wanted to come check out her house. By the time they were at the farm, she felt her old enthusiasm back. "I hope you two won't be too disappointed if I don't marry a rich man." She laughed as they got out. "Because I'd rather be poor and happy in a box than unhappily married in a castle."

It was dark out and both Zinnia and Jake seemed tired. So they all hugged good night and Kate, glad for some alone time, went into her tiny house. What she said was completely true. There might've been a time, a year or two ago, when someone like Glen would've appealed to her. Just for security's sake. But not anymore. Even as much as she liked Hank—and she did—she would rather be single the rest of her days than living in the shadow of his beloved Elizabeth.

As hard as it was to see Jake and Zinnia leave the next morning, Kate was glad to return to her routine. Not that she had that much of a routine, but she was eager to get the rest of her seedlings planted. And she wanted to get ready for a mini open house to show her friends what tiny home living was like. Besides Abby and Aileen, and a guy friend of Molly's, she'd met a young woman at the grocery store who was interested. That was four prospective customers. And then there was Leota.

Kate decided to call her that afternoon. She didn't want to sound too pushy, but she was curious as to how Leota's plans were shaking down.

"I ordered my tiny home on Saturday," Leota exclaimed. "It's one of their more popular models and the factory had several of them almost finished. And since I didn't want any extras, Kirk told me it'd be ready in about three weeks. And he's going to schedule the moving guys to deliver it."

"That's great. I'm so excited for you, Leota."

"Me too. I mean, I vacillate between over the moon and scared spitless, but mostly thrilled."

"I felt like that too."

"Yeah, but you didn't tap all your savings for yours."

"That's true. But won't that make your payments pretty low?"

"Yes. That's the great part."

"And I'm still happy to rent you one of my

lots," Kate reminded her. "It can even be rent to own if you like."

"I don't want to take advantage, but that would be wonderful."

"I'm just thankful to have you for my neighbor."

"Not as thankful as I am." Leota went on to explain how glad she was to give notice on her apartment. "The manager hadn't bothered to renew my lease last winter so they can't even make me stay a day longer."

"Are you going to let your family know about your relocation?"

"I'm going to tell them I'm living in a tiny house in Pine Ridge. But the only forwarding address I give them will be a PO Box. That reminds me—I need to call the Pine Ridge Post Office tomorrow."

"I'm sure you have lots to do to get ready for your move. But at least you have more time than I did."

"I've already started to sift through things. For a small apartment, it's pretty stuffed in here."

"One more thing." Kate explained about Zeb's interest in purchasing a lot. "And he's interested in the one next to you. But I thought I should check with you on it."

"Zeb's so sweet. Why wouldn't I want him for a neighbor? In fact, I kind of like the idea of a big strong guy next door. He could probably come in handy at times."

"For sure. Zeb really is handy too." Kate told her about his help with her mini flower farm.

"He's a good guy."

"I couldn't agree more."

As soon as they wrapped up the phone call, Kate called Zeb with the good news. He let out such a happy whoop that she had to hold the phone away from her ear.

"Leota actually seemed happy about it too," Kate said after he calmed down. "I'm not saying that she's interested in anything more than having a good neighbor."

"Sure, I get that. And like I promised, I won't be bugging her. I'll understand if she only wants to be friends. Disappointed, sure, but I'll understand."

"I'll like having you nearby too, Zeb."

"Cool. And I'm happy to pay you for my lot as soon as possible. Hank told me that if you agreed to sell to me, I could even start building my tiny house right on it."

"You're building your own house?"

"Hank helped me make some plans. It's going to be like a mini log cabin."

"Sounds cute."

"So let me know what the price is, and I'll pay you."

Kate didn't know how much to deduct for his

help with her flower garden project, but she was determined to be generous. Because Zeb really was like family.

And now with Zeb on board, as well as Abby and Aileen and a few others who seemed genuinely interested, she might soon have enough capital to cover the expense of opening her florist business. Perhaps even before August like she'd been hoping. But before she started her search for a small shop in town, she wanted to get her potential customers here to see her tiny home. After a few phone calls, Kate's tiny open house was scheduled for the upcoming weekend. And everyone coming sounded enthused.

For the next several days, Kate went into full speed getting her place looking as good as possible. Both inside and outside. By Saturday, she had an outdoor carpet, a couple of Adirondack chairs and tables, and a few more lovely flower planters set up outside. This combined with some friendly outdoor lights and a few other touches made the whole place magically inviting. And it looked even better on the inside.

Her plan was to serve a casual appetizer buffet and drinks. She'd encourage her guests to stay and visit into the evening. Hopefully, they'd get a feel for what tiny house living really felt like. Tiny house living done right.

By the time her guests started to arrive, everything looked perfect. At least to her. Whether or not it appealed to them was another matter. But as Glen liked to say, "tiny houses were not for everyone." Not that she was in the habit of quoting Glen Stryker. And despite her cool responses to his regular phone calls to "check on her," he didn't seem to be giving up anytime soon. She wondered if he thought she was playing hard to get. But she didn't have time to think about that now. She just hoped he didn't pop in uninvited again. He'd already done that once this week.

"Welcome," she said to Aileen, her first visitor. "Go inside and look around as much as you like. Make yourself at home."

Before long, she had six guests, both inside and outside of her tiny house. They ate and visited, checking out every nook and cranny of her house, even testing out her sleeping loft. Finally, as the sun sank low in the sky, promising a gorgeous sunset, she invited everyone to stroll over to the pond. So much had been done lately that she wasn't too worried about showing it to potential buyers.

Once there, she explained where the access roads went and where the utilities were already being installed. "The lots have all been leveled and, although you can't see it yet, grass seed has been planted. That's why the soil is damp. Soon it'll be green and lovely." She told them a little bit about the vision for the finished development and showed them how large the lots would be. "All the yards will be fenced and pets are allowed."

"Does that mean I have to mow a lawn?" Aileen asked.

"Not if you don't want to." Kate explained how Zeb had offered to be the maintenance man. "What we want to offer is a little more space than you'd find at Pine Ridge Lake Estates for a fraction of the price. And the green grass will make it feel cleaner and cooler."

"And you can have pets?" Abby said happily. "I have a cat."

"Yes. We'll be just like a regular neighborhood. Only smaller homes."

"And all lots look onto the pond?" Bethany asked.

"Yes. That's how Hank's drawn it all out. I'll give you all maps back at my house. We just decided this week to call the place *Aspen Pond*. Hank told me to ask for your response. What do you think of that name?"

They all agreed that it was nice, and then Kate explained about the lots she owned. "I picked the south side of the pond because I love the way the light comes through the trees and seeing both the sunrises and sunsets." She pointed toward the mountains. "I mostly love this side because I think it has the best view."

"Have any other lots sold yet?" Aileen asked.

"I'm holding onto one for a friend of mine.

And Hank has sold a couple. But he really wants to wait until we're fully developed, you know, before he puts it out there in a big way. You guys are just getting a sneak preview." Kate could tell by their expressions and interest that some of her lots would soon be sold. "Also because I want a choice in who my neighbors are." She smiled then pointed to the two lots she'd already picked for herself and Leota. "And I'll be living right here."

By the time her guests left that evening, she had three serious offers to purchase lots. She had to restrain herself from doing a happy dance after the last vehicle left. To make a profit in such a short time—amazing! But seeing the lights on inside Hank's house, she didn't want to draw attention to herself. She hadn't exchanged more than brief greetings with him this past week. Not purposely, it was simply that they seemed extra busy. And she was grateful for that. Her heart needed some distance.

With the sales of three lots finalized the following week, plus the potential for two more offers coming in by next week, it was time to get serious about her florist shop. Even if her blooms weren't ready, she had contacts with flower wholesalers. Not only that, she'd also been scouring garage sales, estate sales, and second-hand stores, looking for interesting containers for flowers, as well as some pieces to use in her shop. So far, Hank hadn't complained about the growing collection of what could be "junk" to the untrained eye. She'd tried to tuck it out of sight between her tiny house and Hank's barn, but she needed it cleared out soon. She was just stowing a box of collectable dishes beneath her tiny home when she heard Zeb call out her name.

"Over here." She dusted her hands on her jeans as he came around the corner.

"Hey, watcha got here?" He peered curiously at her stash of finds. "Looks like a garage sale." He stooped down to examine a stack of wooden milk crates. "These are cool."

"I've been collecting things to use in my florist shop." She removed one of the teacups from her most recent find. "Something like this could make a sweet tiny arrangement."

He chuckled. "The tiny house lady and her tiny arrangements. I like it."

"And I have larger things to put flowers in as well." She picked up a white pitcher she'd found at an estate sale. "This would be nice with irises and forsythia, maybe some twisted sticks and a branch of cherry blossoms. You know, if it was spring."

"I'm not sure what for-cynthia is, but I bet you'll make it pretty, Kate."

She set the vase back in the box then looked curiously at him. Lately, he'd been so busy she'd barely seen him. "So how's Aspen Pond coming?"

"Well, right now, we're waiting for the electrical inspection. But all the cable's laid and looks good. We just need their okay before we connect power to the boxes."

"That'll probably be nice for you. I mean to build your house. How's that going? I noticed you had a pile of wood and stuff delivered there."

"Yep. I was just getting blocks set up. Hank said that as long as I don't make a real foundation, it'll still be considered temporary. But it's okay to set it on concrete blocks. Because those are moveable." He grinned. "Not that I plan to move it."

"Good. I hope not."

"And I even talked to Leota a couple times. You know, on the phone. And I might be imagining things, but it sort of seems like she could have feelings for me." He looked earnestly at her. "Do you think it's possible?"

Kate laughed. "I think it's very possible. I wouldn't want to get in the middle of it, but Leota does speak fondly of you, Zeb."

He sighed. "That's good to know, because Hank was worried. He thought I was blowing this whole thing out of proportion."

"Out of proportion?" She studied his reaction. "Why's that?"

"I think he's worried I could get hurt. And it's probably because that's how his mind works." Zeb peered curiously at her. "Like when I asked him about you, he made it sound like there'd never been anything between you two. Like no big deal."

She shrugged. "That's pretty much true."

Zeb frowned. "Really? Because I could've sworn he was just putting on an act, pretending like he didn't care."

"Why would he do that?"

"You know, so he wouldn't get hurt."

"I don't think he's worried about that, Zeb. He knows we're just business partners. And not really partners now. More like associates. That's all."

"Well, you sure could've fooled me. I saw the way he looked at you real early on. I haven't seen him like that before."

She shrugged again. "Maybe you imagined it."

He looked doubtful. "I don't think so. I know Uncle Hank pretty well."

She didn't know how to respond to that.

"Here's what I think." He lowered his voice as if he expected his uncle to pop around the corner. "Hank needs time to warm up, you know? Like you have to be extra patient with him."

"I think everyone needs to be treated with patience." Kate forced a smile.

"Yeah, you're probably right. But Uncle

Hank's probably a slow starter when it comes to romance."

"He doesn't seem like a slow starter around Natalie Spalding." Kate regretted making this admission. But, really, wasn't Zeb aware? Did he even notice that Natalie's car was parked there this morning?

"That's just business."

"Sometimes business morphs into other things." She tried to think of a way to change the subject. "Hey, that deer fence you made looks great, Zeb. I slept like a baby last night—just knowing the deer wouldn't be foraging my flowers anytime soon."

"They're safe, all right. And some of your flowers are looking real pretty. It'll be fun to see it when everything's blooming."

"I know! Now if I could just find a place for my florist shop." She pointed at him. "You don't happen to know of anything in town? Just a little shop tucked in a corner somewhere? Even a shared space. I won't be picky."

"I don't know of anything. But I'll be on the lookout."

She thanked him and, not wanting the conversation to return to her relationship with Hank, she told Zeb she had things to tend. But as she went into her house, she wondered if she'd been too quick to dismiss a relationship with Hank. Maybe he really did need her to be more patient, or perhaps he needed some encouragement from her.

She glanced out her window, thinking perhaps she should try to reconnect with him somehow. But she looked out just in time to see Hank getting into the passenger side of Natalie's Corvette. She couldn't see his face or expression, but she imagined he was smiling. Why not? As usual, the Corvette top was down and it was a beautiful summer day. Why shouldn't Hank enjoy himself? As she took off, Natalie threw back her head, laughing as she raced her car down the driveway, leaving a cloud of dust behind her.

Well, at least Kate could get in her SUV now, and go cruising around town. Although she'd already asked a realtor for help in finding a shop space—and she checked almost daily with the Chamber of Commerce, and local newspaper ads—Kate still hoped she'd drive through town just as someone set out a sign announcing: COMMERCIAL PROPERTY FOR SALE OR LEASE. Then she would race up to them and make an offer. Of course, that never happened. Today was no different.

Before giving up, she checked in with her realtor again. But the news was the same as last week. Yes, there was still that furniture store for sale with about 8,000 square feet and priced to match. And what had recently been an Asian restaurant was vacant now, complete with its recently remodeled and very expensive kitchen. But nothing that even slightly resembled a florist shop was available. At this rate, it seemed likely her field of flowers would bloom before she acquired a place to sell a single arrangement.

As she drove home, she actually considered constructing a roadside stand. At first, she imagined something like a grade-schooler's lemonade stand. Then she dreamed bigger, imagining it as an attractive mobile unit. Sort of like a super tiny, tiny house. Maybe she'd ask Hank for some design help since she knew he'd already sketched some ideas for tiny homes. Plus that would give her an excuse to reconnect with him.

But as she drove up the driveway, she noticed that, once again, Natalie's silver Corvette was parked in front of his house. And Zeb could be right, it might just be business. But really? Natalie had already been here twice this week, and they were not short visits either. One had gone from early afternoon into the evening. No, Kate decided, this had to be something more. And there was no need to pursue anything with Hank. If he needed patience and time, she would give it to him. Because at the moment, distancing seemed like her best course. She just wished she could move her tiny house a little farther away. It wouldn't be long.

● ● ●

Kate kept herself busy tending her flower field, which got prettier by the day, and collecting items for her "someday" florist business, as well as continuing her search for a shop location. She also did a couple more "showings" of her tiny home. Word was getting around that she had tiny-home lots to sell but they were going fast.

She had sold lots to Aileen, Abby, Bethany, and Zeb. Counting Kate's own lot and the one reserved for Leota, she only had six left to sell. Plus Molly's friend just confirmed his interest. Her funds for the florist business had multiplied. Now she just needed a place. But instead of worrying about it, she'd decided to simply pray. If it was meant to be, God would provide. In the meantime, she'd continue to look and try to be patient.

On the day Leota and her tiny home were scheduled to arrive, Kate put her ongoing search for a business location aside. Eager to welcome Leota and her house to Pine Ridge, she and Zeb had already planned a little celebration for tomorrow night. They'd invited their soon-to-be tiny home neighbors and a few others. Zeb was going to barbecue burgers and Kate was making salads and dessert.

To Kate's relief, Hank was still fully on board with Leota's arrival. He'd even had a plumber out to adapt his garage septic tank so that it could serve both Kate's and Leota's tiny homes. A good thing since Kate's tanks had been nearly full and she'd been unsure of what to do about it—and didn't want to bother Hank with her personal plumbing problems. She'd already been taking super short showers and tossing out her dishwater—just to keep her tanks from filling too fast. But now she could shower for as long as she liked. Truly luxurious!

As she swept off the section of concrete pad that would soon become Leota's temporary front yard, Kate wished their new development was ready for occupancy. It would make life so much simpler when they located over there. She felt certain Hank would appreciate it too. It could be her imagination, but it seemed he was just as uncomfortable as she was about the proximity of their homes. But according to the last, albeit brief, conversation she'd had with him, things were coming together like clockwork. "Mid-July," he'd promised her just yesterday morning when they'd crossed paths in the driveway. "Maybe sooner."

As Kate set the broom aside, she noticed a vehicle turning in to the farm. Hoping it was Leota leading the way for her tiny home processional, she was disappointed to realize it was actually Glen Stryker in his white Jeep Wrangler. She'd noticed he'd called twice on her phone today but hoped that ignoring his calls would help communicate her level in interest.

Still, she forced a polite smile as he pulled up in front of her petite house. Was this man ever going to get the message? His dogged determination was mind-boggling. It was also a little flattering. Especially since Hank seemed cooler than ever. As if he wanted to make it clear to her—their relationship was purely platonic. Well, fine. At least Glen Stryker seemed to appreciate her.

She'd told Leota a bit about Glen on the phone and Leota had actually suggested Kate pursue him. "Are you kidding?" Kate shot back. "I mean he's nice enough, but he's not my type. Not at all! This guy is full of himself, kind of a showoff. I wouldn't call him narcissistic, but he's probably close."

"That's exactly what I was thinking. He probably sees you as a challenge, Kate. Like he wants to win the race and claim the prize. But if you ran after him, he might lose interest. You might even scare him off," Leota had laughed. "Just act like you're dying to get married, that you're already reserving the church and looking at dresses. He'll probably take off running."

But the mere thought of that terrified Kate. What if he liked that?

"Hey, Kate." Glen was out of his Jeep, flashing that confident smile, like she must be thrilled to see him. "I hear you're looking for someplace to open your florist shop business."

"Yeah." She frowned slightly. "I haven't made any secret of it." In fact, she was certain she'd mentioned it to Glen more than once.

"Well, I just might have the answer for you."

"Really?" She led him over to the shade of her front porch. Despite her resolve to hold this man at arm's length, she suddenly felt a bit friendlier. "Would you like something cold to drink? I just made a pitcher of tea."

"Sounds good." He made himself comfortable in a rocker, patting the armrest with satisfaction. "Aren't these the best?"

"Yes, I love them. I'll be right back." She hurried inside, pouring them both a tall glass of iced tea, complete with a mint sprig. "Here you go." She sat next to him, eagerly watching him. Hopefully he wasn't just toying with her.

"So how've you been?" he asked after taking a long sip.

She quickly explained about getting ready for her friend Leota. "She's on her way right now. Driving the pilot car for her tiny house transport. I can't wait to see her."

"But your tiny house development isn't finalized with the city yet. At least that's the scuttlebutt in town. Did something change?"

"No, no, it's not ready for anyone yet." She pointed out the temporary parking spot next to her tiny home. "It's not very big, but it's only temporary."

"Hank's being pretty accommodating with his farm. Two tiny homes?"

"Fortunately, we won't be here for long. Hank estimates Aspen Pond will be ready by mid-July." She set down her glass. "But you mentioned a lead on a florist shop property. Please, I'm dying to hear what you know. You're so much better connected with the business world than I am. Please, let your cat out of the bag."

He ran a finger down the sweating glass with a sly smile. "It just so happens that no one knows about this particular spot yet. I mean that it might be available. Well, except for me that is."

"Okay." She nodded eagerly. "Are you going to spill the beans or do I have to twist your arm until you squeal?"

"That'd be interesting." He chuckled. "So, as it turns out, this property is mine."

"Really? You own a piece of business property in town?"

"Well, it is and it isn't."

"Is or isn't what?" Why did he like making everything into a cat and mouse game? So he could have the upper hand and watch her squirm? Maybe he really was a narcissist after all.

"It is a business property." His eyes twinkled. "But then again, it's not."

"Is your goal to frustrate me?" She suppressed

the urge to sock him. "Can't you just tell me what you're talking about?"

"I bought this little fixer house about twelve years ago, I guess. Property was still cheap back then. I'd just started to develop Pine Ridge Lake Estates and I figured I'd use it as an office to sell lots. Then, as it turned out, my lake development took off so fast, and sales were so great out there, I never needed the place in town. It wasn't too long before I built the lodge with loads of office space.

"I decided to keep that town property for an investment or even a tax loss if necessary. Mostly it's been an affordable rental for low-income tenants. But the last renters were pretty rough on it. It's too run-down to rent to anyone, and I've been too busy to do much about it. It's sat vacant these last few months."

"Where is this place?"

He described the location. "It's just one block off of Main Street, right next to the library."

"You don't mean that little red and white gingerbread house?" She leaned forward with interest. "With the big porch and overgrown patch of weeds in the front yard?"

"Yeah, that's the place." He chuckled. "Someone else called it a gingerbread house too. But the condition of the house suggests a child-eating witch might actually live there."

"Why that's a cute little house, Glen. And it

would be a sweet florist shop." She felt her hopes elevating.

"It would take a lot of work. Not work I care to invest in."

"Are you willing to sell this house?" Even as she asked this, she wasn't sure she could afford it. She'd been hoping to lease.

"I don't know for sure."

She sighed. "Then what do you have in mind? You obviously aren't just telling me this to torture me, because I'd love to have a place like that for my florist shop."

"I didn't come here to torture you." His brow creased. "And I wouldn't string a friend along."

She grimaced at the way he said this. Was he referring to her? Suggesting she'd strung him along? She'd dropped him hints left and right. But maybe she'd been too polite about it. Maybe he was a guy who couldn't take a hint.

He reached for her hand, something he often did. And, she'd noticed, not only with her. Glen was a hands-on sort of guy with everyone. "I do consider you my friend, Kate. And since you're my friend, I'd consider giving you a year's lease on that house."

She felt her eyes grow wide. "You would?"

He nodded. "Yep."

"That's wonderful." She paused. "But I have to ask, would there be any strings attached? I mean I like you, Glen, as a friend. But that's all. I'd want this to be strictly business. You know?"

"I know, I know. You've made your position clear. You want to be just friends."

She felt a wave of relief. "I'd really, really love to lease your house."

"But you haven't even been inside it. That's no way to make a business decision. What if the floors are falling through and the ceiling leaks?"

"Does it?"

"Well, no. But you don't know that."

"That's true." She nodded. "But I do know the place would have to be really atrocious for me to say no. And I wouldn't expect you to offer me something that's about to fall down or needs to be torn down. That's not what friends do."

"You're right. But as someone who wants to become a good businesswoman, and I think you do, you should learn to keep your cards closer to your vest."

"It's only because I feel desperate. I've got flowers ready to sell, and lots of things to put in my shop. I just want to get it going." She confessed her idea for a roadside stand. "Even a very run-down house would be better than that."

"I guess so."

"And besides a solid roof and floor, I assume the house has plumbing and electric, right?"

"Yes, of course. But it's about a hundred years old. Electric and plumbing were updated in the fifties. And I had it re-roofed several years ago. Even so, it needs some serious TLC."

"I can do that," she said eagerly. "And besides, I was hoping for a place that would look sort of rustic and old fashioned." She could already imagine buckets of flowers on the shady porch. Maybe some antiques here and there. She could make it so charming.

"And you're okay if I can only commit to a one-year lease?"

"One year's better than none."

"And any improvements would be on your own dime, Kate."

"I think that'd be okay. Unless there's something major. Of course, I'd need to see the house first." She tried to look like a formidable businesswoman.

"Want to go now?"

"I'd totally love to." She checked her watch. "But Leota and her tiny house will be here any minute."

"Right." He slowly stood.

"Tomorrow?" she asked.

"Sure. Tomorrow's fine. How about I pick you up around noon? We'll get a bite to eat, catch up some more, and then I'll take you to see it."

Kate really thought that sounded a bit like a date. But then she realized it also sounded like something friends might do together. Or business acquaintances. "Sure, that works for me."

"Then it's a date." His grin looked slightly smug, like he'd just won this round. Or else he was just pulling her leg.

She forced a smile. "A business date, right?"

"Yeah, of course." He handed her his empty glass. "By the way, you should try answering your phone more often, Kate. I wouldn't have to drive out here so much. Not that I don't enjoy the drive or face-to-face visits."

As she walked him to his pickup she explained about her phone's lack of connectivity, as if that was the main reason—and sometimes it was. "Anyway, I don't see the point of keeping it on me all the time."

"What about your development?" he questioned. "Will that have better phone reception?"

"Yes. Of course. I can hardly wait for that."

"See you tomorrow." He reached for her hand again, clasping it warmly. "I think we'd make good business partners."

"Well, I, uh, I hope so." She felt uneasy. "I would love to lease your house, if it all works out." Just then she noticed movement inside Hank's house, going past the window. Was he watching this encounter? And, even if he was, did it really matter? She thanked Glen, waving as he drove away. She really didn't believe she was leading him on by simply agreeing to a business deal. But at the same time, she didn't know what went on inside that brain of his.

It really did seem like Glen thought of her as a challenging game. The way his eyes twinkled when he said, "It's a date," suggested as much. And she had no doubts he was used to winning. As she walked back to her porch, she remembered Leota's suggestion. What would Glen do if he thought Kate was after him? If he thought she had a wedding in mind? Would he take off in the opposite direction? Even so, she wouldn't attempt something like that . . . at least not until she'd signed that lease.

She was just going up the steps when she heard another vehicle coming down Hank's driveway. Hoping this really was Leota, Kate ran back out to see. But it was just that overly familiar silver Corvette again. As usual, with the top down, and Natalie's platinum blonde hair blowing in the wind, like she thought the cameras were rolling. And, really, the scene was picture perfect. That was probably why Hank had been looking out the window earlier. He hadn't been watching Kate and Glen, he'd simply been looking for Natalie. Although he didn't seem to be looking now.

Chapter 25

Kate had only experienced a few encounters with Natalie Spalding and, unfortunately, none of them had been particularly pleasant. Even though Kate tried to remember what Glen had told her, that Natalie had grown up poor, which had probably affected her attitudes toward wealth and prestige, it was hard to tolerate the somewhat snooty woman. But seeing that Natalie was parking her car dead center of the driveway, like she often did, Kate knew someone needed to intervene. And she didn't see Hank making an appearance.

"Hey, Natalie." Kate waved, forcing a tolerant smile. "You can't park your car there."

"Why not?" Natalie frowned as she closed her door. As usual, her makeup was perfect, her tousled hair looked like someone had styled it, and with shoulders back and head held high, she strode up to Kate. This woman either had excellent posture or a superiority complex. Kate could never be sure.

Stifling irritation, Kate explained about the imminent delivery of a tiny home, glancing toward Hank's house in the hope he'd pop out and back her on this. But his front door remained closed. And, oddly enough, Zeb didn't seem to be nearby. Odd since Kate had expected him to wait for Leota with bated breath. Hopefully nothing was wrong.

"Why is a tiny home being delivered here?" Natalie sounded territorial, as if she thought this was her property.

Kate quickly explained about the holding situation, just until Aspen Pond was ready. "And then everything will return to normal." She glanced toward the house, hoping Hank would come intervene.

"So you and your friends plan to turn Hank's beautiful farm into a shabby old trailer park?" Natalie shook her head with a look of distaste. "Too bad."

"They aren't trailers," Kate corrected. "And I'm only talking about one more tiny home. And for a very short while."

"It's bad enough he's got to have *that* parked here." Natalie pointed to Kate's sweet little house. "But another one as well?" She looked thoroughly exasperated as she got back into her car. "This is getting ridiculous."

At this juncture, Kate wanted to suggest Natalie just leave her car there—let the semi-truck plow right over it. But she knew that wasn't merely childish, it was mean-spirited. Fortunately, Natalie started the engine. But as Kate watched Natalie drive, too fast, to the garage area where Hank's truck was parked, she really did feel mean-spirited. What was wrong with that woman?

For a moment, Kate stood there gazing at the two vehicles parked side by side. Could there be two more completely opposite automobiles? She didn't think so. In fact, that was exactly how Hank and Natalie seemed to her. Total and complete opposites. Of course, some people believed opposites attract.

Natalie strolled up to Hank's house, went up the porch steps and walked right through the front door—without even knocking. Kate wasn't really surprised. Just irritated. But why should she care? If Hank was seriously interested in a woman like that, it explained everything. Natalie and Kate were as different from each other as . . . as Hank Branson was different from Glen Stryker.

Fortunately, a distraction was rolling down the road to the farm. Kate felt a rush of happiness to see Leota's light blue Mini Cooper now turning down the long driveway. Followed by the hefty diesel semi-truck with her tiny house (looking quite large) trailing behind it, they made an interesting procession. Kind of like a circus parade where a clown led an elephant.

As Kate waved to them, she wondered if Hank would come out to greet Leota. She remembered how he'd been on hand when she'd arrived and how he helped out when her house was being set up. But with Natalie inside his house, well, it looked like Kate and Leota might be on their own this time.

Kate was pleased to see the same transporters that had delivered her house. She showed Tony where Leota's house was to be placed and where the hookups to water, sewer, and electricity were waiting. And the two guys just took over from there. Just like before, they seemed to know exactly what to do and how to do it. All they wanted was for the "ladies to stay outta the way."

"This is so exciting," Leota gushed after they'd exchanged hugs and greetings. "I thought we'd never get here."

"Did you get scared leading the way?" Kate asked.

"I'm embarrassed to say, I was terrified. I kept looking in my rearview mirror, almost certain my little house was going to careen over a curve and land in the river, taking the poor moving men with it."

Kate nodded. "I felt just the same when mine was brought over."

"But we made it here." She hugged Kate again. "I still can't believe it."

It took more than an hour for the house to be put in place and set up. But the movers were barely down the driveway when Leota started showing Kate her house. "I know it's more modern looking than yours, but I totally love it."

"I think it suits you." Kate nodded approval. "I

314

can't wait to see it all put together. Do you need help unpacking?"

"I'd love help." Leota pointed to a box. "That goes in the kitchen."

The two women chatted as they unpacked and stowed things away. Kate told Leota more about her kids' visit and how they had all been in better communication since then. "I think they respect me more." She put a lampshade on a lamp, tightening it.

"Not ready to throw you in the old folks' home quite yet," Leota teased.

"Not yet."

"So, how are things with you and Hank?" Leota sounded cautious. "I've been almost afraid to ask since you never seem to mention him anymore."

"Oh, we're on good terms," Kate said a bit tersely. "Friends, of course."

"Just friends?"

"That seems to be how he wants it, and I'm fine with it, really."

"Really?" Leota paused from hanging a bright colored modern art painting on the wall.

"Really." Kate nodded firmly. "At the moment, Hank has company. A lady friend named Natalie. You might've noticed that flashy silver Corvette parked by the garage. It's hers. And it's been here a lot."

"Oh?" Leota's brows arched. "So it's a serious relationship?"

"She's his client. Hank designed her house. It's being built now. But she just keeps coming over here. And sometimes he goes with her. So, yes, I think it's serious. Well, as serious as someone like Hank can be."

"Someone like Hank?" Leota frowned.

"You know, he's still in love with his departed wife. I already told you about that."

"Zeb mentioned it too. But I assumed he was moving on."

"I've had moments when I thought that too. But if he's moving on, it's not with me. To be honest, Hank's a hard guy to figure out." Kate tossed a striped pillow onto Leota's creamy white sofa.

"So what about your friend Glen? Did you propose marriage to him yet?" Leota chuckled.

Kate rolled her eyes then, with more enthusiasm, shared the news about Glen's gingerbread house. "It's very exciting." She carefully unloaded a box of glasses. "I get to see it tomorrow."

"Oh, I hope it works out. Maybe you'll hire me." Leota set a cobalt blue vase on the countertop. "Although Molly might throw a fit. Did I tell you she wants me to start work on Saturday? That gives me the rest of today and tomorrow to get settled."

"Well, we seem to be moving pretty quickly in here. And I'm not surprised she needs you so soon." Kate told her how busy town had been. "Which makes me even more determined to get my florist business launched. Wait until you see my field of dreams."

"Field of Dreams?" Leota looked confused.

Kate told her about her three acres of seedlings and plants. "Everything is growing so well. I jokingly call it my field of dreams."

"What will you call your florist shop?"

"I'm not sure yet. I've jotted down a number of ideas."

"Maybe it should be called *Field of Dreams*."

"Interesting." Kate nodded. "I'll put that on my maybe list."

Together they worked and visited until most of Leota's things were put into place and everything looked very neat and tidy—and attractive. "You're lucky not to have as much stuff as I did." Kate closed a closet that was only half filled. "You actually still have room for more."

"I got rid of a lot of things." Leota adjusted a colorful area rug in front of the sofa. "I decided on a very simple criteria for what would be allowed in my tiny house."

"What criteria?"

"I had to either love it dearly or use it daily."

"Seriously—that worked?"

She nodded. "Absolutely."

"Well, I'm impressed." Kate looked around

the clean looking modern home and smiled. "It's really lovely in here, Leota."

"Thank you." She flopped onto the sofa, arms spread wide, and smiled even wider. "I'm happy as a clam."

Chapter 26

Kate was ready and waiting for Glen the next day. As she climbed into his Jeep, smiling brightly, she greeted him. He looked slightly surprised, and she hoped he hadn't mistaken her enthusiasm as a romantic gesture. But maybe it didn't matter so much. Especially if Leota's theory was right. Maybe Glen would back off if Kate warmed up. Not that she planned to start discussing engagement rings anytime soon.

As they had a nice outdoor lunch at Pine Lodge Inn, Kate visited congenially with Glen. She told him about Leota's arrival and how happy she was in her tiny new home. "It's nothing like mine." Kate described the modern design and clean lines of Leota's house. "I wasn't sure I'd like it, but I really do."

"So Hank's going to allow people to put any kind of tiny house they like on his property? That seems a little risky to me."

"Well, not any kind. Hank's developed some pretty simple CC&Rs that our homeowners must agree with. Just basic things like yard maintenance, garbage bin storage, house size, parking cars, and whatnot. And all tiny houses must be approved before placement. Mostly for safety, although Hank reserves rights of refusal. But he said he'd only use it if a tiny home was decrepit or just too weird." She chuckled. "I've seen that TV show, and I know there are some pretty bizarre looking tiny homes out there. I saw one called *The Yellow Submarine*. And that's exactly what it looked like."

"Yeah, that's my point. I'd hate having those monstrosities on my land. I hope Hank's not sorry about this."

"We realize there will be some different styles of homes. Our goal is for it to feel like an old-fashioned neighborhood where people's personalities can be expressed through their homes. Where Leota's house is modern, Aileen's will be more traditional, mine is like a little chalet, and Zeb's is going to be a mini log cabin. I think it's fun. And no one will accidentally go into their neighbor's house because they all look alike."

"But won't it look hodgepodge? All those different kinds of styles? I sure wouldn't like it."

"No, you probably wouldn't." She poked him in the arm. "But some people wouldn't like *your* development, Glen. Not everyone wants to live in a house that looks exactly like all their neighbors' houses."

"I let them choose a different color for their doors and shutters. That distinguishes them a bit."

"And you have how many colors they can choose from?"

"Three." He bristled. "No one has complained yet."

"Your resort is charming," she reassured him. "I loved it the first time I saw it."

"Just not enough to live there."

"Well, you know why. We've been over that." She smiled as she pushed her empty plate aside. "As you say, tiny homes aren't for everyone. And tiny home developments aren't either. We like being able to give people options. And you shouldn't be concerned, after all, we're not stealing any business from you."

"That's true." He wiped his mouth with a napkin. "Now, let me guess, Kate. You're probably chomping at the bit to see my poor old ramshackle house."

"You guessed right." She nodded eagerly. "Take me to the gingerbread house."

"I just hope that child-eating witch isn't inside." He grimaced. "I'm warning you, Kate, the place is in shambles. I doubt you'll want any part of it."

"Let me be the judge of that." Kate reached for her bag and stood. Glen could talk the house down until he was blue in the face, but until she saw it for herself, she was not giving up. And, she hoped and prayed, he was probably exaggerating.

As Glen drove them across town, he made a few more disclaimers about the property. "I just don't want you to be too disappointed."

"Don't worry. I'm already bracing myself for the worst."

"And one more thing. It stinks in there," he finally said as he parked in front of the charming structure. "I mean it really stinks."

"Well, smells can be eradicated."

"I don't know." His expression was grim as he handed her a tarnished brass key. "But, if you don't mind, I'll take a pass on showing you the place. You go ahead and poke around, for as long as you can stand the stench in there."

"Thanks." She grasped the key like she'd caught the brass ring on a merry-go-round and, bracing herself for a bad smell, she hurried across the narrow weed-infested yard and on up to the porch. There were a few rickety boards, but nothing particularly dangerous. She took in a deep breath as she stood in front of what could be an attractive door—with a little TLC. The glass knob was probably original and worth preserving. And the door beneath layers of crackling paint had raised wood panels and a leaded glass window that someone had painted over. She put the key into the lock and turned. With the door barely opened, the smell came wafting out. It was bad.

She stood there for a moment, holding her breath and looking inside the good sized front room. The wide planked floors were so dark, they looked almost black. The walls were painted in awful neon shades of pink, orange, green and yellow. But that was an easy fix. Now, taking a deep breath of fresh air, she hurried inside. The windows in here were leaded too, but also painted, giving the room a weird almost spooky look. Maybe a witch really did live here.

Still holding her breath, she hurried on to the little kitchen in the back. There she opened another door, hoping that a cross breeze might help freshen the air. But first she stuck her head out to get a breath of fresh air. Glen hadn't exaggerated, the stench in there really was sickening.

She surveyed the kitchen from the opened doorway. It was even more old and worn than the living room. Probably little changed since it was built—what, a hundred years ago? But the painted cabinets, an awful mustard color, looked fairly solid. And the farmhouse porcelain sink, if it was clean, might be white. And it was large enough to use for flower arranging and could probably be quite charming. The filthy linoleum on the floor and countertops looked disgusting and would have to be replaced. She turned around in the doorway, trying to catch another breath of fresh air. Would she really be able to eradicate this stench? A stinky florist shop wouldn't be popular.

She went back inside, this time checking out the two small bedrooms. One could be used for storage with a flower fridge. The other could be a workroom or office. She looked at the bathroom, which was bigger than she'd expected, but looked like it needed to be gutted. How much would that cost? Afraid she might lose her lunch, she hurried back out through the front room, gasping for a breath of fresh air.

But as she stood on the porch, she noticed the front room didn't smell quite as bad as it had earlier. Or was she just getting used to it? Trying to ignore the stench, she gazed inside again . . . and suddenly she could see it. She could imagine those wood floors refinished. Not to look like new, but with their old patina gleaming. And the walls painted a clean soothing shade of creamy white. She would bring in antique tables and shelves and fixtures.

This room would be partly a gift shop and partly a florist shop. She'd already been searching wholesale companies online. She'd found things like soaps, linens, candles—pretty gift items that would be attractive alongside her lovely bouquets. Yes, she could see it!

"It's perfect," she whispered aloud. Then, holding her breath, she made another quick run through the house, closed and locked the kitchen door, then hurried back through the front room. Outside again, she was able to breathe as she locked the front door, pausing to admire the wraparound porch. It was perfect to display plants and flowerpots and perhaps even garden things and seedlings. Not only that, she would also transform the small weedy lot into a lovely garden. This would become a mini version of her "field of dreams." *Yes,* she thought, *this is it, my little field of dreams.* And that's what she was going to call her shop. *Little Field of Dreams.* It might take some explaining for people to grasp its meaning, but that was okay.

Feeling excited over the prospects, she hurried out to the Jeep where Glen was talking on his phone. Not wanting to eavesdrop, she stood outside, fondly gazing at the little gingerbread house from a distance. Really, other than the horrid smell and the work that needed doing, the place was absolutely perfect. It was truly an answer to prayer.

"So what'd you think?" Glen called to her. "Did it make you sick?"

She was about to burst into effusive praise for the perfect place, but then remembered his counsel about being a savvy businesswoman. She shouldn't lay her cards on the table.

"Well, you were sure right about the stench." She wrinkled her nose as she got into the Jeep. "I can't believe you let me eat lunch before going in there."

He chuckled. "Didn't really think about that. But I figured if you saw the house first, you'd probably bail on lunch."

She nodded. "Yeah, you're right."

"So then you're not interested?" He didn't seem concerned as he started the engine. "I thought it'd be too much for you."

"I didn't say that." She buckled her seat belt. "It's just that it will take so much work to make it habitable for a flower shop. And a lot of money too."

"I told you that already, Kate. And like I said, I don't plan to invest anything more into it."

"But you don't want to sell it to me?"

He pursed his lips, as if thinking.

Even if he did want to sell, she wasn't sure she wanted to be that deep in debt. "So, if you do want to lease it, I have an idea. What if I do the improvements and cover the expenses in lieu of paying rent? I'm guessing that everything I'd like to do would be a fair exchange for about, say, a year's worth of rent." She wasn't really sure about that, but it sounded good.

He slowly nodded. "I think we could work something like that out."

She hid her surprise. "That'd be great."

"You really think you can get that stench out?"

"I honestly don't know. I plan to go online and look for suggestions. But for starters, I think a thorough cleaning, painting, and refinishing those floors could make a big difference."

"Yeah, I guess." He shook his head. "That family had pets. Too many pets."

"I could tell."

"And then you saw the paint in there." He growled. "Place looks like a circus. And painting the windows too. What a mess."

"It was, uh, interesting." She glanced at him. "So what kind of rent did you charge for a place like that anyway?"

He shrugged. "Not much. And they didn't even pay me half the time."

"Oh?"

He sighed. "But they were having a pretty rough year. The dad got sick and the mom's job was just minimum wage."

She smiled at him. Despite his tough business-man exterior, it seemed Glen had a heart. That was nice to see.

"So, if you're serious about this, I'll get my lawyer to write up a lease agreement."

"Great." Kate hoped that she hadn't bitten off too much with this, but something about it just felt right.

"I'll make sure that he understands you're only responsible for cosmetic changes. If there's anything wrong that we can't see, well, I don't expect you to cover that."

She felt a wave of relief. "Okay, that seems fair. And I promise your house is going to look way better when I'm done."

He nodded. "I know it will." He pointed to the ice cream shop. "Hey, want to pop in there for dessert?"

"I'd love to, but I really need to get home. We're having this welcome party for Leota tonight, and I still need to put some things together."

"A party?" His eyes lit up and she suddenly realized her mistake.

"Yeah, nothing big. Just a few tiny house neighbors stopping by. And Leota's new boss, Molly."

"Oh, yeah. Molly McIntire." He nodded. "I just saw her yesterday, she said she had some sales help coming. So that's your friend Leota."

"Yeah." She glanced at him. He seemed overly interested in Leota's little party, but maybe he didn't understand it was really small potatoes. "I doubt you'd want to come tonight, Glen. It's really just a gathering of a few tiny house friends, but you're more than welcome to—"

"I'd love to come. And I'd love to meet your friend Leota. What can I bring?"

Surprised by his enthusiasm, she suggested he bring an appetizer, reiterating that it really was just a very small get together.

"A tiny party for your tiny homeowners." He laughed. "I might have to steal that idea for my own place. Tiny parties could become a big deal."

She couldn't help but smile as he continued toward the farm. Not over his tiny party joke, but because she was daydreaming about her little gingerbread house and all the plans she would soon be implementing to create her Little Field of Dreams. It was truly exciting!

Kate was still in high spirits as she set out food for Leota's welcome party. Thanks to Hank, they were expanding the gathering to his covered porch. "Thank you for letting us enjoy your shade. I didn't realize it would be such a warm evening." She set out a plate of deviled eggs and another plate of veggie sticks and dip. "It's so much cooler over here."

"No problem. Zeb is sure excited about having Leota here." He tipped his head toward the barbecue grill where Leota was assisting Zeb. "They seem to have really hit it off."

"Yes, it's sweet. It'll be interesting to see where it goes."

"I've never seen Zeb so energetic. I was actually getting concerned. He's doing so much these days. Helping with Aspen Pond, building his tiny house . . . I was worried he might burn out. But then I realized he's just happy."

"So is Leota." Kate smiled. "I don't know if I've ever seen her this happy."

"You seem happy too."

"Really?" She looked at him, surprised that she'd even been on his radar. "Well, I guess I am feeling pretty happy today."

"I saw you and Glen go somewhere again today. You two seem to be spending a lot of time together. Is that why you're so happy?"

"That's part of it." She noticed a car coming up the driveway. "Looks like guests are starting to arrive. And, uh, speaking of Glen, he'll be coming too."

"I thought this was just for our tiny-home folks."

"He heard that Molly was coming, and she's not a homeowner."

"But her sister is. And she's Leota's boss."

"Right. But Glen wanted to meet Leota and I figured it was as good a time as any." Kate felt taken aback by Hank's resistance toward Glen. Not very hospitable.

"Sure. Of course. The more the merrier." But his tone didn't sound too merry.

She was about to tell Hank the real reason she was happy—about finding her florist shop property—but she noticed another vehicle was turning off the main road. "Looks like Glen's not the only person who's not part of our tiny-home community."

"Huh?" Hank turned.

"Natalie Spalding." Before he could respond, she went out to welcome Abby and Molly. And, not eager to be around Natalie, she led the sisters directly over to the tiny houses. "I know you've both been wanting to see Leota's house," she told the women. "It's just perfect."

Leota came over to join them, welcoming them

330

into her new house. Molly and Abby oohed and awed, admiring everything.

"This is so cool. I think I could live in a house like this," Molly declared.

"Give up your full-sized house?" Abby challenged her.

"You know my house, Abs, it's pretty small and cramped. I realize it's maybe three times as big as this, but with these tall ceilings and simple lines, well, Leota's house lives bigger."

More guests had arrived . . . Grayson, followed by Aileen were heading up to the porch. Then Glen showed up and Kate, still concerned over Hank's negative reaction, went out of her way to make him feel part of the group. Leota looked amused as he shook her hand, warmly welcoming her to Pine Ridge. And then, right there in front of Leota and everyone, Glen produced a lease agreement that his lawyer had put together that same afternoon.

"We've got plenty of folks to witness this thing," Glen told Kate as they took turns signing the contract. And then he produced a chilled champagne bottle, urging everyone to toast both Kate's new business venture and Leota's happy arrival.

Before long, Zeb was announcing the burgers were ready and people fixed plates and found places to eat and visit. All in all, it was a congenial gathering and everyone seemed to be enjoying themselves. But Hank and Natalie both seemed to have vanished. Kate tried to appear untroubled by this, but underneath she felt seriously aggravated.

Since the Corvette remained in the driveway, Kate figured the two were inside. She couldn't imagine Natalie wanting to be part of their gathering, especially considering her attitude toward tiny homes in general. But it seemed rude on Hank's part. Still, this wasn't his party. He'd already taken time to get acquainted and welcome Leota. So maybe it didn't matter. Well, except to her.

By the time the party started to wind down, Kate's patience with Glen was winding down too. Oh, it wasn't his fault. It's not like he was being anything other than *Glen*. But she was tired of him sticking to her like flypaper, acting like they were something more than just friends. She could tell Leota found this very entertaining and suspected she'd hear more relationship advice from her later, but at the moment Kate was fed up.

"I'm going to start clearing things," she told Glen. "If you'll excuse me."

"Need help?" he offered.

"That's okay." She forced a smile as she gathered up some things from the picnic table. "You stay out here and enjoy the party." She wasn't eager to walk into Hank's house, but Zeb had told her to take things to the kitchen, promising that he'd do the major cleanup.

"But I'm happy to help," Glen insisted, opening the door so she could take a load inside.

"Oops!" Natalie jumped from the other side of the door. "Didn't know anyone was coming in."

"Hey, Natalie." Glen grinned as he held the door open. "I thought that looked like your car out there. What're you doing here?"

"Just visiting with Hank." She backed up into the house so Kate could carry her load inside. "Hi, Kate." Natalie's eyes narrowed slightly at the load of dirty plates. "That looks, uh, interesting. Are you giving those to Hank?"

"Well, they're his dishes. Zeb said to take them to the kitchen."

"Right." Natalie held her head in that superior position again, stepping away as if she thought the dishes might soil her pale blue sundress.

Ignoring her, Kate continued on into the kitchen. The sooner she got the cleanup out of the way, the happier she'd be. She could hear Natalie and Glen visiting in the other room, and grateful for this reprieve from Glen, she decided to go ahead and rinse the dishes and load the dishwasher. Zeb had already done a lot for this evening.

"What're you doing in here?" Hank suddenly emerged from the other end of the kitchen with a curious expression. "I thought Zeb was on KP tonight."

"Zeb did a lot to get this set up. And he grilled the burgers. I just thought it was only fair that I helped." Kate ran water over a messy plate.

"Then let me help." He took the rinsed plate from her.

"But Natalie's in there," she said quietly. "You should probably—"

"She's still here?" He frowned.

She glanced at him as she rinsed a glass. "You didn't know she was here?"

"Well, I could've guessed. But I was in my office. Revising her fireplace wall. For the umpteenth time." He sounded clearly aggravated. "First she wants built-ins then she wants an eighteen foot tall rock wall. Then she wants both."

"You've been working this whole time? That's why you weren't at the party?"

"Sorry about that. But Natalie's contractor needs my revisions ASAP. He's tired of all this indecision too. Her change orders on the kitchen set him way back."

"You're saying Natalie just sits around, waiting for you to finish your revisions while you work?"

"Pretty much. She usually hangs out in the living room. I won't allow her in my office any-more." He loaded another glass then lowered his voice. "I actually have to lock the door."

"You're kidding." Kate couldn't help but giggle.

"Yeah, it's pathetic." He glanced toward the kitchen door that led to the dining room. "Do I hear voices?"

"Natalie and Glen are in the living room. Sounds like they've been having a nice little visit."

His mouth twisted to one side. "If you and Glen weren't involved, I'd love to sic Natalie onto him." He laughed then grew sober. "Sorry, that was my frustration talking. I shouldn't have said that. I apologize."

She blinked, nearly dropping the platter. "That's okay. As a matter of fact, Glen and I aren't involved. I keep trying to make that clear to him, but he just doesn't get it. And he won't give up."

"Then why do you go running around with him?" Hank frowned. "Like today. You looked pretty happy when you jumped into his Jeep."

So he *was* watching. Kate felt a happy rush. He did care. She quickly explained about the stinky gingerbread house, about how thrilled she was to get it, and her exciting plans to restore it. "And that's the only reason I went with Glen today. And he knows it. I keep making myself clear. But that man is super stubborn."

"Glen Stryker's used to getting what he wants." Hank closed the dishwasher and looked at her. "And he obviously wants you, Kate."

Kate heard Natalie's and Glen's voices getting closer. "They're coming."

Hank grabbed her hand. "Come with me."

She didn't resist as he led her through the back doorway, down a dim hallway and into what had to be his office. Woodsy and masculine, with a large desk and oversized computer screen and a handsome drafting table on the other side of the room.

"What a cool working space." She nodded. "I like it."

"Me too—and now you're stuck with me." He grinned as he locked the door.

She tilted her head to one side. "So you're locking me in?"

"I'm locking them out." Hank ran his fingers through his hair then looked intently at her. "So you're honestly not interested in Glen? You're serious?"

"I'm one hundred percent serious." She laughed. "When you offered to sic Natalie on him, I almost jumped for joy."

"Natalie might go for it. I know she'd be impressed by his net worth. Money means a lot to that woman. Problem is, I doubt Glen would go for her." Hank sighed. "You present serious competition. Nat wouldn't have a chance."

Kate didn't know what to say, so she simply murmured a quiet *thank you*.

And then Hank reached out for her hand and in

one swift and unexpected move, he took her into his arms and tenderly kissed her. She couldn't have been more surprised, or pleased. And she happily kissed him back.

Chapter 27

Kate and Hank were pretty much the talk of the town the next day. Nobody knew the original source of the gossip trail—it could've been Glen or Natalie, or perhaps Molly or Aileen since they were both socially active in Pine Ridge—but neither Kate nor Hank much minded. Probably because the rumor was partly true. And the rest of it, well, it would sort itself out later.

The basic scuttlebutt circulating through the community was that two hosts of the party at Hank's ranch suddenly made themselves scarce. But no one suspected they had disappeared together. Their so-called "dates" (Glen Stryker and Natalie Spalding) were reported to have been "scandalized" when Hank and Kate emerged from Hank's lovely home, holding hands and grinning at each other like love-struck teenagers. Of course, Natalie was quick to throw out a disclaimer, stating she hadn't actually been "dating" Hank at all, that he was simply her architect. But Glen wasn't saying anything.

Kate knew the main reason for so much interest was the fact that everyone in town had considered Hank Branson "off the market." A lonely widower who would never recover from losing his beloved wife. Even when he'd been seen around town with Natalie, no one had taken it seriously. Well, except for Kate. But not anymore.

"So what about Elizabeth?" she asked Hank the following morning. Holding hands, they had strolled down to the pond to check out her field of flowers and the new trees recently planted in Aspen Pond . . . but, as they sat on the new bench under the aspens, she knew it was to be alone.

"I need to explain something to you." Hank spoke with an intensity that got Kate's full attention. "Elizabeth is part of my past. A part that I can let go of now. That I want to let go of." He turned to her. "You're a part of my future, Kate. At least, I hope you are."

"I want to be." She reached for his hand. "But only if you're really ready, Hank. I don't want to rush you."

He leaned toward her. "I'm ready," he whispered, sealing it with a kiss.

Kate remained determined to lay low the following week. She knew people in town were curious about how she'd "hooked" Hank. Leota, though thrilled for Kate, had confided how Molly and Abby were both a bit jealous. Giving Kate even more reason to keep a low profile until the rumor mill ground down.

Fortunately, she had her stinky gingerbread house to distract her. She'd researched a number of natural scent-removal remedies online. Everything from lemons and vinegar to baking soda and hydrogen peroxide. But plain old soap and water seemed about as effective as anything. And lots of elbow grease. After scrubbing the mustard colored kitchen cupboards, she discovered they were actually painted a buttery yellow and not unattractive. They'd come in handy for storing vases and supplies.

Hank, eager to spend time with her, came in to help during the first few days. Despite the uninviting aroma, he quickly caught the vision for her Little Field of Dreams. He helped her rip out the nasty linoleum from the kitchen and bathroom to discover the same wide plank wood floors ran throughout the entire house. He proclaimed them fairly solid too. And so he'd rented a floor sander and, certain the floors were the source of the worst smells, he donned a face mask and went to work. By midweek the wood floors were all down to clean looking raw wood. And the smell was nearly eradicated.

He and Kate covered the wood floors in protective heavy paper so she could continue to clean and paint without messing them up. Then after the walls were in good shape, Hank would help her to stain and seal the floors. In the meantime, he needed to devote some time and energy to the tiny house development. Something Kate completely understood since the city had suddenly become a bit difficult. Hopefully it wasn't related to Abby—since she worked there. Was her nose out of joint over Kate and Hank's budding romance?

Even though Kate missed Hank's help and companionship, getting their development back on track was as important to her as anyone. And she was praying that the bumps in the road would soon be smoothed out. But on Friday morning, with her gingerbread house nearly stench free with all the surfaces cleaned, she happily commenced to painting. Everything would be the same milky shade of white. Besides being simple and less expensive, it felt fresh and clean and would contrast nicely against the soon to be stained wood floors and baseboard.

By afternoon, she was just finishing up the front room when she heard someone call her name from outside. Hoping it was Hank, she set down her roller and hurried out—only to find Glen standing on the porch with a hard to read expression. Hopefully he wasn't planning to tear up her lease agreement and kick her out. Would that even be legal?

"Oh." She smiled stiffly. "It's you. Hello."

"Thought I'd come check on your progress." He wrinkled his nose. "Still smell like a pig pen in there?"

"Come and see for yourself." She opened the door wider, waving him inside.

He stepped in and looked around then slowly shook his head. "Not bad. Not bad at all."

"Thanks." She told him about the sanded floors beneath the paper then, feeling awkward, bit her lip, trying to think of the right thing to say. "Glen, I've been wanting to talk to you about—"

"Don't say anything, Kate." His smile seemed deflated. "I get it. You kept telling me we were only friends."

"I'd like to still be friends."

He made a halfway shrug. "And, really, I'm not surprised that you're attracted to Hank. A lot of single women have chased after him. But I never thought Hank would come around like that, you know, that he'd get over Elizabeth. I thought he was a hopeless case. But if anyone could bring him around, well, I guess it would have to be you." Now his smile looked more like the old Glen and he jutted his chin out just a little. "And I like to think I had something to do with it, Kate."

"How's that?"

He chuckled. "Natalie blames me for making Hank jealous. If I hadn't been going after you, Hank wouldn't have jumped in like he did."

"Really?" Kate felt amused.

"Of course, in hindsight, she thinks she should've gotten to me first, that I could've made Hank jealous for her sake." He shrugged. "But I doubt it would've worked like that."

Kate couldn't help but chuckle. "That is one persistent woman."

"Tell me about it." He rolled his eyes.

"So she's pursuing you now?"

He nodded. "It's not so bad. You know, for a rebound romance. I suppose I could do worse."

Kate stuck out her hand. "I hope you'll still consider me your friend, Glen."

He shook it. "You bet. So, tell me, when are you and Hank tying the knot?"

She felt her cheeks warm. "Let's not get carried away now."

"Aw, Kate, you know he's going to ask."

"No hurry for that." She nodded back to the gingerbread house. "I've got plenty to keep me occupied."

"And I won't distract you from it." He tipped his head. "Keep up the good work, Kate."

Despite Hank's diligence with the city, there continued to be a few holdups with the opening of the tiny house development. As it turned out, Kate's Little Field of Dreams flower shop opened up first. And the response to her grand opening was far better than she could have imagined. Oh, she knew the shop looked great, even better than her dreams for it, but she never expected many people to show up for her grand opening. She was glad that Leota had taken the day off from Molly's Mercantile to help. Plus Zinnia had come over too. Not that she was much help. But Kate appreciated her being there.

Of course, Zinnia had been a bit dismayed to witness Zeb's devotion to Leota last night at dinner, but she quickly got over it, admitting to Kate that he really wasn't her type after all.

"Maybe I should give Molly my notice," Leota said as the three of them were closing up the shop.

"I know she'd be sad to lose you." Kate locked the door.

"Yeah, and it's been barely over a month." Leota straightened up what remained of the soap display.

"If I lived here, I'd work for you, Mom." Zinnia sat down on the bench by the door.

"That'd be fun." Kate patted her head. "I'm just glad you came today."

"Jake wanted to come, but he had a previous commitment." Zinnia kicked off her shoes and leaned back.

"Hopefully he'll come sometime when it's not so busy." Kate picked up some flower petals that had fallen onto the beautiful, gleaming wood floors.

"And I forgot to tell you. A woman named Susan said she's going to call next week about flowers for her parents' anniversary party. Cool, huh?"

"There were several people talking about

making floral orders," Leota told Kate. "You're going to be busy."

"It's so amazing." Kate slowly shook her head.

"But I'd like to be the first person to actually place a flower order." Leota grinned at her.

"Really? What do you want?" Kate asked.

"Wedding flowers!" Leota held out her left hand to display a diamond engagement ring.

"Leota!" Kate hugged her.

"Really?" Zinnia popped up from the bench to see.

Leota just nodded with tearful eyes. "Zeb asked me last night after dinner. I was going to tell you both, but I didn't want to steal any thunder from the grand opening today."

"This is wonderful, Leota. I'm so happy for both of you." Kate glanced nervously at Zinnia, wondering how she was taking this news.

"This is so cool!" Zinnia hugged Leota. "Zeb's really a great guy."

"I know." Leota was beaming. "He wants us to get married in the community area at Aspen Pond. We're thinking late summer or early fall."

"That's so exciting." Kate nodded. "I can just imagine how beautiful it will be."

"Where will you live?" Zinnia asked. "You have your tiny house and it looked like Zeb's was almost finished."

"We decided to keep both our tiny houses.

We'll take turns staying in them. But, like I told Zeb, a girl needs her space."

Zinnia laughed. "Good for you."

"It's fortunate that I sold Zeb the lot next door to you, Leota. Less running back and forth that way."

"He hopes to have his house finished a week or two before the wedding." Leota sighed. "And you really will do my flowers for me?"

"Of course!"

It was mid-August by the time Aspen Pond was finalized with the city and officially open for occupancy. Zeb's tiny home was the only one in place and not quite finished. But as Hank and Kate, with Chester leading the way, strolled around the pond-side path, there was no denying that the place looked fabulous.

"This is so exciting," Kate told Hank. "Everything about it, the design of the lots and their charming fences, the footpaths and access roads, the new trees, the thinned-out aspens . . . it's all just perfect."

"Thanks." He squeezed her hand. "But you get some of the credit."

"Not really. The design is mostly yours. And pulling it all together like you did. Well, it's really something."

"Did you arrange for the movers yet? To get yours and Leota's houses into place?"

"They'll be here Friday morning."

"Great. And I've started to schedule the others too. Making sure that we don't get a traffic jam. But I expect we'll have everyone in place before Labor Day."

"How many do we have now?" She bent down to pat Chester.

"A grand total of fourteen."

"That's nice. I'm glad we're not completely filled up yet. Might make for a smoother transition." Kate wasn't sure how she'd feel to see every lot filled.

"Yeah, my thinking too. And I have three more lots sold and with folks waiting for their houses to be built. And two sales that are pending."

"I've got a couple sales pending too."

He peered across the pond. "I think everyone is going to like it here."

Kate looked over to the community picnic area. "You did a great job on that structure," she told him. "I love how it looks like a giant gazebo. It's going to be so perfect for Zeb and Leota's wedding."

"Hard to believe Zeb's getting married." Hank sighed. "Chester and I are going to feel pretty lonely over there."

She gazed over toward his house and barn, wondering about how her life would change when she moved over here. Having morning coffee with Hank and Chester had fallen into a sweet routine. She would miss it a lot. "Well, you'll just have to come visit us," she said quietly.

He nodded. "Count on it."

Zeb and Leota's wedding was small and sweet. And in Kate's opinion, the flowers were spectacular. By now, with fourteen different tiny homes in place, Aspen Pond felt like a real community. A tiny community perhaps, but a pleasant one. Everyone seemed to be genuinely happy to be there. Oh, sure, there were some adjustments. But nothing too concerning. The only thing Kate missed about it was Hank. And Chester.

"That was a good wedding," Hank said as he joined her on the perimeter of the small dance floor. "I've never seen Zeb happier."

"I'm not sure his parents are as happy." Kate frowned over to where Zeb's family was clustered together.

"That's just the way they are," Hank reassured her. "I wouldn't concern myself over it." He reached for her hand. "Besides, we're Zeb's family. And now, Leota's too."

She smiled at him. "Thanks for saying that, Hank. To be honest, I'd been feeling a little, uh, disconnected lately."

"Disconnected?" His brow creased. "But you're over here with your tiny house community. You have your shop in town." He pointed over to where Zinnia and Jake were eating at a table with

Molly and Garson. "And you even have your kids here today. How can you feel disconnected?"

She wondered how candid to be then decided to just toss it out there. "I mean from you, Hank." She smiled. "I miss you. And Chester too."

His eyes lit up. "And I've been feeling sorry for myself . . . feeling lonely over there in my big house. And I was disappointed that your kids declined my invitation to stay with me."

"That's only because Zeb and Leota offered them the use of their tiny houses during the weekend. Since they'll be off on their honeymoon. Both Jake and Zinnia are excited about staying in a real tiny house."

"So the kids have fully come around."

She peered curiously at him. "But what you said. Are you really lonely over there now?"

He nodded somberly. "I miss you being nearby."

"I miss watching sunsets with you."

"You do?" He sounded surprised.

"Of course, I do. And I miss our morning coffee. And I miss Chester. I miss everything, Hank. Mostly I miss you."

"Do you miss me enough to give up living in your tiny house?"

"What are you saying?" A rush of excitement went through her as she studied him closely. "What do you mean?"

"I mean . . . what I'm saying is . . . Kate, I love

you. I want to marry you. Would you be willing to give up your tiny house? Will you marry me?"

"I love you too, Hank. And I *do* want to marry you. But do I really have to give up my tiny house to do it?"

He laughed as he wrapped her in his arms. "No, you wouldn't have to give it up completely. After all, it would make a nice little getaway sometimes."

"Our home sweet tiny home getaway," she agreed.

"Sounds perfect." They sealed it with a kiss. And not a tiny one either.

Books are produced in the United States using U.S.-based materials

Books are printed using a revolutionary new process called THINKtech™ that lowers energy usage by 70% and increases overall quality

Books are durable and flexible because of Smyth-sewing

Paper is sourced using environmentally responsible foresting methods and the paper is acid-free

Center Point Large Print

600 Brooks Road / PO Box 1
Thorndike, ME 04986-0001 USA

(207) 568-3717

US & Canada:
1 800 929-9108
www.centerpointlargeprint.com